Δ'ΑΙΟΣ

A Call Me Icarus Novel

First paperback edition October 2023

Book cover by Sarah Mason Art

ISBN 979-8-9892830-0-2 (paperback)

ISBN 979-8-9892830-9-5 (hard cover)

ISBN 979-8-9892830-1-9 (ebook)

www.andromedaruins.com

CONTENTS

Dedication   V

Content Warnings   VI

Epigraph   1

Ten Years Ago   3

1. The Rooftop   16

2. The Break In   29

3. The Dream   37

4. That Night   44

5. The Coffee Shop   59

6. The Tattoo Shop   69

7. The News Cast   83

8. The Question   97

9. The Plan   109

10. The Grocery Store   124

11. The Need of a Name   133

12. The Rescue   148

13. The Aftermath   161

14. The Nightmare   171

15. The Elysian   183

16. The Shutdown   196

17. The Aquarium   210

18. The Dance   225

19. The Next Morning   237

20. The Argument   250

21. The Meltdown   261

22. The Exchange   272

23. The Pain   287

24. The Vow   301

25. [REDACTED]   313

Index of Greek Terms Used   315

Acknowledgements   320

About the Author   322

Also By Andromeda   323

THIS BOOK IS FOR THE KIDS WHO WERE TOLD
THAT THEY WERE NEVER ENOUGH.

THEY LIED. YOU ARE MORE THAN THEY DESERVE.

This book contains depictions of:

Immolation, Child Abuse, Death, Hallucinations (both visual and auditory), Violence, Gore, Slut Shaming

Read at your own risk.

Here is what they don't tell you:

Icarus laughed as he fell.
Threw his head back and
yelled into the winds,
arms spread wide,
teeth bared to the world.

(There is a bitter triumph
in crashing when you should be
soaring.)

The wax scorched his skin,
ran blazing trails down his back,
his thighs, his ankles, his feet.
Feathers floated like prayers
past his fingers,
close enough to snatch back.
Death breathed burning kisses
against his shoulders,
where the wings joined the harness.
The sun painted everything
in shades of gold.

ANDROMEDA RUINS

(There is a certain beauty
in setting the world on fire
and watching from the centre
of the flames.)

—Fiona, @wearealsoboats on Tumblr

TEN YEARS AGO

...AM I DEAD?

No. I can feel far too much for this to be death.

I can feel the burning, the agony of my skin melting. I can feel my vocal chords tear. I can feel hatred pooling deep in my bones.

What is death, anyways? What will happen when I cease to exist? Do places like Elysium and Tartarus exist? And if they do, would I go there?

I don't think so. Elysium is a paradise for heroes and those who have done good in their days on Earth, and I can't say I've done that.

On the other hand, I don't believe I've done anything to warrant being exiled in Tartarus for eternity. I haven't had the most glamorous life, but I don't think I should be lumped in with some of the worst souls in myth.

Maybe when I appear before the triumvirate of Kings—Minos, Rhadamanthys, and Aeacus—they will tell me that I'll spend the rest of time unbound as a nameless and faceless shade doomed to roam the fields of Asphodel.

I suppose I'll have to die to learn my fate, and so far that hasn't happened. Why is that?

A burning sensation engulfs the right side of my face. My cheek feels like it is boiling, the skin pulling itself taut and straining as pain wreaks havoc in my body. The pain builds itself up, adding layer upon layer of pain until I am screaming and thrashing.

Why is my face burning?

That's right...

I was training with *him,* and he never takes it easy on me during training. Throwing everything he can at me. He thinks I can withstand it because I am his child, that somehow the fact that his blood runs through my veins makes me special.

But, just like every other time, it was shown that I am not special. That I am just a kid and not his perfect creation.

Through the haze of pain, I try to recall what weapon he used against me. This is the worst, most excruciating pain I've ever felt, it must have been one hell of an invention. Of course, there is the burn that tells me the weapon has fire elements, but that doesn't narrow it down at all. Everything made by his hands uses fire.

I will never forget a single one of the weapons he used against me. The blistering and bubbling of my skin is something that will haunt me for as long as I live, the putrid stench of burning hair and clothes follows me.

Sometimes I catch a whiff of that smell when my mind wanders. It catches me off guard every time, rips my mind away from whatever it is that I'm working on.

The searing pain coursing through my body tells me that it was a long range fire weapon he used. There are no sharp pangs—a tell of a blade or serrated weapon. There are no dull, yet overwhelming pulsations—a tell of blunt weapons hitting their mark repeatedly.

No, I can only feel the tightness of blistering skin being pulled taut over poorly wrapped—if wrapped at all—wounds.

It doesn't matter how hard I try to recall the training session, though. I cannot remember what happened. I can't even remember what lead to the training session, why I was training in the first place. I can't remember anything...

"Icarus?" a soft voice, muffled by the pain that I'm drowning in, drifts through the haze.

"Are you back yet?"

Back yet? What does that mean, am I not in the training room still? That's not right, I'm never brought to my room after training. If anything, I might be in the infirmary. I have woken up there a time or two. Normally, though, I return to consciousness in the middle of the training ring. If I can't hold my own in a fight, then I am not worthy of the treatment and care of the on-site nurse.

The discomfort of pain makes me to groan as I force my eyes open. Everything hurts, it feels like my bones are hollow but at the same time weigh thousands of pounds.

I fight to move my arm, using them to push myself into a sitting position. My joints protest the movement, they creak and pop relentlessly. It takes a moment, but I do get myself up and to the edge of my bed.

My room in the dormitory isn't large. I can reach the door from where I sit on the bed with minimal stretching. My breath hitches as I lean for the doorknob, but my hand misses the mark. For a moment I cannot move, cannot breathe, as I try to push through the blinding pain the movement caused.

I force myself to take a breath as I re-adjust, aiming my body more towards the door as I reach for the doorknob once again. My hand lands, then slips, falling uselessly back onto the mattress. I can feel my fingers twitch and spasm as they try to follow the command my brain gives them. I contract the muscles, balling my hand into a fist just to prove that I can. Then, I reach back out for the handle.

The door flies open as soon as the latch clicks. In the doorway stands the human embodiment of the sun, a person that I have become very close to in my time here. Someone who can light up any room he's in with his smile and his kinds words. Just his presence is enough to soothe my pain, allowing my lungs to take in more air as I catch his worried gaze.

"Sunny," I say, my voice hoarse and throat sore. "What are you doing here? You're gonna get in trouble."

The rules of this place are strict. Even more so when you're the 'prodigal' son of an Elysian, if my experience is anything to go by. They strip away your freedoms to the point where you're not allowed to leave your room unless it is to go to class or to training. It's like a damn prison in here.

"Doesn't matter, we need—"

"Doesn't matter? What do you mean 'doesn't matter'? You know what they'll to if you get caught here again." Not only that, but it matters to me. I won't tell him that, not out loud, but his safety matters to me.

"That doesn't matter right now Icarus!" He puts his hand on the left side of my face and leans in to rest his forehead on mine. In a softer voice he says, "We need to get you out of here, okay?"

A moment of silence washes over us as I try to process what is happening. Why do I need to get out? Why did I wake up back in my room? *What is going on?*

I'm not going to get answers just sitting here. I take a deep breath before looking up into the burnished gold of my sunshine's eyes.

"Okay," I mutter.

Some of the tension in his face dissipates, the corner of his lip twitches up for a brief second. He leans away from my face, patting

7

my cheek as he does. Then he turns away from me, looking into my closet.

"Cool, I don't have much time before they realize I'm not in the training room. Are you able to help me pack your things?"

The relentless pain I have been ignoring still courses through my body, telling me that I won't be able to stand. I try anyways.

My joints are still upset from sitting up, I can feel my muscles scream and strain with the effort to pull my weight off the bed. I almost make it to a standing position when I feel a stabbing sensation in my side that makes me gasp and fall back onto the bed. I'm about to try standing again when my sunshine turns back to face me.

"Whoa, Birdie. Don't hurt yourself." He looks like he wants to reach out to me, like he wants to make sure that I'm okay. But he doesn't.

"Why don't you stay there and tell me what to pack?"

I nod and make myself as comfortable as I can on the edge of the shitty dormitory bed. I don't have many belongings, here or otherwise. Part of the Elysian Program is learning to live without attachments. Something I excel in.

I give him a list on what to pack of my meager belongings: two of my hoodies, my blades, and a few keepsakes he has given me over the years. Nothing too big and heavy, everything else can be replaced.

When he's done packing, he hands me the backpack. He doesn't say anything, but I can tell from the set of his shoulders and the slight frown on his lips that there is no getting out of this.

It is time to go.

He helps me stand up. My arm loops around his shoulders and his arm wraps around my torso. It isn't an ideal situation, to have to leave when I'm this injured. But we are going to make it work.

This whole thing is weird. What happened to me in training? Why do I have to leave right now? Can't we wait for some of my injuries to heal? Why is my sunshine so anxious?

I can feel his rapid heartbeat from where I am pressed into his side. Honestly the entire reason I'm going along with this is because he's so frantic. My sunshine is the one that stays calm, this is unusual for him. He's trying to hide it, which makes the whole situation weirder, but he should know that I can read him better than that.

"Why?" I whisper as we round the first corner. Every step we take away from the room is like a stab in my heart. That room has been mine for as long as I can remember. It's not much, just a shitty little dorm room with a ratty twin size bed and barely enough room to stretch. But it's mine. It's all I've ever known.

"Why now?"

"Birdie we don't have time for this. We need to get you out first," his reply is rushed as we make our way through the hall. Silence envelopes us again before my sunshine gives in.

"Fine, but you have to keep moving even after I tell you. Daedalus is trying to kill you."

Of course this is about *him*. I know he goes too hard on my in training, but that's because I'm his successor! I was created to live up to his expectations, so it's okay for him to push me a bit harder than everyone else. I haven't managed to impress him yet, but I will! I just need to get stronger, work on my agility. Then I will live up to his expectations. I just need more time!

My mind is so loud that I almost miss what my sunshine whispers next, "I can't lose you."

I wish I had missed it. I don't know what he means, the words add a whole new layer to the mess we're in. One that I cannot bear to think about.

"Why would he want me dead? I've tried my best. I train and study and I even got told that I'm a promising candidate for the Elysian Program." I want to scream so bad right now, just vent all my frustrations into the air, but I can't. This is all too much.

There is one thing bothering me that I haven't yet voiced; "I am his son, for the Gods' sake. He can't just throw me away!"

Silence falls over us again, but this time neither of us break it. The winding corridors of the Academy keep us distracted, this place is built like a maze. I have always thought it was a nod to the myth of the Labyrinth, but as we try to escape the building I realize it's more than that.

The Academy may as well have been a re-creation of the Labyrinth. It's twisting halls and classrooms designed to keep the students contained in their walls.

Our escape is interrupted by a loud BANG—the guards must have realized that my sunshine isn't where he is supposed to be. It's too late for them, though. We're standing in front of the exit, the door loom over us.

Once through the doors, it's a short trip to the chain link fence surrounding the property. The fence I have never seen the other side of.

My sunshine places a hand on my cheek and turns me to face him before we leave.

"You cannot die," he commands in a low voice. His hand shifts a bit, trying to avoid when I assume are some disgusting pits of boiling skin on my face.

"Icarus. Promise me. Promise me that you will not die." Why does it sound like he's saying goodbye?

"You're coming with me." There is a flash of something—pity, my mind supplies—in his eyes before he looks down the hall.

"You are coming with me, right? I can't do this without you." At this point, I am begging him to answer and say that he won't abandon me.

He doesn't respond, instead tensing before turning to open the doors. There are footsteps echoing down the hall. We don't have long before the guards catch up to us.

It will be quicker for him to get away without me, I am slowing him down. Just as I go to say that he turns and slides his arm under my knees, picking me up and running.

"Please don't leave me alone," I whisper, wrapping my arms securely around his neck. If I cannot die, then he needs to be there with me. He needs to make it out because I don't think I can survive without my own personal sunlight to keep me sane.

"Birdie," his voice trails off. He finally looks down at me, his eyebrows pinch together and his lips set in a frown. Tension thickens the air between us.

My eyes drift to his throat where his throat bobs. His mouth opens as if he wants to respond before a shout cuts him off.

"There they are!"

The guards found them. My sunshine's golden eyes widen, his mouth snaps shut as he sprints the rest of the way across the lawn.

How did the guards find us so quickly? That building is massive, it should have taken them longer. Are we going to make it out? Thoughts race through my brain and distract me.

"Icarus!" My sunshine's voice snaps me back to the situation at hand. We've stopped moving, I'm sitting on the ground next to the fence.

"We're here. I need you to climb this fence, okay? Once you get over the fence you have to run. Can you do that?"

My mind is still reeling from the sheer amount of information this situation has dumped on me, but those instructions I can understand. I nod. Yeah, I can run. We can run.

The guards are getting closer, close enough that I can hear the rustling fabric of their uniforms. My sunshine helps me stand and grab onto the fence. Thank the Gods that adrenaline exists, it's the only reason I am able to pull myself up the chain links.

With his help, I am able to reach for the top of the fence. It takes me a moment, but once I get a good grip on the bar I begin to pull myself up.

As soon as I flung my leg over the fence I heard a pained yelp. I stabilize myself where I sit and look back to the ground, where I expect to see my sunshine climbing up after me. Instead I find a nightmare come to life.

He's fighting the guards. My sunshine is fighting the guards that are twice his size and losing. He's hurt, down on one knee. That must be why he cried out, knee injuries are a bitch.

And yet he's fighting. He can't move much from where he's kneeling, but he is still holding back the guards. Giving me time to get out.

But I can't leave him. He is supposed to come with me, make sure that I get out of here safe and stay alive. He can't do that if he's fighting the guards.

"Go, Icarus! Run and never look back!" I can't. I can't just leave without him. I need to get down there and help him. I need to—

"RUN YOU IDIOT!"

I never was good at disobeying orders. Even if I want to do nothing more than stay and help him, I have to leave. Tears start to well in my eyes as I swing my other leg over the fence. Climbing down isn't an option with my vision blurred like it is so I jump. It's going to hurt like a motherfucker when I wake up tomorrow, but right now the only thing I can feel is the strain in my throat from the tears that want to be spilled.

Blood drips a path down my leg. I must have gotten caught on a stray wire in the fence. I want to look back so bad, but I have to keep going. I can't stop now or they'll catch me and my chance at escape will be gone. All the pain that my sunshine has gone through will have been for nothing if I am caught out here.

I need to run. I need to get into the trees. They aren't that far away; I just need to run to them. The guards will lose sight of me in the forest then I can disappear.

Just before I get to the forest, I hear another shout from my sunshine. This one is much less pained and I don't know if that is a good thing or not.

"I will find you again! I will find you out there!"

I believe him. He will find me, I just have to make it out. I have to get out of here and stay alive. Then my sunshine will make it out and find me and we will be together once again.

With my hopes high I dart into the woods. I can't look back, I don't know if the guards are following me or not. I just have to make it out...

THE ROOFTOP

ICARUS STARTLES INTO CONSCIOUSNESS, quickly sitting up as he struggles to catch his breath. He raises his trembling hands to his face, covering his eyes and pressing against his temples. The only sound he can hear is his own shuddering breaths and the distant sound of cars on the streets outside.

Gods, he hates that dream. Well, it's more of a nightmare at this point. He hates that nightmare, hates the reminder of where he came from and who he left behind. Icarus takes in a heaving breath as he slides his hands down his face.

The worst part about waking up like that, in his opinion, is the sweat. Now that he's starting to calm down, he can feel how his sheets are soaked with it. The kind that'll make you change your clothes to escape just how uncomfortable and upset you are. His skin starts to prickle from discomfort as the damp sheets cool.

He wastes no time in throwing his legs over the side of the bed. The cold floor beneath his feet helps to wake him up a bit. Taking a moment to fully disentangle his mind from the nightmare that has been plaguing him, he stands up and makes his way to the closet. When he gets there, he peels off the large shirt that he had worn to bed. It clings to his figure and feels gross and sticky.

He stands there for a moment, trying to think of what he should put on. *Gods*, he thinks, *it's too early for this shit*. Deciding to just grab the nearest hoodie—city weather be damned—he turns around and heads towards the kitchen.

If Icarus is going to stay awake—and he is going to stay up, he isn't going to go through that nightmare again—then he's going to need some caffeine. He yawns as he reaches across the kitchen counter to grab an energy drink. He cracks it open and takes a mouthful of the delicious carbonated energy in the can. It's exactly what he needs right now.

Taking a moment to indulge in the sweet taste of the drink, he thinks over the nightmare. He hasn't had that particular nightmare in a while, so why now? Why—after ten years—is he being haunted by that night all over again?

Fuck all of this. Icarus needs some fresh air. He pushes himself away from the counter and towards the front door, briefly stopping to consider putting on pants and shoes. He chuckles, he's just going up to the roof. No need to get dressed to the nines for that.

Icarus steps into the hallway and pulls his door closed before shoving his hands in the pocket of his hoodie and heading towards the stairs. His apartment is on the top floor of the run-down building, he only has to go up a single flight to reach the door to the rooftop. He turns the handle and tries to open the door quietly, but it has a mind of its own and slams against the brick wall. One of these days Icarus is going to bring something to cushion the wall so it isn't so loud.

It's a beautiful night out. The stars are as visible as they can be in the city—that is, to say, not very visible—and there isn't a cloud in sight. There's a nice breeze keeping the hot and humid air moving. He knows shouldn't be wearing a hoodie in this weather. Especially after having to change out of one sweat-soaked clothing item, but he needs the comfort and sense of calm that the hoodie gives him.

"I will find you again, my ass," he mocks. "It's been ten whole years and I haven't seen hide nor hair of the bastard." It's not like Icarus misses him or anything, with his infectious laughter and ability to light up any room he was in... Okay, maybe he does miss the man just a bit.

But it's been ten long years. Icarus is a different person now, someone his sunshine wouldn't recognize. He has different aspirations and goals. He can't keep waiting around.

Icarus takes another swig of the energy drink as he walks to the edge of the roof. Standing up here—alone—he feels free. He feels like he can do anything, like he can make the world bend to his will.

Who knows, maybe he can...

Icarus lets his gaze sweep out over the sleeping city beneath him before sitting down on the ledge of the roof. The best part of this particular apartment building is that it is old. Granted, the dust and decay aren't great, but the rooftop access and lack of safety rails more than make up for it. Icarus just wants to be able to sit on the ledge, dangling his feet 20 stories over the roads below him. Is that too much to ask?

He's happy to be back in this building, even with how decrepit it is. This place is the closest thing he has to a home. He had to leave for a couple months thanks to someone recognizing him in a local shop, but he's finally back.

It's perfect timing too, from what he's heard on the streets. It seems like there is all kinds of new information for him to find. Citizens who have first-hand encounters with the Elysians, new Elysians coming out on the scene, and new gossip in his favorite tattoo parlor. He hasn't had the chance to stop in yet, but apparently one of the clients with loose lips had a run-in with a bigwig that went south. That's amazing news for Icarus. If random people on the streets are starting to see the Elysians for what they are, it makes it much easier for him to get the information he needs to bring them down for good.

The fresh air is much needed tonight and with the prospect of having a way to move his plan forward Icarus is in high hopes. He doesn't need anything dragging down his mood, much less a memory of a boy he used to know. He raises his hand to idly trace the scar on his cheek. The one that the boy was so careful not to touch before. He knows why; even now with years of healing it looks disgusting. The skin is rough and ragged even if it doesn't hurt anymore.

Icarus is snapped out of his thoughts by the sound of the roof door banging against the brick wall. Dropping his hand, he quickly turns and looks at the stairwell. He is not prepared to see another human being, didn't anticipate anyone else coming out onto the roof at this hour.

The person standing in the doorway doesn't look like they would hurt him, so at least there's that. Well, by society's standard they look like they might hurt him. But being as much of a social outcast as he is, Icarus can recognize when someone is mean and when they just like the edgier aesthetics. This person doesn't look mean, they just happen to have a mohawk, tattoos, and piercings. Not too dissimilar to Icarus himself.

"Sorry," they say, "I didn't think anyone would be up here at this time of night. It's usually just me and the stars up here."

"Don't let me stop you, then." It won't hurt to have some company. It's not like Icarus has much of a social life, having to stay on the run from ATLAS and all.

"Can't sleep?" they ask, sitting down on the edge of the roof next to him. Their sock clad feet hang over the edge, swinging lightly in the breeze.

"Neither can you, it seems." Who is this person? He hasn't seen them around the building before. He's sure he would have noticed and remembered someone like them. They seem almost ethereal, like they aren't meant to walk amongst mere mortals like him.

"I don't think I've seen you around here sweetheart, did ya just move in?" Even their voice, light and airy, holds an air of grace to it. It's a voice that seems to know all. As if they would know when Icarus lied or bent the truth, even though there was no way that anyone besides Icarus knew his story.

As if they can hear the thoughts going through his head, they turn to look at him. If their voice is hard to hold the truth from, it is damn near impossible with their eyes. They seem to pin Icarus in place, almost looking through him into the very depths of his soul.

Realizing he has yet to answer, Icarus looks away from the stranger and says, "I guess you could say that. I've had the place for a while, but I just moved back to the area." This isn't a lie, per se, but he's not about to tell a stranger that he was on the run and couldn't stay in one area for too long.

"Same goes for you, though. I haven't seen you in the halls since I've gotten back."

"I guess that's fair. Trying to stay hidden from an almost omnipresent government does tend to make you a bit of a shut in." A small laugh follows their words. The melodic sound drifts off, mixing with the sounds of the sleeping city.

Silence falls over them as they sit on the roof, enjoying each other's quiet company. It's too early for the birds to start their morning calls. That is, if there are any in the city. Icarus has never seen one, but he remembers a time when facts about the winged creatures became a staple in his everyday conversations. His sunshine had always loved them.

Instead, the sounds of cars driving down the streets and the nightlife going about their business—both human and machine—fill the air. When Icarus looks down to the streets he can see the light trails of the cars zooming past and the ant sized people going about their nightly business.

It doesn't take long, though, for Icarus to become interested in what the stranger had said. They had mentioned that they were on the run from the government as well, but why did they tell him this? They don't know each other, so why?

Icarus debates how to bring this up. *If* he should bring it up. It isn't his place to needle this unknown person to telling him their life story, but they had brought it up. Deciding to do something before he chickens out, he settles on, "Hey... Can I ask you something personal?"

The question is so quiet that he thought they might not be able to hear him over the idle sounds wafting up from the streets. He supposes that was how the universe would decide whether the question should be asked: whether they heard it or not.

It seems that they did hear it, as they responded with a light, "Sure kid, what's up?" It almost sounds like they knew what the question would be.

As if they were just waiting for Icarus to make the first move and ask, "Why are you running from the government?" The air between the two falls silent, like a bubble had formed around them and cut off the sounds of the roadways below. Even the air stops flowing, if the stranger's hair coming to a rest over their shoulder is any indication. Icarus looks up for a brief moment, meeting their gaze before looking away as they answer.

"I suppose I could ask the same of you, huh stranger." Icarus' breath catches in his throat at the answer. How does this person that he had never met before know that he is also running from the government? Is he that obvious?

He's about to ask when the stranger says, "Relax, kid. Us outcasts have to be able to judge who we're safe with. Your whole being screams 'I have an issue with authority'. It's kinda hard to think you're anything but an outcast like me."

Icarus lets out the breath he's holding. He is just that obvious, but only to people like him. He can live with that.

"To answer your question: it's because I know too much." That hits close to home for Icarus. If you're too smart in this world, you become a target. They don't want you learning their secrets, they'd rather have mindlessly loyal dogs to do their work. It didn't take him long to figure out that his curiosity was the reason why Daedalus wanted him dead all those years ago. Icarus likes to learn, and that's not what ATLAS is looking for in candidates for the Elysian Program.

"They really don't like it when you're privy to their secrets, huh?" Icarus adds, thinking back to the nightmare that led him to the roof in the first place. He would say that it was a coincidence that dreaming of the reason he was on the run led to him talking to a stranger about why they were on the run. But there's one universal constant that he still believes in: There is no such thing as a coincidence.

No, the universe isn't kind enough to allow for coincidences. If something seems too good to be true, it is. People don't just show up, and they aren't just kind right off the bat. No, that only happens when they are trying to get information from you.

"You know," he starts, "I'm going to be really sad when I find out that you were sent by ATLAS to locate me." The corner of Icarus' lip tugs down as he says it. He really hopes that isn't the case, but one could never be too sure. It would be in the government's niche to send such an ethereal being to do their dirty work. Someone who could get through years of carefully crafted and erected mental walls that stood between the outside world and his mind.

"Oh? What an honor! And here I thought I was just a stranger to you," they respond lightly.

Icarus grins at this. They are a stranger to him. They quite literally just met on this rooftop. And yet, he feels like he could talk to them. Not necessarily trust, as trust is something that he struggles with, but he feels as though one day he would be able to trust this person. And boy, does that thought scare him.

He's been alone for so long, just surviving as best as he can. It's easier that way. Icarus has a hard time understanding people, so why should he be around them? That just leads to misunderstandings and hurt feelings.

But maybe, just maybe, it has been long enough. Maybe he has been through enough on his own. Maybe he wouldn't mind the company this time around. He doesn't have to trust them. At least, not yet. He can just enjoy this run-in on the roof of an old building in the middle of the night. Maybe he can even make a friend if they saw each other again.

He smiles as he thinks about these possibilities. Maybe this time, he can allow someone into his life without having to punish himself for leaving them behind. "You're right. But it'd still suck if the first real person I've talked to in ten years were a narc."

Letting out a half-hearted chuckle, he looks down towards the streets below. There aren't many people out at this time of night.

Just the occasional drunk person stumbling home from the bar, really. It's nice, being able to take in the city while it sleeps.

There's no societal expectation when facing the sleeping city. No need to put on a mask to get through the day. No need to even put on pants! He is allowed to take it all in without the judgment of everyday folks.

He can just sit up here on the rooftop of an old apartment building and exist. No repercussions or needing to run, to hide. Just existing for once in his life. Maybe that is why he keeps finding himself up here when he can't sleep.

Even now, with the addition of the stranger, he is still just existing. They don't seem to care either. Hell, even they showed up with no shoes on.

Icarus looks over at the stranger as they stand up, taking their time to stretch after sitting for so long. The crackles and pops that their joints make blend in with the sounds of the waking city below. Icarus can't remember ever having a discussion as peaceful as this one had been. It was a rather nice turn for the night compared to when he first woke up.

Before turning to leave the rooftop, they look over the city. To their left, the first rays of morning sunlight were beginning to creep over the city skyline. While businessmen and government officials alike are waking, they say, "My name's Andromeda. I have a feeling we'll be talking again soon."

Icarus doesn't look away from the sunrise as he hears their footsteps receding. He doesn't look away even as the door to the rooftop slams shut. As he is taking in the breathtaking scene, he can't help but think about the interaction he just had with the stranger—*Andromeda*—again. It looks like things are about to get very interesting from here on out.

Even as the logical part of his brain is telling him that he needs to keep his distance from this new variable in his life, he can't help but want to run into them again. If he can get a feel for them and whether he can trust them, he would be set. After all, the hardest part of his plan is doing it alone.

He is going to need someone there to be his rational thought, to stop him from doing anything too out of the box. He is going to need someone who makes sure that he comes back in one piece. Even though he was trying to forget the boy in his nightmare, Icarus still made him a promise to stay alive. And he is going to need someone to keep him accountable with that.

There's no reason to think too hard about it right now, though. Icarus still has to figure them out. How did a stranger who was also on the run from the government end up in the same building as him? There are too many coincidences that had popped up in their conversation for Icarus to just blindly leap into trusting them. He needs to figure out how they got here and how they found him before he can do that.

After taking one last look at the people starting their daily routines on the street below, Icarus stands up and turns to head back inside. Back to the grind of finding information about the Elysians. Back into the cacophony of madness that he has made his life into since leaving the academy that day.

THE BREAK IN

THE MUFFLED SOUND OF his neighbors waking up fills the quiet hallway as Icarus makes his way inside. The whirring of blenders and the shuffling of tired feet leak through the paper-thin walls, the heavenly smell of breakfast being made complements it.

Briefly closing his eyes, Icarus takes a deep breath. He could go for some real food right about now. *Unfortunate.* He will have to make do with whatever leftovers are in the fridge. *If* he has any leftovers in the fridge, that is. It has been a hot minute since he's gone grocery shopping, what with having to leave the city for a time.

Icarus loses himself in his thoughts, imagines a delectable home cooked meal waiting for him just inside his apartment. He pictures himself pushing open the door he left ajar and being greeted with a banquet of food: fluffy pancakes drenched in sticky-sweet syrup, crispy potatoes, creamy yogurt with fresh berries mixed in, just a vast display of every food he had been craving for the past months. He nearly starts salivating at the thought.

...Wait. The door he left ajar? Icarus was sure that he had closed the door before heading up to the rooftop after his nightmare. His hand stills mere inches away from the wooden door, where he was about to push it open.

He racks his brain, trying to sort through the haze of the events that occurred that morning. *Woke up, panicked, grabbed a drink, left, closed the door, said fuck it about locking the door, went to the r oof.* Yeah, he was sure that he had not left his door open.

He hadn't locked the door, but it was the middle of the night; no one else in the building should have been awake! Well, that new person—*Andromeda*—was awake, but no one on this floor is ever awake that early. No one should have known that he had left the door unlocked, no one.

So why is his door ajar?

Something is wrong, he can feel that truth sinking into the pit of his stomach. Of course this had to happen today, the day that he had been so out of sorts that he had not grabbed his blades before leaving. This was the first time in years that Icarus had left himself vulnerable, and of course it was after that *damn nightmare*.

It's not like he can stand here and think about it, though. At this point, if anyone was still in his apartment, they would know that he was standing outside. Then again, if there was someone in there, they would have tried to attack him by now. There is no target easier than one standing idly with no weapons.

Fuck, no matter how he cuts it, Icarus is in a bad position.

Accepting that he doesn't have much choice in the matter, Icarus pushes the door open. He scans the entryway: his posters on the wall are still there, the coat rack is still empty, there are no signs of damage, the kitchen looks the same as he had left it, and *oh*—the bureau.

Stepping through the threshold, Icarus makes his way towards the repurposed entertainment center that sits in his entryway. His switchblade should be in the top drawer, that's where he puts it every time he enters his apartment.

Icarus grabs the blade, feels the comfortable weight settle in his palm as he moves further into the apartment.

From here, he can see around the corner into the living room: empty. He quickly checks the bathroom to his right then ducks into the spare bedroom. There's nothing, no one hiding under the bed or in the closet, no sign that anyone had been in the room.

His left eye twitches as he crosses the living room to check his bedroom. Walking up to the door, Icarus mulls over the situation.

There's no telling what he'll find in his bedroom, he only hopes that it will be nothing.

The door opens, pushed forward as Icarus peeks through the frame. There's his bed, his dresser, his chair covered with clean laundry that he had yet to put away. Everything is the same as it was when he left that morning.

Glancing under the bed reveals nothing, just some stray socks and an abundance of dust. He stands up and moves towards the connected bathroom. *Nothing.*

Icarus is puzzled as he steps back out of the bathroom and into his bedroom. His eyes scan the room one final time, this time landing on a piece of paper sitting on his bed—half tucked under a blanket and not easily visible from the entrance.

He picks it up before leaving the room. He didn't need to check the kitchen on his way in since it is connected to the living room, but now that he knows there's no intruder he should. First, though, he needs to close and lock the door. He had left it open when he entered in case there was an intruder present. Now, though, he can close up.

A pause, hand hovering over the locked deadbolt. All of the adrenaline Icarus is running on is starting to dissipate. *God, he's exhausted.*

Turning, he runs a hand over his face. Will he ever get a moment of peace? That's all that he wants at this point as he walks back into the kitchen to find an envelope sitting on the counter.

He stands there a moment, staring at the unassuming manila envelope. Waiting for it to become something more than what it is, feeling as if the other shoe will inevitably drop if he touched the damn thing. His eyes scour every square inch of the envelope, desperately searching for anything that can tip him off as to what it contained.

There is nothing. No writing, no blemishes, nothing. It is just a manila envelope. *A manila envelope that someone broke in to put on the counter,* his mind supplies. He will have to actually open it and see what's inside, gut feeling of impending doom be damned.

Flipping over the envelope, Icarus is faced with his own name in a scrawling script. The gut feeling returns with a vengeance. Clearly, the person who left the envelope knows that Icarus lives here. That's a problem.

He doesn't know what else he could do to cover his tracks. He lays low, doesn't cause a scene, follows the laws as best as he can. He had even left a few months back because someone recognized him in a local shop! There should be no trace of him in this city, he has been so careful.

And yet, someone knows he lives here. Someone broke in just to leave an envelope with his name on it, taunting him. Telling him he isn't safe here.

He sets the piece of paper from his bedroom down with the envelope, deciding to deal with them later.

Right now all Icarus wants is to relax, to feel the stress of this whole situation melt away. He double checks the lock on the front door—it's still locked, exactly in the same position as he had left it.

He sighs in relief as he turns around, heading back into the bedroom. As the adrenaline fades it is replaced by a pounding headache. He shakes his arms out, trying to dislodge the tired ache from his bones. When that doesn't work, he resolves to at least try and be a functional human being by taking a shower.

As he passes his bed, he lifts the hem of his hoodie over his head and flings the fabric onto the mattress. He had only worn the hoodie for a bit on the roof, it should be fine to keep out of the laundry. He stretches, feeling his back pop and crack as he groans.

The lights in the bathroom are still on from his check earlier, the harsh fluorescence sends a wave of nausea through him. His eyes squeeze shut as Icarus blindly gropes the cold tile wall for the light switch.

As the lights switch off, he cracks his eyes open and looks in the mirror. There are signs of exhaustion all over his face, the heavy purple bags under his eyes and the crinkle of tension between his eyebrows give it away. *Gods, I look like shit.*

He can't stand to look at himself any longer, instead opting to turn on the shower and step in.

The water is warm as it slides down his body. The rivulets wash away his worries and stress as they track their path down past his collarbones, his top surgery scars, his tattoos.

Icarus leans forward into the overhead stream of water, letting it run down over his head and soak his hair. The weight is almost uncomfortable, his hair has grown considerably in the months that he was gone. He hadn't noticed until the strands were heavy with water. *I'll need to cut it soon*, he thinks as he washes himself.

Before long, Icarus runs out of excuses to stay under the warm water. After stepping out of the shower and drying himself off in the humid air of the bathroom, he heads to the closet to throw on some clothes.

He always hates having to decide what to wear. If he could, Icarus would wear the same hoodie and shorts everyday. Unfortunately, he does have to go out in public, which requires real clothes. And it is too damn hot in the city to wear a hoodie out of the air conditioning.

Grabbing a pair of black jeans and a cut-off tank, Icarus thinks about what he's going to do that day. After the scare of his apartment being broken into, he doesn't think he'll be able to sleep. He should look at that manila envelope and piece of paper resting on his kitchen counter, but he just doesn't want to. He needs to do something to keep him busy, keep him awake.

I can try and find leads, he thinks. Now that Icarus is back in the city, he can start digging into the leads on the Elysians that he had before leaving or even try to find new ones.

Yeah, maybe that's what he will do. Spend the day hitting up the areas he knew would hold rumors and people who have seen too much. Then, he can end the day at the bar, grab a drink or two to help soothe him into a restless night of sleep.

Yeah, that sounds like a good idea.

The sun is fully up and glaringly bright as he walks out of the bedroom into the living room. Icarus squints from the pain of the harsh light, quickly moving to close the blackout curtains he has hanging in front of the glass sliding doors.

He won't be able to do anything with this headache, won't be able to even think clearly once he leaves the apartment. Icarus decides to fuck it and take a pain pill and some sleep aids before sitting down on the big comfortable chair in his living room, staring across the room to where he can see the manila envelope resting on the counter.

If he can't go out and get information, then he should at least look at what's in it. His legs don't seem to get the memo, though, as he stays firmly planted in the comfortable plush of the chair. He can feel himself sink into the inky abyss of sleep in the warmth and comfort of his seat.

Icarus is so fucking exhausted. Maybe, just maybe, he should take a nap.

His eyes slowly close as his consciousness begins to fade. He's going to be in pain when he wakes up, the position he's sitting in and the jeans he's wearing will make sure of it. But none of that matters as he pulls the closest blanket over his body and loses the battle with sleep.

THE DREAM

"I FOUND YOU!"

I can't help but smile as the kid yells from the doorway. I giggle as I respond, "You sure did kiddo! Good job!"

He is getting good at this, though I still like to make it easy for him to find me. Today I hid myself in a janitorial closet, or what would be a janitorial closet if it wasn't completely empty and unused. We don't want the kid getting lost in the halls of the Academy, after all.

I'm glad I get to have moments like this. I don't know how it happened, but the kid latched onto me as soon as he saw me that day. Now, I'm essentially a glorified babysitter. It beats being stuck in classes, though.

"We've been playing this for a while, what d'ya say we take a break and get some lunch?" I ask the small bundle of energy in front of me.

He nods, his blond locks bobbing with the movement. His hair is starting to get long, the dean is going to make him cut it soon. A shame really, the soft locks are something that I love playing with and braiding.

I guess the nod is as good of an answer as I'm going to get. As I stand up, I lean over to pick the kid up. He sprints away from me, stopping a good distance down the hall before turning to run back towards me. I brace myself as he launches his full weight onto my back.

I stumble but manage to catch myself with a hand on the wall next to me. It's still enough to make the little gremlin start laughing, though. Gods, this kid is going to be the death of me.

As I stabilize myself, I reach back to grab the little shit's legs. Have to make sure he's not going anywhere. Not that he needs my help to keep from falling with the absolute death grip he has around my neck right now.

I can't breathe, but before I can do anything to get him to loosen his hold a voice calls out from down the hall.

"Stop choking him, Achilles. He can't carry ya if he's dead!"

I turn around—a smile already growing on my face—to see my sunshine walking towards us. I wasn't expecting to see him today, what with classes and training and all. I'm not going to complain, though. I will take any moment with my own personal source of sunlight that I can.

The good mood doesn't last, however, as he leans to whisper in my ear. "I'm taking over looking after the kid. Daedalus wants to see you."

The smile falls off my face at the words. What do they want with me today? I'm not supposed to train, and I have been excused from class to watch Achilles.

"Okay, and?" I whisper back. That man can wait, I would much rather go to lunch than deal with his bullshit.

"Birdie, you can't ignore this. Nyx wants you there too."

"Well, why didn't you say that?" He shoots a look at me, silently judging me for my disregard of the summons when they came from Daedalus. I roll my eyes, leaning away from his warmth to break the news to the kid in my arms.

"Hey kiddo," I say, maneuvering Achilles so that I am holding him in front of me. I reach up to tuck a stray strand of hair behind his ear. "I have to go talk to some people. Apollon is gonna take you to lunch today, okay?"

Uh-oh, he does not look happy at that. "I'll be right back! I won't take long! Just go with Apollon for now and before you know it, I'll be there. I promise."

39

I hate making false promises, but it's the only way to get the kid to go with my sunshine. I will just have to deal with the repercussions later, after I talk to Nyx and Daedalus. Gods, I wish I knew what they wanted.

The kid takes a moment to think about what I said before nodding and detaching himself from my body. After I set him down, he walks over to Apollon, who has his arms out ready to pick him up. Achilles stands there, judging the arms that are waiting before letting out a huff and crossing his arms. He then turns to walk down the hall towards the cafeteria, not even waiting to make sure Apollon is following him.

I shoot an apologetic look towards my sunshine, patting his shoulder and mouthing a quick 'good luck' before turning and walking the other way. I shove my hands into the pockets of my pants as I make my way to the training room. That is the only place we are allowed to go as students besides our rooms and the classrooms, so they must want to meet me there.

Every step I take towards that room makes me more nervous. Why do they want to see me right now? This is highly unusual of them. The sound of my boots hitting the floor accompanies my thoughts as I make my way through the winding corridors. Before I know it, I'm rounding the corner to see two large arched doorways before me.

They don't like it when we are even a second late, so I don't have much time to dawdle or worry about what might be awaiting me.

Well, here goes nothing, I think as I open the large wooden doors in front of me.

Whatever I was expecting, it was not Nyx berating Daedalus. Seeing the tall and otherworldly woman demeaning and belittling someone was not something I thought I would ever see. I have always seen her as graceful and elegant, and this is anything but. Her face is sharp and pointed as she spits insults down at my father. Though, it does feel good to see Daedalus get his comeuppance. He deserves to be knocked down a peg.

As the door slams closed behind me, Nyx straightens herself and turns to look at me.

"Child," she says as if she was not just yelling, "thank you for coming so quickly." I don't know what they were arguing about, but for Nyx to lose her composure like that it must have been something serious. But it's not my place to know.

I bow my head out of respect for her as I say, "Of course, ma'am. I came as quickly as I could." I don't have much of a choice in being here, but I greatly respect her and would never be so rude as to ignore her summons.

Daedalus, on the other hand... Well, I push the rules as much as I can when it comes to him.

Speaking of the Devil, he seems to finally compose himself enough to step forward, taking his place next to Nyx. I look up at him as he clears his throat, trying to find his voice. After a moment, he growls out a simple, "Training. Do your best."

I let out a sigh, I was really looking forward to not having training today. But it's not like I can say no. I nod once in acknowledgment before I turn and make my way to the wall where the weapons are resting. I am just a few steps away when I hear rustling and the sound of a flamethrower heating up. I barely have time to think before I feel the searing heat tickle the back of my neck. Why is he already attacking? I haven't even grabbed any weapons yet. He shouldn't be attacking!

I duck and roll away to the side, barely missing another lick of flame sent my way. Shit, I don't know what to do. I can't get close enough for a bare-handed attack with him using the flamethrower, but I don't have any weapons on me. I have to get a weapon.

When the flame dies down, I decide to make a dash for the wall. I was only a few steps away from it before I rolled, and now I just need to get there. Lady Luck is not on my side today, as I am knocked over by Daedalus. He has come to stand between me and my only chance at winning.

He points the flamethrower at my face. Surely, he'd call it here and let me get a blade so we can properly train, right?

Time slows to a crawl as I hear flint striking from within the flamethrower. I look up at Daedalus, up at my father, with my eyes blown wide. What is he doing? I am prone and clearly not going to win this battle. That doesn't seem to matter as the flames reached my face, hot and burning. I can feel the fine hairs on my face catch on fire, my skin blistering and boiling as the flames quickly spread to my clothes and my hair. I scream.

What have I done to deserve this?

What did I do wrong?

The pain is too much to bear as I slip into unconsciousness.

THAT NIGHT

ICARUS JOLTS AWAKE WITH a cry, tears streaming down his face. He hates crying, hates that he can cry oh-so easily when he has a nightmare about his father. He didn't cry when he dreamed about leaving his sunshine, why is this one different?

He gets up from the chair as he wipes away stray tears, taking a moment to stretch. His neck and back hurt from sleeping in the chair and as he reaches up he can hear his joints crack.

"What I wouldn't give for one night of goddamned peace," he mutters. The dim red light coming in through the windows lets him know that he slept longer than expected. It would be a good time to head to the bar. His nap doesn't leave any time to scout out other sources of information, those will need to be visited at a later time.

He grabs the clothes draped over the arm of the chair and heads to the bathroom to freshen up. The cold water feels amazing as he washes his face before heading back out to the living room. On his way through the bedroom, Icarus grabs his flannel to tie around his waist and a pair of boots.

Icarus sees the manila envelope sitting on the kitchen counter as he passes the island. *Those*, he thinks, *are a problem for future me*.

He reaches over them to grab an energy drink before heading out. Should he be drinking a highly caffeinated energy drink before going to the bar? No, but that isn't going to stop him from doing so. He can barely function without the energy, symptoms of caffeine addiction rule his life and at this point it is easier to just give in to them and drink the overly sweet drinks.

The crack of the can opening is a welcome sound as Icarus turns to face the fridge. The sweet taste of artificial sugar coats his mouth as he decides what he wants to eat.

The fridge is just as bare as it had been earlier. A trip to the grocery store will need to happen, soon. For now, he grabs some leftover pizza and ranch. There are only two pieces left, but that's more than enough knowing that he is going to be at the bar. If he really needs anything more than that then he can buy it there.

On his way out the door, Icarus grabs his blades. With every-thing that has happened recently, he doesn't feel comfortable leaving without them.

His eyes scour what's visible of the apartment one last time before closing and locking the door. With any luck, the door will remain locked while he's out and he will return to an empty and untouched apartment.

The hallway is void of any signs of life. No sounds of people shuffling in their homes, no smells of food being cooked, nothing. Icarus makes his way towards the elevator at the end of the hall, carefully stepping over the oddly shaped stains that litter the carpet. He can barely see them under the shitty fluorescent lights, but he *knows*. They've been there for as long as he has lived in this building and, to be quite frank, he doesn't want to know what they might be from.

One of the stains sits as an obstacle before the elevator spanning from one wall to the other. It's one of the reasons he so rarely used the death trap other than the fact that it was so rickety and could not possibly be held to safety standards.

Given the day Icarus has had so far, though, he'd rather risk his life in the rickety metal contraption than deal with ten flights of stairs. It would be just his luck to fall and tumble down the concrete stairwell. He is already in pain, he does not need to add that to it.

After pressing the button to call the elevator, he contemplates which bar he wants to go to. There are only a handful in the area that will let him in with no state-issued ID and even fewer that don't host Elysian regulars. The ding of the elevator arriving briefly distracts him as he steps into the metal coffin and presses the button for the lobby.

If he's being honest with himself, Icarus does not want to walk all the way across the city. His muscles are already stiff and screaming from the nap he took, a long walk is the last thing he needs.

That leaves the bar around the corner. Everything else is too far away. At least that bar is small, it's a hole-in-the-wall type shop that not many people frequent. The bar is about a block's distance from his building. It's the first place he found in the city that would serve him without an ID. Good news, seeing as he hasn't had one since his escape from the Academy.

Not that he hasn't tried to get his hands on one, but there is always an issue with the paperwork whenever he makes time to go to the BMV. The last time he was in, he asked the kind lady behind the counter and all she could tell him was that they can't issue identification to the dead. He isn't sure what that means, since he's fairly certain that he is very much alive.

But that's fine. Icarus shouldn't have a paper trail anyways if he wants to keep out of the eye of ATLAS. It hasn't been too much of a detriment in his life thanks to his ties to former Elysians. He can get pretty much anything he wants if he goes to the right person, and this bar is no exception to that.

He's been coming here for a few years at this point. He remembers being so scared the first time he came here. It's a small enough joint that they don't have a bouncer so he had no trouble getting in, but he would have to show ID to the bartender. When he sat down, though, they didn't question him and just served him. A perk of having body modifications, he supposes. The galaxy of scars, piercings, and tattoos adorning his body give credence to the idea that he isn't a child.

It doesn't much matter, though. He's just glad that he has a place that he can reliably go. It helps when he needs to release tension and get information, those two go hand-in-hand anymore.

The stench of sweat and alcohol radiates from the building as he approaches. One perk of this place is that there are relatively few flashing lights at any given moment.

It is like he walked into a wall of sound, throngs of people litter the building. Odd given the time. The music is already blaring, playing whatever popular song the last patron to use the jukebox queued.

Icarus squints his eyes, tensing the muscles in his jaw in an attempt to alleviate some pain as he makes his way towards the bar at the back.

There is one seat open at the very end. He makes a beeline for it, passing through the crowd of people without sparing any of them a second glance. It doesn't matter who's here so long as someone talks to him.

A couple people whistle as he passes by, trying to catch his attention. He rolls his eyes and keeps pushing through until he makes it to the open bar stool and sits down.

The bartender looks over and nods before he can even think of flagging him down, giving Icarus some time to glance out over the crowd while he waits for service.

There are a lot of regulars from the area lining the bar, familiar faces that he's glad to see. People he knows will talk to him once they get a bit of liquor in their system.

There's also a lot of underage kids here, someone must have spread the news about the bar again.

It's not surprising in and of itself, but what is interesting is the sheer number of people packed into the room. This place has always been more of an underground shop, it isn't designed to hold so many people.

If this keeps up, Icarus will have to start looking for a new bar to frequent. With an uptick in patrons comes people who could recognize him and his scars, and Icarus cannot have that.

The bartender taps the bar top next to him, dragging Icarus' attention back.

"Hey feathers, want your regular today?" she asks, spoken just loud enough to hear over the blaring music.

Icarus nods and the bartender turns to grab the liquor needed to make the drink. He doesn't know what his regular is, just that it tastes amazing and has alcohol in it. When he first started coming here he didn't know anything about alcohol and left his choice in drink up to the bartender. He doesn't need to know what it's called. He likes it and the bartender knows what it is, that's all that matters.

The drink is set down on the counter in front of him, the glass of the cup clanking against the polished wood. As soon as it touches down, Icarus grabs it and downs it. If he is going to make it through the impending overstimulation, he needs to get some liquid courage in him.

The bartender chuckles as she turns to make another drink, setting a second glass down where the first was just a moment ago. Icarus thanks her as he sets down the empty glass.

He picks up the full glass, sipping at the deliciously sweet drink as he turns to watch the crowd. It's hard to hear anything over the music, the conversations going on around him blend together.

He is straining his hearing trying to pick apart the words, but that only makes them fuzzier. A tap on his shoulder breaks his concentration, drawing his attention to a person standing just a hair's breadth away. It takes a moment to recognize them in the dark, but there is no mistaking the stocky build and long dark hair: his favorite source of information has found him again.

Icarus is at a crossroads. He could blow off his informant and continue the night as he had started it, straining to possibly overhear anything related to the Elysians in the packed bar. Or, he could trade favors like he used to.

Neither option sounds great right now, so he might as well have fun while listening to gossip.

He forces a mask of sultry intrigue into place and grins as he looks up at the informant. "Long time no see, Alkibiades," he purrs, reaching out to play with the fabric of their shirt.

They smirk, tilting their head towards the door behind the counter. Inviting him back for some privacy while they 'talk'.

Alkibiades has ties to the owners of the bar, Icarus had found out when he asked them if there was somewhere nicer for them to enjoy each other when they were still hooking up in the dingy bathroom.

Icarus downs the last of his drink, slamming the glass on the counter and throwing down a twenty before standing up to follow the informant into the back room. As soon as he walks through the door he is pushed up against the wall, a hand coming to rest against the wall by his head while the other goes straight to his hip.

A deep, raspy voice whispers in his ear, "Been a while since I've seen ya, where'd you go?"

Icarus tilts his head back against the wall, opening his neck up for the mouth that does not hesitate to start licking its way up his throat.

"Had to go out of town for a bit. Didn't miss me, did ya?" he taunts. The informant bites down hard, and he can't help but moan at the pain.

The pain lets up as they lick their mark. Icarus bites his lip to stop himself from groaning, from sounding too needy from his months away.

"What are ya here for? What do you need?" they mumble, diving back into the sensitive spot just below his ear.

"Heard rumors 'bout the Elysians." The hand on his hip started moving, lazily sliding down to cup his ass through his jeans. His own hands clumsily reach in front of him, searching for the informant's belt in a hurry to unfasten it. "Thought you might fill me in on what I've missed while I was gone."

The click of the belt coming undone is all Icarus needs to hear before he sinks down to his knees. The hand that is braced against the wall drops to tangle in his hair as Icarus undoes the button on their pants and pulls them down. He licks his lips before looking up, locking eyes with Alkibiades and mouthing the growing bulge in front of him.

The informant lets out a breathy *fuck* before saying, "I'll tell you what I know as I wreck your beautiful mouth."

Icarus hums, agreeing to the exchange as he pulls their underwear down and frees their erection. He runs his tongue along the underside of their shaft, taking his time to pay special attention to the piercings lining it. The informant grunts, tightening their grip in his hair before saying, "Rumor has it a new class just graduated."

He cocks an eyebrow and stops his ministrations, that isn't new information. He wants new information, not a graduation announcement.

The informant pushes his face into their groin, trying to get him to continue as they say, "That's normal, what's not normal is one of the graduates."

Icarus turns his head and kisses the base of their cock, moving a hand from their thigh to stroke them. The pressure in his hair lessens to let him move back and he wastes no time in licking around the head of their cock. He hollows his cheeks and rests the head on his tongue, locking eyes with the informant as they groan.

"There's a pretty blond kid, graduated two years ago and already in the top five. Always had a little redhead following him, though the kid dyed their hair black recently."

Now that is information that Icarus can work with. He rewards Alkibiades by sinking down on their cock, taking the entire length in his mouth. He gags as the tip of their cock hits the back of his throat and starts to pull back. The feeling of the metal piercings dragging along his tongue draws out a moan, the vibrations of which he can feel through his lips.

Alkibiades moans and bucks their hips before tightening their grip in his hair once again to hold him still as they fuck his mouth. Icarus slackens his jaw, opening up wider for them as their thrusts become sloppy. A trail of spit connects his tongue and their cock when they pull out.

Without warning they pull Icarus up, turning him around and pushing him against the wall. They use one of their calloused hands to hold his wrists above his head while the other hand roughly pulls at his jeans, forcing them down over his hips.

Icarus begins to object—this wasn't the deal, he didn't plan on getting fucked tonight—but is cut off as the warm and spit slick cock penetrates him. His cheeks burn as he lets out a rather pathetic and needy moan, it has been so long since he had gotten laid and *Gods* does it feel good.

He succumbs to the heat building inside him, lets himself be fucked without resistance. The slight pain of the piercings entering him with each thrust makes Icarus' mind melt, they feel so good.

The hand holding his wrists lets go, instead moving to wrap around his throat. Alkibiades tightens their grip, restricting his breathing as they pull him flush against their body. The change in angle sends waves of bliss through Icarus, each thrust hits his g-spot making him see stars. He is close and the informant fucking him knows it.

Their free arm wraps around his body, their hand moving to play with his clit. That additional stimulation is enough to send him over the edge, his legs trembling as he tenses and comes with a cry.

The informant lets out a deep and guttural moan at the constriction around their dick. They thrust once, twice more as they come inside him. His vision is swimming as he comes down from his ecstasy to their soft puppy thrusts as they ride their high.

After a moment, they pull out and help Icarus turn around and rest against the wall. Icarus looks up at Alkibiades through tear-stained eyes. The warm trails of cum making their way down his legs are a welcome feeling as he tries to calm his breathing.

"Thanks for the info. Let's do this again sometime."

That is all the informant needs to hear as they pulled their underwear and pants back up, fastening their belt before leaving the room. Icarus is left alone in the back room, giving him privacy while he composes himself. They have done this tango enough times for him to know that no one outside of this room would have heard them, and if they had they wouldn't say anything about it. That doesn't stop him from worrying about it, though, as he struggles to stand up and make his way to the small coffee table on the other side of the room.

Icarus grabs the wet wipes that he had left there the last time they exchanged information, using them to clean himself up before relieving himself in the attached private bathroom. He is not about to get a UTI from an unplanned hookup. No way in hell.

He looks in the mirror, fixing his clothes and running a hand through his hair to make himself look somewhat presentable before walking out of the private room and into the throng of people in the bar.

He starts to push his way through, not stopping at the bar on the way out. He wants to go home, and needs another shower after that. *And a nap,* he thinks as he pushes out into the night time air. Nothing beats a cool breeze after getting fucked in the hot ass back room of a bar.

The walk back to his apartment passes in a blur, his mind too busy rotating the new information to notice the city he is already extremely familiar with. He laments over the fact that his unit is so high up, sometimes he wishes that he had chosen a unit on a lower floor so that he wouldn't have to worry about choosing between the metal death trap and climbing ten flights of stairs.

Sucks, he thinks, *it's safer to be on the top floor. I'll just have to deal.* The elevator dings and he steps through the open doors. He wants nothing more than to be in his apartment, curled up in his comfiest blanket after a nice long shower.

His plans are delayed as the elevator makes a stop on the seventh floor, doors opening and letting the stranger from the rooftop steps into the metal box. Hopefully, they won't talk to him and it'd be an uneventful ride up.

"Oh, hey! You're the guy from the roof last night!" Nope. The universe officially hates him.

He takes in a deep breath before turning to them, managing to cobble on some semblance of a mask as he says, "Hey! That's me!"

The elevator coming to a stop gives Icarus a blissful reprieve as the doors open on the 9th floor and Andromeda makes their way off the elevator. Before the doors close, they turn around and cheerily say, "Have a nice night! Try not to have too much fun." The last thing he sees before the doors fully close is the cheeky wink they throw at him.

It isn't long before the elevator pulls up to the tenth floor, dinging as the doors slide open and Icarus exits into the stained hallway. He hops over the stain directly in front of the elevator and silently makes his way to his door. Thankfully, it is still closed and locked. He lets out a sigh of relief, Icarus isn't sure what he would have done if someone had broken in again.

He unlocks the door and hurries inside, taking off his boots before rushing to the bathroom.

He needs another shower, he feels disgusting and grimy. Icarus' body is on autopilot as he strips and steps under the scalding hot water.

The information he had gotten from his informant is back in the front of his mind. There is no way the 'pretty blond' is who he initially thought it was. No way, it couldn't be.

The more he thinks about it, though... No. It's impossible. Who would the other kid be?

A redhead kid that dyed their hair black. There's a stirring in his gut, telling him that he should know exactly who it is, but no names come to him. As far as he knows, he was the only redhead in the program and it sure as hell was not him.

He steps out of the shower, drying himself off and grabbing a hoodie from his closet to throw on. After making himself comfortable, he goes back out to the kitchen to grab something to drink, he was parched after being active. He grabs a jar from the cupboard and fills it from the tap.

As he downs the water, he turns and leans against the counter. On the island across from him sits the manila envelope and letter from earlier.

Icarus sighs, he really should read those. He pushes himself off the sink, heading back to the bedroom to grab a pair of shorts.

If he is going to stay up and read what was left in his apartment, then he is going to need some coffee.

He grabs the envelope as he heads back out of his apartment, making sure to lock up again as he leaves. There's a café about two blocks away that's open 24/7, he'll go there. Maybe that will give him the motivation he needs to actually read the documents.

He wants to know who broke into his home and why these papers are important enough to track him down to do so. What about him, after living under the nose of the Elysians for ten years, made him a target for a home invasion?

THE COFFEE SHOP

MOONLIGHT FILTERS THROUGH THE front window of the café illuminating the papers Icarus has laid on the table.

They are... confusing to say the least. Multiple pages of sensitive information about the Elysians face him—information that even he had not known. Sure, there is the basic stuff: names of the top Elysians, their ranks, their weapon specialties.

The rest of the information though? That's what's confusing Icarus. Who could possibly compile this kind of information? And why is it in his possession? No one should know who he is, much less know where he lives. So why were these documents left with him?

And who left them? Did they search for him just to break into his apartment and leave a file of classified documents? Were they going to come back for them?

He groans, trying to find words to express his confusion but is met with nothing. There is so much information swimming in the files that his sleep-deprived brain cannot process. He closes his eyes, laying his head onto the cool surface of the table.

The soft sounds of the coffee shop are comforting, the grinding of the coffee beans and the whirring of the steam wands create a beautiful melody that mixes with the ambient music coming from the hidden speakers. The cherry on top of the sensually pleasant atmosphere is the delectable aroma of fresh brewed coffee.

Icarus is nearly lulled to sleep by the white noise. He can take just a quick nap, can't he? Drift off into the clutches of sleep and forget about the mess that his life has become...

He pushes himself off the table, standing up and making his way towards the short line at the other end of the store. If he is going to actually read and attempt to process the files, then he needs to get some caffeine in his system.

"That'll be five forty-five, please!" Icarus sighs, he's too tired for this. Too tired for the shrill voice of the overly friendly barista taking the order of the person in front of him. Too tired to be standing in line, his knee wobbling under the effort of keeping him standing. Too tired to form the words he knows he will need to say when he steps up to the register.

More than ever he wishes he had been able to fall asleep instead of coming here. He knows it would have been a fitful sleep filled with nightmares and memories, though. At least he is being somewhat productive here.

A step forward and Icarus is greeted with, "What can I get started for you, sir?"

"Can I get a mocha please? With caramel?" he forces out. Words are not his friend right now, his ability to speak diminishing with every word forced to take shape. The barista is staring at him, waiting for him to finish his order as he realizes he forgot to tell her a size. He fumbles over the word for the size he wants, his brain not willing to supply the word 'large' so he points to the large cups on the cup rack next to her.

Thankfully, she understands what he means. "Awesome! A large cafe mocha with caramel will be..." her voice drifts off as she types the order into her register. "It'll be six dollars even!"

How can she be so... awake? It's way too early for this. Icarus pulls out his wallet and hands her a ten. He waves the barista off when she tries to give him the change. It isn't much, but he likes to tip service workers whenever he can.

"Thank you, sir! Your drink will be up at the end of the bar in just a moment!"

He nods his thanks before returning to his table. The paper he should be most interested in reading is on top of the others. It sits there, mocking him and his inability to gather the courage to actually read it.

The name at the top, bold and caps locked, was one he thought he'd never see again. One he had naively hoped he would never see again.

DAEDALUS
#1 Ranked Elysian

Icarus' eyes skip over the section labeled 'Family'. He is not ready to see his own lame listed there, not ready to see what notes they have on him. Instead, he looks over the 'Run Ins' section:

SAVED CITIZEN
Friend of a Criminal
2020

- Insulted the civilian
- Pushed to the ground when asking a question
- Caught in the crossfire of an invention

Yeah, that sounds about right for his father. That old man can't seem to hold his tongue, he's always lashing out at everyone including the people he is supposed to be 'saving'. Icarus is a bit concerned about the last bullet point. Getting caught in the crossfire is likely a literal statement on this sheet. It would be a good idea to figure out who this 'Saved Citizen' is, see if he can't talk to them about their experience. At the very least, they'd be able to commiserate over their burn scars from a shared tormentor.

There are two more encounters listed below it, but before Icarus can read them over he is distracted by a flash of gold entering the shop. His eyes shoot up, latching to the new patron standing in line with their back to him. It's normal for bright colors and movement to grab his attention, but this time something feels *different*. He can't put his thumb on it, but his brain is telling him that he should recognize them. It's screaming that he should know who they are.

But for the life of him, he cannot make out who it is. *Whomst? The fuck?* From this distance, he can't see anything that might tell him who they are. Their plain black clothes could be the tell of an Elysian, but that isn't a guarantee. The only truly identifiable trait is the halo of blond curls cascading over their shoulders. *Why do I feel like I know them?*

A shadow falls over the table, dragging his attention away from the captivating patron as a cup of coffee is set down on the table in front of him. He looks up to find Andromeda standing at his side.

"Well, fancy meeting you here stranger!" they chirp, a bright smile gracing their face. They sit down across from Icarus as they continue, "Didn't think I'd see ya again so soon, didja get any sleep?"

Sleep? Had Icarus gotten any sleep? He scoffs, as if he'd be so lucky. The coffee on the table must be his, Andromeda has another cup in their hands. He tentatively reaches for it, bringing the cup closer to cradle it in his hands. The warmth permeating the cardboard sleeve brought comfort to Icarus. He takes a deep breath, relishing the moment of peace as Andromeda moves to take a seat across from him.

The sticky sweet taste of the caramel mocha was exactly what he needs right now, it takes everything in him to not burn his tongue from drinking too fast.

"Hun," their voice is laced with concern, "you look like you're gonna fall asleep at any moment." Andromeda's eyebrows pinch together, a deep crease appearing between them. Icarus keeps his eyes trained on the crease, knowing that they are trying to catch his gaze. He is too tired to maintain eye contact right now, instead he sets his mocha down and picks up the dossier on Daedalus.

Silence stretches between the two, the air growing thick with Andromeda's unspoken plea for him to talk about what's on his mind. Something about them makes him want to talk and that scares him. He doesn't understand why they are such a comforting person, what makes them so easy to be around?

The words don't come to him, though, and he has no way to tell them that. He doesn't know if they know ASL, doesn't know if they'd even understand why he has to switch to the non-verbal language.

He's not reading anything on the page, too focused on his growing anxiety and the mounting tension in the air. Then, like a violin string being plucked, the tension is gone.

"Alright, not gonna talk about your fucked up sleep schedule." He lowers the paper slightly to see them lean back in the booth, sighing before saying, "Got it. Whatchya readin?"

Icarus contemplates whether he should answer that question. It has only been a day since he met them. He has no reason to trust them, especially with documents as damning as these are. *You don't have a reason not to trust them, either.*

His eye twitches as he debates himself on whether to share or not. For their part, Andromeda sits quietly in their seat, letting him come to his own conclusion instead of pressing the issue.

That makes it seem like they are genuinely interested, not trying to get him to reveal information. They are also a runaway. They escaped the clutches of ATLAS just as he had if what they said on the rooftop is true.

Not only that, but they are seemingly friendly and have made it a point to ask about his well being on more than one occasion. He knows he can't take down the Elysian Program on his own, that would be a suicide mission.

They're just one person, right? Icarus can take a chance on them and if it bites him in the ass, then it bites him in the ass. It would be easy enough for him to disappear again, this time with the docket in hand and the knowledge that ATLAS is looking for him.

His eye twitches. He looks over the top of the paper he's holding and he sees Andromeda calmly waiting for his answer. They are leaning back in the booth with their arms up as they braid their mohawk. They smile at him as they tie it off in a ponytail.

He really hopes he's making the right decision. Before he can change his mind, he sets the paper he's holding on the table and slides it towards Andromeda.

Words have not returned to him, but they are unneeded as he watches Andromeda's eyes widen in shock at the information on the page.

"Holy shit," they say under their breath. They look up, locking eyes with Icarus. "Holy shit, how did you get this?"

Icarus struggles to maintain eye contact. It ends up being too much and he turns away, deciding to focus his vision on the necklace they are wearing instead—a choker adorned with a beautifully intricate Celtic knot that he can't help but trace with his eyes.

Now that he's not focusing on the eye contact, he can process what they said. *How did I get this?* He shakes his head, they need to have an actual conversation about that. One that cannot take place in a public café.

He reaches a hand out, silently asking Andromeda to return the document they were reading. There is a nagging voice in his head telling him that he should really just talk to them, tell them to meet him somewhere safer so they could speak freely about the information. It's telling him to just say *something*, but he can't. His eyebrows scrunch together from the effort, his mouth opening in an attempt to give shape to his thoughts.

They hand the paper back and he puts it in the manila folder with the rest of the documents. "No problem! I can imagine you've had a long day," they say, a soft tone of care lacing their words. "Why don't we meet for dinner at your place tonight?"

Relief runs through him at the words and he releases a breath he hadn't realized he was holding. He hopes they can see how grateful he is for their understanding, even if he can't tell them.

He grabs the manila folder and holds it against his chest as he stands up, one hand hovers over the cup of coffee as he mentally debates whether he should take it with him or not.

Before he can decide, Andromeda reaches over and puts their hand around the cup. "Don't worry about the cup, I've got it!" they say, smiling up at him. He's not sure how much more he can handle, tears threaten to spill at the amounts of care they have shown him.

He swallows the lump of emotions in his throat and turns to leave the shop. His eyes scan the room on his way out, searching for that tug of familiarity from earlier. There is nothing, no sign of the blond person at all.

The bell above the door signals his exit as he steps into the crisp morning air. He needs to rest, needs to get himself back in order so he can speak to Andromeda tonight. Sending a look of longing towards his apartment building, he heads further into the city.

He has someone he needs to talk to, someone who will hopefully be able to help Icarus figure out where the manila envelope came from.

The Tattoo Shop

Gravel and glass crunch under Icarus' boots as he makes his way through the dark alleys of The Flats. The neon lights of the shop signs do more to illuminate his path than the rising sun does as he winds his way past piles of trash. Mounds and heaps that may or may not be hiding people who were forced out of their homes by the greed of ATLAS.

The pungent smell of stale beer and dry blood fills the air. Not uncommon for the area, but that doesn't make it any more pleasant. It doesn't matter how many times he walks this path, Icarus still cannot bring himself to get used to the smell.

The shop is in the basement of a run-down hotel. It isn't easy to find, the only sign of life is the shitty neon sign nestled into a cutout in the rough brick. Neon litters the streets of the new city, but it's rare to see this far into Old Town.

The sign makers don't like to travel this far out, they stay in Ohio City as much as they can. It takes a lot of sway to get any of them to cross the river.

This shop is one of two that have a sign. The owner is a big deal, a former Elysian. He retired from active duty a few years back. His name still holds gravity in conversation, even years after his 'disappearance'.

Rumor has it that no one knows how he got his in with the sign maker. Icarus knows better, though. He's well aware of how much his name means, and though he does not use that power often he did use it to get the sign. It's a fitting name, too.

Τελεταί. The Mysteries. Not just an allusion to what surrounds the shop and it's owner, but also a nod to what he deals in. Revelries in the shape of public orgies, maddening rituals, and raucous parties.

Icarus knows first hand what kind of mischief the owner deals in. He shudders as he remembers the time he walked in to get information and was instead met with a cocaine fueled orgy. He had wasted no time in turning on his heel and walking right back out the door. There weren't many things in this world that Icarus vehemently did not want to see, but his tattoo artist's dick is definitely one of them.

Icarus takes a moment to gather himself before opening the door. He sends a small prayer to whatever higher being exists that there's no wave of sweat or weird sounds coming up the stairs before starting to head down the stairs into the small front room.

It feels weird being here with no plan other than to get information. Walking into body modifications with no plan is not something he normally does, but with the lack of sleep he hasn't been able to sit down and think it through.

The hum of the tattoo machine is surprisingly calming. He closes his eyes and lets the monotone hum wash over him and work to loosen the headache mounting at the back of his skull.

With his eyes closed, he walks back towards the private room. He has been here so many times that he knows where everything is, can imagine it as he passes by. With the first few steps he walks past the ratty armchair. Then, the banged-up coffee table. He can even picture the book on the table, where there'd normally be an artist's portfolio; there is instead a raggedy book of Greek Mythology. The paperback book's cover is torn and sticking out at an odd angle as if it is barely being held together by spite. He always found that funny. Spite is what's holding Icarus together, too.

A few more steps and Icarus opens his eyes. The door is cracked open today, he can see the edge of the tattoo bed from where he's standing. As he pushes the door open to the dimly lit room, he can see his artist hunched over a person laying on the bed.

Their back is illuminated from the headlamp the artist is wearing, revealing an intricate pattern of confusing halls and pathways being drawn on the skin.

Ah, it's Ariadne. He hasn't officially met Ariadne yet, but he has heard his fair share of the artist gushing about the tattoo and the person it was going on.

Icarus knocks on the door frame as he fully enters the room, a signal to the artist telling him that he has company. The buzzing of the tattoo machine stops and the light of the headlamp swings up, blinding Icarus.

"Hey kiddo, wasn't expecting you today!" Icarus is silently relieved when the artist greets him, his tone is friendly. *He isn't mad at me.*

He's tempted to leave the overhead light off as he passes the switch, but decides to flick it on at the last minute. He hates using overhead lights, they're too bright and an affront to the gods for no reason. But, it definitely beats having the headlamp shining into his soul as he talks to the artist. Headache be damned, he is stuck between a rock and a hard place on this one.

Ariadne groans as she moves to get off the bed. She looks up at him, groggy from the nap he rudely woke her from. Icarus doesn't understand how anyone is able to sleep through a tattoo. They don't hurt like some people say, but the vibration of the needle is too stimulating to let him rest.

SORRY UNANNOUNCED ME, he signs. There is a thump as Ariadne rolls too far and ends up falling off the bed. Icarus glances over to make sure that she is okay before returning to his conversation with the artist. **RETURN-TO CITY**, he idly wiggles his fingers as he thinks what he wants to say. How long has it been since he returned to the city? Two days? Three? He furrows his brow, **MAYBE THREE DAY?**

The artist holds up a finger as he turns to Ariadne, whispering something to her that makes her get up and start collecting her belongings from the chair. Then, he turns back to Icarus and says, "You know you're always welcome here kid, welcome back to town. Now show me the back piece." With the overhead light on in the room, he reaches up to turn off his headlamp.

"Have you been nice to my baby?"

Icarus lets out a breathless chuckle. Of course the first thing his artist would want to know is if he took care of his tattoos. He turns around, reaching over his head to pull the back of his hoodie up exposing the deep red wings spanning the length of his back.

Ariadne whistles, a long and appreciative sound as she sees her husband's work. The tattoo had been a beast to heal, but the hours of torturous pain and restless nights of endless itching had been well worth it. He spent days ogling the tattoo after it had first healed, the feathers look so real that you can almost feel them when running your hands over the inked skin. It is everything he wanted and then some.

A feather-light touch runs down the etched skin. There is only one person who had ever touched him with that kind of reverence, his artist must have gotten up to inspect the tattoo. He is admiring his art—*as he should*—when he says, "Looks like you should have used more lotion."

He lets go of one edge of the hoodie to flip him the bird. It's impossible to hide anything from his artist, of course, and he knew that his lackluster care would be noted. There are likely small splotches where the ink had fallen out due to his poor moisturizing regiment, but it's not like he has much of a choice in that.

Icarus drops the back of his hoodie with a sigh as he turns to face the artist again. **YOU KNOW? HARD REACH AREA ALONE**. His eyebrows raise as he speaks, his signs becoming large and boisterous. He then mimes trying to reach the middle of his back. That gets a chortle out of his artist and Ariadne. He hadn't thought to consider how he would need to reach every part of his back before getting the tattoo, and the fact that he doesn't have anyone in his life to help him makes it that much worse.

"What're we doing today, kid?" he asks.

He sighs and taps his fingers against his arm as he thinks. He really doesn't have any set plans for a new tattoo, he'll have to come up with something on the fly.

SLEEVE MAYBE FIRE? SMOKE? He gestures to his right arm from his hand up to his shoulder. A long time ago he had wanted a tattoo like this, branding himself with flames in a vain attempt to make his father proud of him. Things are different now, though, and the thought of twisting that tattoo idea into something that represents who he is now—a survivor, someone who escaped and doused the flame—sounds great.

"Oh-ho ho that's gonna be sick!" The artist turns back to the tattoo bed, grabbing a paper town and disinfectant to quickly wipe it down. Once he's done wiping it down, he crouches down to mess with some settings and configure the bed into a chair position.

"Hop up! Just gotta get the bench cleaned up real quick and we'll start." Icarus pulls the hoodie up and over his head as he makes himself comfortable on the chair.

He watches Ariadne walk up to the artist and kiss his cheek before turning and leaving the room. It's nice to see the two together. Ariadne was deeply entrenched in the depths of ATLAS, his artist had only managed to get her out recently. He was supposed to be here for that, but his close call meant that he had skipped town and left the rescue in the hands of the artist.

He's not sure what the whole story is with those two. Surely they met when his artist was an Elysian, but beyond that he has no idea. The man refused to tell him anything, simply saying that he was 'too young' to be burdened with the knowledge. That he has already been through too much, he didn't want to pile more trauma on top.

That didn't stop Icarus from helping with the rescue planning. Before he had to leave town, they had found out that Ariadne was on Brunot. Just left on an island in the middle of the river with no way to get back to the city. One day he hopes he will hear the whole story, but for now he's glad to see them both whole and okay.

The door closes with a thunk behind Ariadne, leaving Icarus and the artist alone. The hulking man gets up and walks over to switch off the lights before saying, "So, why are you really here?" His stool groans under the weight of him sitting down. "We both know it's more than just pleasantries."

TOO-MUCH KNOWLEDGE, of course the old man knows he's not here to idly chat. **HEAR ME RUMORS.** The artist grabs the arm he's signing with, positioning it on the arm rest so he can start tattooing. Icarus makes a face, he hadn't thought about what it meant to have his dominant arm tattooed while he's non-verbal.

He looks up at the artist, **RUDE.** The older man chuckles before motioning for him to continue as he grabs a marker to start sketching the design. **fs-ELYSIAN WHAT?** Signing with his non-dominant hand is clumsy and slow, and he hopes the artist will understand what he's saying.

NEW GRADUATE. FIRST, BLONDE. He can't move to point at his first finger, instead opting to slightly curl it in an attempt to get his counting across. **SECOND, REDHEAD. WANT-TO KNOW.**

Icarus watches the artist clench his jaw as he signs. There is something wrong, the tension in the older man's body screams that he had touched a nerve.

The man starts to draw on Icarus' arm when he's sure that Icarus is done speaking. Silence stretches between the two as purple strokes of smoke take shape. When he speaks again, the artists' voice is hushed, "Kid... are you certain you want to know?"

He almost sounds remorseful. "Are you sure you want to hear that information?" The artist looks at him again, his eyes betraying a deep seated guilt. It's enough to make Icarus realize that no, he doesn't want to know. He doesn't want confirmation on who the Elysians are. He doesn't want to see behind the curtain.

And yet, he has to. He needs to know, needs to hear their names said out loud by someone he trusts. There is something weird in the works and he needs to figure out what it is and why it involves him.

YES. WANT-TO KNOW fs-DIO. The artist sighs at his use of the nickname. They fall into silence once again as he rolls his stool over to the workbench to grab his machine. It's not an uncomfortable silence, but one that speaks more than words ever could.

The repetitive buzzing of the tattoo machine fills the air. The design on his arms isn't terribly intricate, and yet as it is permanently etched into his skin it speaks to him in a way that only art can. It speaks to a part of Icarus that he had buried for so long, only to have it resurface in his nightmares. A part of him that he now realizes he will never be able to get rid of, no matter how hard he tries.

The artist doesn't speak until he's done blacking out his hand, "Icarus... where do I even start with this?

"A lot has happened. Ari's here, she's safe." He pauses, turning to smile at Icarus as he says, "You're here. You're safe." The buzzing picks up again as the artist returns to the tattoo. "That's all that really matters."

Nothing is said as the artist tattooed around his elbow. A good thing, Icarus isn't sure he'd be able to pay attention to what was said while trying to sit still. The pain is awful, definitely among the worst tattoo pain he's had. It takes everything in his power not to flinch, that would only make the pain worse.

Even still, the pain is a good escape. It keeps him from thinking about what will inevitably be said. Stops him from tipping over the edge into overwhelming grief.

Because that's what it will be. Once the words are put out there, he will grieve what could have been. Then he will have to move on.

"The two you asked about? The blond and the redhead?" The pause between the artist's words is accentuated by a flick of the wrist. The last few tendrils of smoke start to curl up around his shoulder.

Icarus braces himself. He knows what's coming, he needs to be prepared to pretend like they do not affect him.

"Kid, it's Apollon and Iapyx. Your brother, well, he graduated this year." He sits up, scooting away from the tattoo bed and looks at Icarus. "I guess in a way, he followed a bit too close to your footsteps."

He grabs soap, starting the process of cleaning up the tattoo as he continues, "He's dyed his hair. Apparently some news stations were calling him 'The New Icarus' so he got rid of the one thing that made him look like ya. Daedalus, the bastard, supported the decision and announced his debut as Iapyx about a month ago.

"And Apollon, he... Well, he has made quite the name for himself. Graduated two years ago and hasn't known a day of rest since. Started his own outpost out the gate and broke the top ten in a year. Just last week he was announced as the new number two."

Icarus can't breathe, he struggles to get any air in. It feels like someone reached into his chest to squeeze his heart. He can't let his face betray his feelings, but he knows that the artist heard him gasp.

As the man puts the last ink bottle away, he whispers, "Sorry kiddo."

Icarus closes his eyes, leaning his back until it rests against the chair. He cannot lose himself in his thoughts, cannot spiral. *I'm not home,* he reminds himself. *Just wait until I get home.*

His eyes snap open and he moves to stand up. The artist is watching him as he calmly walks to the full length mirror in the corner. The tattoo is perfect, it feels like it's always been there. An extension of his soul, made tangible on his skin.

"Thank..." his voice is scratchy, roughened from overwhelming emotions and the strain of forcing its use. "Thank you." He doesn't know how to express just how much he loves the art, how much it feels like the artist reached into his very soul to create the tattoo.

His throat hurts, a tell-tale sign that he is just moments away from breaking down in tears. He needs to leave. Now.

There's one more question he needs to ask the artist before he leaves, **BREAK-IN MY HOME, LEAVE ENVELOPE. YOU KNOW?**

If anyone would know how the documents got in his possession, it would be the artist. His knowledge network is vast. There is nothing that happens in Cleveland that he does not know.

A brief flash of shock crosses the artists' face. Icarus grabs the envelope out of his backpack and hands it to him. He watches the artist flip through the contents, letting out a low whistle as he looks over the documents.

"Kid, I don't know what you did to get on Mother Nyx's good side, but you better do your damndest to stay there. This shit right here is *gold*."

Fs-NYX? YOU CERTAIN? That doesn't feel right, why would she break into his place? She could knock on the door and Icarus would gladly let her in.

"As sure as I can be. This shit reeks of her, down to the way it's organized."

His brows raise, **LEAVE WHO?** Someone else had to have left the envelope. There's no way in hell Nyx herself had made the trip and risked being seen in public.

The artist tilts his head at the question. "Could it be one of her kids? She's got a couple of those, doesn't she?"

Now that is a question, does Mother Nyx have kids? If she did, they would have been in the Elysian Program, right? Icarus mentally flips through the Rolodex of information on Elysian prospects, searching for anyone that could have been her kid.

Nothing stands out. No names, nothing.

"Well, I guess that doesn't much matter. Go home, kid. Get some sleep."

He groans, grabbing the folder from the artist. It seems that everyone is out for blood, trying to make him actually take care of himself.

He hands the artist the cash in his bag, a stash he keeps for situations like this. It should cover the tattoo. He'll stop by later and double check that it does, after he's calmed down a bit and can speak again.

A hearty laugh fills the shop as he makes his way up the stairs, as if the old man is laughing at his suffering. A small smile creeps its way onto his face. It's nice to hear the artist laugh.

The alleyway is just as dark as it was on his way in, but this time his heart holds both more joy and sadness. *It's time to go home.*

THE NEWS CAST

THE INKY BLACK COVER of night has fallen over the city by the time Icarus makes his way home. The neon lights of the shops illuminate the streets, giving light as he walks.

It must have rained while he was in the shop, the sidewalk is still damp with puddles strewn about. He pulls his hood up and keeps his head down. Normally the lights would be a nuisance to him, mildly infuriating him at best and inducing a migraine at worst. In the rippling reflections of the puddles, though, they provide entertainment and a sense of calm in the otherwise busy city.

It's a nice reprieve as he tries not to think about the information he had received. It is nice to know where the information in the manila folder came from, and as far as Icarus is concerned that is all the tattoo artist had told him.

After all, it's not like the ranks of the Elysians don't normally fluctuate based on how well they do their job and how much the public likes them. It's inevitable that a graduate would come along and climb the ranks. Sure, it's unusual for it to happen so quickly after graduation. And it's really weird to see the long standing top ten be rearranged, but it was bound to happen!

Maybe the artist has the wrong person, it can't possibly be the one person in this world that Icarus has been hoping and praying to see again. But it couldn't be like this, never like this.

He had hoped—still hopes—that he would see him again. Maybe he'll help his sunshine escape ATLAS just as he had all those years ago.

Icarus knows he had high hopes. He was left with a promise, *I will find you again*, but that hasn't happened yet. It's been ten long years. Ten years of running. Ten years of hiding in plain sight. Ten years of bitter loneliness.

Even still, he has managed to hold onto that hope. Just an inkling of hope that somewhere out there, his sunshine had managed to escape and was looking for him. Since his nightmare that spark had started to dim, then it froze over at the tattoo shop. Now, as he walks back to his apartment, that frozen spark has begun to crack.

A flash of light to Icarus' right catches his eye. He turns and finds himself in front of one of the many news screens implemented throughout the city. They were a motion from ATLAS in an effort to share the most pressing news with the public, no matter where you were in the city. Right now, though, they only share pain.

His eyes are drawn to a figure on the screen, standing in front of rubble and wreckage. He knows not to doubt his artist, especially when it comes to information about the Elysians. He knows better, and yet the little frozen spark of hope in his heart managed to create just enough doubt.

But now? Now that spark is shattered. How could it not be when the person he had been so hopelessly in love with for as long as he can remember is on national television as the new #2 Elysian?

He should have snuffed out the spark years ago when he realized no one was coming for him. Hell, he should have snuffed it out that day ten years ago when he realized he was leaving the program alone.

A single warm tear rolls down Icarus' cheek, snapping him out of his thoughts. He hastily wipes the tear away, mentally pulling a mask of indifference back over his face. He doesn't have time for a breakdown right now, much less a breakdown over a boy. He swallows down the emotions before turning away from the torturous screen and hurrying back towards his apartment.

The rippling reflections of the neon lights mock him, the splotches of color replaying the scene he saw on the screen over and over again. He can hear the news anchor reporting on the tragedy;

news of the bloodshed, news of the people that could not be saved, news of the new rankings.

The world feels so far away and yet so close. Everything is closing in on him, but he is watching from outside the crushing pressure. He can't hear anything, the heavy silence crushing him until suddenly it explodes.

The sound of the cars on the street that he had forgotten about greets him. The footsteps of the people walking down the street join. The drip, drip, drip of water falling from the rooftops into the puddle below. The neon lights that every shop has sitting bold and bright to announce to the world that they are open buzz with electricity. The smell of stale beer and dried blood. The heavy, stagnant air that the city is made out of now that the wind refuses to visit. The droning of the crosswalk signals that never seem to change. The blaring horns of cars cut off as Icarus becomes too impatient and overstimulated to stay waiting for the light to change for even a second more.

It is too much. Too much noise, too many sounds, too many eyes on him as he stumbles his way through the door of his apartment building. Too many stairs, too small of an elevator, too many people judging him.

His shoulder stings as he runs into someone on the way to his apartment, but he can't tell who it is. Everything's blurry and it's too much to handle, he needs to get inside. He wants to curl up and turn it all off, no he needs to curl up and turn it all off.

The only thing standing between him and the blissful release of emotions is the *damned front door* that he can't unlock. He can't get the key into the lock, he can't get the door open, and he's about to kick down the door.

There's a gurgling sound behind him. Someone is attempting to speak to him but all the words blend together. He just needs to make this fucking key work, why isn't it working?

Warm hands wrap around his, prying his fingers off the key as he fights to keep it in his grasp. Nothing can be easy, can it? Someone *had* to come and take his key from him, didn't they?

He's about to fall apart in front of his apartment when he's pushed through the now open door. His mind is focused on one thing and one thing only as he makes a beeline for his bedroom, flopping face down on the bed. He doesn't have his headphones to help him calm down, he doesn't know where they are. But that's okay, he just needs to calm down. Everything will be better when he *calms down.*

He needs to breathe. He's hyperventilating, can't get a breath in. Being face down in the bed does not help, so he turns his head to the side. *Breathe, Icarus. Remember what they taught you.* Breathe in, two, three. Hold. Release, two three. Again. Breathe in, hold it, release. Again.

The fuzziness of the air lessens as he breathes, the panic and fear reside. He can hear the gargling from earlier start to separate into their own words; headphones, blanket, hug. He's not sure what's going on, everything still feels warped and wrong, but if a hug is on the table then he is absolutely going to take it.

Icarus struggles to push himself into a sitting position. The movement hurts, makes his vision swim, so he closes his eyes. The voice is becoming clearer and he begins to recognize its tone—Andromeda has found him.

He is glad that he at least somewhat knows them, it would have been much more concerning and embarrassing to break down in front of a total stranger. Their presence is just as oddly comforting as it was on the roof and in the coffee shop, and Icarus can definitely use the physical grounding.

It isn't difficult to find where they are sitting on the bed, the dip from their weight gives them away even through closed eyes. Icarus leans towards them and hopes it is enough of a gesture for them to understand that he is open to the idea of a hug. Words still have not returned to him, this will have to be enough.

There is a brief moment of doubt as the ever-flowing stream of words coming from Andromeda's mouth stops, but it's gone as soon as he feels them wrap their arms around him. They are hesitant, as if they are scared that he will run away at any moment. They don't know just how little energy he has, most of it going to keeping him sitting upright. Eyes remain closed as he presses his head into their shoulder. His head is pounding and the pressure makes it feel better.

They realize that he isn't going anywhere and tighten their arms around him. It has been so long since Icarus has been held, so long since anyone has truly cared about him. The ever-present white noise is starting to dull, emotions and thoughts he has been suppressing come flooding back all at once. Everything that he has been trying not to think of, everything he has been avoiding.

The warmth of his tears running down his face isn't unexpected, the itch and strain in his throat told him he was going to cry. He hates crying, but he can't hold it in anymore. Icarus has reached his limit, he has ten long years' worth of emotions and cruel thoughts built up and he can't take it anymore!

He wants to talk, needs to talk, but he can't. The words betray him, leaving him a garbling mess on Andromeda's shoulder and he cries out every emotion he has carefully hid away. He grabs at their shirt, holding them close and praying that they don't abandon him like so many have done before.

It isn't long before the inky black abyss of sleep claims him, exhausted from crying and clinging onto a near stranger for dear life as he is.

Icarus wakes up to someone running their hand through his hair. He's curled up in his bed, a blanket thrown over him as his head rests in someone's lap.

What? Oh. He remembers what happened, how he fell asleep and why Andromeda was in his bedroom running their hands through his unkempt hair.

He doesn't want to move, he doesn't want to face reality. He knows that he will have to talk to Andromeda, he will have to explain what happened and why he is such a mess. He will risk pushing away the one person he had decided to let into his life because he couldn't control his damned emotions.

"I know you're awake, my guy."

He curls up into a ball, his voice hoarse as he replies, "Unfortunate." Silence falls over them like a warm blanket. *They're waiting for me to talk.*

The gesture warms his heart and gives him the motivation to sit up. If they can be so kind and considerate to him even after seeing him fall apart, then he can talk to them about it. Explain himself to them.

So he talks. He talks about everything. About the Elysian Program and the torture it entailed. About his sunshine and how he helped Icarus escape ATLAS. About the hope he has held on to for years that his sunshine would escape and find him. About the love that was always there, deep down, but had blossomed in the years apart. About the unease and doubt that had started to creep in when he started hearing rumors about a new blond Elysian. About the newscast on the way home from Τελεταί. About the hope that had held him together through the past ten years of solitude and loneliness shattering beyond repair. About how he was shattered beyond repair and how he doesn't know who he is anymore.

Time seems to blur as he speaks, he's not sure how long he talks or how long he was asleep. No white noise comes back to greet him, no tears well up in his eyes. All that exists as he speaks are the two of them sitting on his bed as the words tumble from his mouth.

The world slows as his words taper off. The buzz of emotions quell leaving him with an overwhelming sense of calm. A deep breath in, leaning away from Andromeda as he breathes out.

"Sorry for dumping all that on you," he says, his voice returning to its serene monotony. He angles himself to stand up, aiming to grab some new clothes and head to the bathroom to change when he's interrupted.

"Absolutely the fuck not. Keep your ass on this damned bed, we are talking about this." They aren't going to take any of his shit, are they?

He knows he will have to talk to them, answer any questions they have about what they just witnessed. Still, he hopes that he can push it off a bit. Now that he's talked through his immediate thoughts, he's become numb.

"I'm gonna change, get out of these clothes." He pushes himself off the bed, moving to stand in front of the closet. If he cannot avoid confrontation, then he will at least make sure he is as comfortable as he can be during it. He kicks his jeans off as he considers which hoodie to throw on. The one he is currently wearing must have gotten wet while he was out of it, it feels *wrong*.

The closet is rather bare, he doesn't own much of anything that would fill it up. That should make the decision easier, and yet Icarus was torn between two hoodies. He needs to decide which one is the biggest and comfiest since his go-to hoodie is down for the count.

"Look," Andromeda levels at him, voice growing in intensity as they say, "I understand that you don't quite trust me yet. I mean, we just met yesterday. Hell, I don't even know your name yet! But-"

"Icarus." He grabs the hoodie on the left and pulls it over his head. He takes a moment to pull his hair up and fasten it in a ponytail before turning and leaning back against the closet door. "My name is Icarus."

"Okay. Icarus. Y'know, that fits." Their voice is calmer, quieter, as if that piece of information is enough to placate them.

Icarus huffs. The name really does fit him, doesn't it? Always jumping into things without thinking of the consequences, taking risks, and keeping shit close to his chest until he gets a bit too close to hubris and starts to fall apart. Falling in love with the sun personified. Burning, falling, crashing, drowning. Yeah, the name fits him.

The only difference between him and the Icarus of myth is that he died at the end of his story. Icarus has no plans of dying. No, he plans on making it out the other end of his story and living to tell the tale.

"Icarus, I'm going to ask you a question and I need you to be honest with me." Andromeda stands up and walks to him. They reach a hand out, moving to touch his face before dropping their hand as he flinches. "Can you do that?"

He doesn't like it when people ask him to be honest. Not only does it mean he has to be honest with them, but that he has to be honest with himself. And yet, he nods. He owes it to Andromeda after forcing them to witness his mess.

"Are you okay?"

His breath catches in his throat. That is not the question he had expected. Hell, he didn't even know what he had expected and yet he knows it wasn't this.

Tears threaten to spill and he looks down at the hem of his hoodie. He owes them honesty, but he doesn't know if he can bear the honest answer. His entire life, he had been taught that showing weakness to others was the worst thing a person could do. That once you admitted that something was wrong, you became broken goods. That there is no place in the world for broken goods.

And yet, here Andromeda was asking him to bare his weaknesses to them. They clearly care, that much is obvious to him. Maybe, just this once, he could allow himself to break. And maybe this time when all is said and done there would be someone there to help him pick up the pieces.

He doesn't have to say anything as Andromeda says, "I get ya." They turn around to grab a blanket off the bed—the fuzzy one that Icarus loves the texture of.

To say he is confused would be an understatement. Are they not going to ask him more questions? Are they going to just move on like none of this happened?

"Come on, kiddo. We're making dinner." That doesn't answer his question. At all.

His stomach rumbles at the mention of food. He can't remember the last time he ate, it must have been before he went to the bar. Yeah, he really shouldn't turn down the chance of eating a home cooked meal.

Pushing himself off the closet door, he follows Andromeda out to the kitchen. As soon as he crosses through the doorway a blanket is thrown over his head. He panics, he can't see, he can't breathe. His muscles tense as arms wrap around him.

"It's me," Andromeda's voice calms him. He knew it was them, yet his body couldn't help but react. As his breathing slows, the arms around him move until he's being picked up and carried bridal style.

He counts their steps. One, two, three, four and they stumble. The arms shift him in their grasp before continuing. Five, six, seven, eight sounds different. They must be in the kitchen, the linoleum floor sounds different underfoot. Nine, ten, eleven, and he's being put down.

The island is cold, the chill permeates the fuzzy blanket he is wrapped in. He pulls the blanket back and off his head to be met with a smug grin from Andromeda. He doesn't know what to make of the situation and shifts uncomfortably.

"You're gonna sit there and look pretty while I make dinner. Then, we're gonna talk through some shit, yeah?" While they talk they turn and grab a wooden cooking spoon—Icarus' sauce spoon—and point it at him. Icarus snatches the sauce spoon from their hand, pointing it back at them in a threatening manner.

"Fine. But you aren't allowed to use my sauce spoon for whatever it is you're making," he says, setting the spoon down on the counter next to him. The edge of the counter is uncomfortable under his thighs as shifts himself. He pulls his legs up to sit cross legged. Sitting like this takes up the majority of the counter space. It doesn't look like Andromeda needs the room, Icarus watches as they set everything out on the island across from him and start cooking.

If they are going to do this, he's going to make sure he's as comfortable as possible. "Where do you want to start?" he asks.

Andromeda turns to face him, a puzzled expression on their face. Their eyebrows furrow as they say, "Oh. I wasn't expecting it to be that easy. Hold on."

Icarus snickers, of course they thought it would be harder to get information from him. Normally, it was. However, this is not a normal situation and they had just held Icarus through one of his most vulnerable moments. He might as well fill in the gaps that he stumbled over earlier.

Plus, they're stuck with him now. They are his and he is theirs.

He watches as they raid his cupboards, pulling out a pot and a pack of noodles. Looks like they are making pasta for dinner, not that he would complain about that. Pasta is food for the soul.

"I guess we should start at the beginning." They fill the pot with water and set it on the stove before turning back towards him. "Who are you, Icarus?"

THE QUESTION

WHO IS HE?

Now, that is a hard question to answer. Who is Icarus?

Is he the little redhead boy from the Elysian Program? The one that strove for excellence in everything he did to make his papa proud? No. No, he is not. But, that would be the easiest answer.

Is he a runaway child desperate to find a *home*? A kid burnt and battered to hell and back searching for somewhere to belong? Well, yeah. But that's not all he is.

Icarus isn't sure he knows who he is. He's not sure that he'd be able to explain it to someone else, even if he knew who he was.

A finger pokes him between the eyebrows. "Okay, that was too much. I can hear your brain overworking itself from here," Andromeda jokes. They return to the pot of noodles, stirring it as they say, "We're gonna do this twenty questions style, got it?"

Icarus nods before realizing that they can't see him, shooting them a soft, "Yup."

"Gonna start it off real easy, kid. How old are ya?"

He had expected the questions to start off more difficult to answer, something more along the lines of the 'who are you' question from earlier. This, though, is something he can easily answer. "I'm twenty-three. Are you a cat or a dog person?"

"A cat person. What kind of question—you know what? Nevermind. How do you know the Elysian you cried over?"

Ah. There it is. "We grew up together. Is your name actually Andromeda?"

"That's what they told me. You were in the Elysian Program, then?"

"Yup." Icarus drums his fingers on the counter next to him. The texture doesn't feel right under his fingertips, much more slippery than he remembers. He looks down as he asks, "Were you?"

Shit, he forgot about the paper he found after the break in. He had left it here on the counter when he went to the coffee shop, deciding that it would be better to read it here instead of mixing it with the contents of the manila folder.

"Yeah I was, up until two years ago." He looks back up at them, watches them stir the packet of fake cheese into the cooked noodles as they say, "Food's done, where are your bowls?"

Icarus reaches up to the cabinet behind him and pulls out his favorite soup mug and a bowl. He hops off the counter to set them down as Andromeda brings the pot of mac 'n cheese out.

"I'm using that as your question."

"What? No, that's not part of the game! No, my question is—"

"Sucks, my turn now," Icarus says with a smile. "What's your specialty?"

Andromeda shoots him a glare as they settle down at the table. They serve dinner into the bowl and the mug, chuckling to themselves as they do. "Medicine, I don't fight." They hand him his mug, asking, "What are you gonna do with the information you showed me?"

"I want to ruin them. Burn them to the ground until there is nothing left." He can feel their eyes on him, watching him as he speaks. Their gaze burns as he holds a spoonful of noodles in front of his mouth and blows on it, it makes him doubt their intentions. He had assumed they wanted to act against ATLAS as well, and had thought that was why they had brought up that they were a runaway.

"Cool. We're on the same page, then." A wave of relief washes through him. He eats the now cool noodles as he waits for the next question.

He doesn't have to wait long. "What's next?"

Instead of responding verbally, Icarus stands up to grab the paper off the counter. He sets it down in front of Andromeda on his way back. He hasn't read it yet, doesn't know what it says or who it's from.

Now, though. Now that paper is important. He has a gut feeling that their answer lies somewhere in the writing.

"I found this letter yesterday after our talk on the roof. Came back and my apartment was broken into." They look up at him, concern weaving its way into their facial expression. "Nothing was missing, but that information and this letter was left."

They turn their concentration back at the piece of paper in front of them, reading it since Icarus had not. He will need to read it, he had only glanced at it while they were making dinner. Even then, the only information he had gathered was who the letter was from. And, oh boy, does Icarus take pleasure in knowing that their next step is to steal ATLAS' golden prodigy from under their noses. If only he could see the Big Three's faces when they do.

"Do you know what they mean by 'I thought he was dead, are you telling me they lied'? Who are they talking about?" Andromeda asks. Icarus has no idea what they are talking about and motions for them to hand the paper over to him.

███████

What do you mean he's alive?

There ain't no way he made it out that night. You heard the story just as much as I have. Hell, even the dick thinks he's dead.

I thought he was dead, are you telling me they lied?

You can't get my hopes up like this. If he is still alive, can you get him a message?

I want out. I'm done.

He will know what that means if you can get it to him. Not that I believe it.

Especially now that they've separated me and Pat. Can't get my hopes up now when I'm trying to get him back.

Tell your twin I said hey,

Achilles

"He's talking about me," he breathes. The handwriting is as sloppy as it always was and hard to decipher in some places, but he knows they are talking about him. Knows that the only person Achilles would get so worked up over is him.

"You?" Confusion thickens Andromeda's voice as they ask, "Why do they think you're dead?"

"I don't know. As far as I know, I'm not dead. Though, that does explain why he never tried to find me. Why neither of them tried." Why did they think he was dead? He knew he was worse for wear when he had run, but he had escaped. He doesn't remember anything after entering the woods. But he's here now, he had escaped.

Icarus shakes his head, he can't think about that right now.

"Well, you've got that folder of information, right? Maybe there's something in there?" It is useful having Andromeda here, they are great at distracting Icarus when he needs it most.

He nods, standing up to grab the manila folder from his backpack. They're right, maybe there is information in here that will explain this whole mess. He had skipped over the family details when reading the document earlier, there must be something there.

He hands two of the four sheets from the envelope to Andromeda as he returns. The two he keeps are information sheets on his father and Sisyphus, the third of the top three Elysians.

"This is all information I already know, I know how these monsters treat civilians." He still can't bring himself to look in the family section, he doesn't want to see his name. The section looks short, anyways, so there likely isn't anything useful there. "You find anything?"

"Yeah, think I did. I'm assuming you kept your dad's sheet?"

Icarus sets the sheet between the two of them as Andromeda sets the sheet for Cassiopeia down.

"This is my bitch of a mother. Ignoring the blatant disregard of gender, there's something wrong." They tap the sheet of paper a few times before sliding it across the table. "Says I'm dead."

They look up from the table, catching Icarus' gaze as they say, "So, how'd you die?"

He cocks his head and looks down at the documents in front of him. Sure enough, Andromeda is listed as DECEASED in the family section of Cassiopeia's dossier. Why would they be marked as dead?

"Holy shit," he whispers, "we're dead." That explains so much. Why Icarus can't get a form of identification. Why his tattoo artist told him to lay low. Why he was told to avoid being recognized. It isn't because ATLAS is looking for him. No, it's because he is a dead man walking the streets.

For a moment Icarus is relieved. If they are legally dead, that means they can just leave. That is why his sunshine never came looking for him, why he will never come for him. He—and Andromeda if they so wish—can just leave the city. Make a life somewhere where no one knows their past. Make a humble life for themselves instead of risking everything to abolish the systems that harmed them.

His breath shudders as he allows himself to explore that fantasy. It doesn't last long, though, as he is reminded that a life like that isn't possible for someone like him. He would be riddled with guilt if he were to leave Achilles behind. Especially now that he has physical evidence that the kid made an attempt to find him.

"We're dead." He repeats, his voice filled with the heartbreak and grief of a future that could have been. "We're dead, but that doesn't matter."

He returns to the letter from Achilles. In the grand scheme of things, being legally dead might actually help them. Being dead means that even if they leave DNA behind while breaking the kid out, it would be useless. After all, how could a dead kid leave DNA?

"What matters is getting the kid out," he forces his voice to sound more confident, sound like he isn't falling apart as everything crumbles around him. It's just one thing after the other these days, it seems.

He looks up at Andromeda. They look sad, their eyes burning holes into the paper that said they are legally dead.

"I can't leave him behind, I have to get him out." He can see conflicting emotions at war in their eyes. Can see them work their way from a hopeful shine to a dull resignation before settling on cold determination.

They softly nod and say, "Okay, yeah. We're gonna get the kid. What's the plan?"

Isn't that always the question. What is next? "We're going to need more information."

"And I take it you know how to do that?"

"I think I can figure out who this letter was addressed to. I'm gonna go to them." The name at the top has been scribbled out, the black smudge makes any text he could have read indecipherable. However, he has the lead from the tattoo shop to run on. With the addition of a supposed twin, it would not be difficult to pin down who the letter was addressed to.

Andromeda stares at him for a moment, the gears in their brain rotating what he said. They look like they want to ask him a question, but when they open their mouth they instead say, "Cool, we'll deal with that tomorrow."

"Nah, lemme get changed into real clothes—"

"We're dealing with this tomorrow," they say sternly. "I swear to all that is holy if you stand up right now." If looks could kill, Icarus would be severely harmed, if not legitimately dead.

"Eat ya damn food."

"Damn!" Icarus sits back down in the chair he just stood up from. "Okay! I'll eat the food first!"

"And then?"

Icarus pauses. He wants to go back to the cafe, there is something there that he missed. He knows it, can feel it deep in his gut. But the look on Andromeda's face says that that is not an option. The glare they are sending him says that he will need to actually rest for the night if he wants them off his case.

"Fine! I'll sleep too!" He dramatically throws his arms in the air before crossing them. "Are you happy yet?"

That seems to placate them for now as they lean back and move their attention to the now cold mac 'n cheese that had been dinner.

There is a moment of silence between the two. Icarus really doesn't want to re-heat his bowl, he doesn't have the energy for that. Andromeda must not want to, either, as they say, "I'm ordering pizza."

Icarus picks up their now cold dishes and takes them out to the kitchen. "Cool, dairy-free please."

He throws what's left in the bowls into a container. Those will make for some good lunches for the next couple days. At least, until he can convince himself to go to the grocery store.

"Who the fuck eats pizza with no cheese?"

"Someone who's allergic to cheese, I guess. Also, order from Hestia. She knows my order and has dairy-free cheese options." Icarus turns on the tap and lets it run for a bit until the water is just hot enough to wash the dishes in.

"Order from—Hestia has a pizza shop?"

"Best pizza in town, just about everything is grown in her roof-top garden and she has one of those ancient brick ovens."

"Damn, and I'm just now hearing about this?" There's a thunk in the middle of the sentence. Icarus chuckles as he imagines Andromeda slamming their hand on the table, upset that they missed out on some good pizza.

"Well, she does tend to keep everything on the low since she's on the run. Elysian things, y'know?"

"No, that makes sense," they grumble. Icarus finishes washing the dishes and setting them to dry. He turns and leans back against the counter.

"Are you going to mope all night, or are you actually gonna order some food?" he teases. He's curious why they haven't left yet. The shop isn't far, but the only way to order is to physically walk into the shop and order.

"I thought the whole 'Oh, Hestia has a pizza shop?' ordeal would tell you that I have no idea where to go."

Huh, yeah, that should have clicked with him. It's not like they could search up directions, they likely don't have a phone just the same as him. Can't risk having a way for someone to use GPS to locate him. It's not like he has anyone to keep in contact with, anyways.

"It's just down the street. Go out the front of the building and head down West Saint Clair, it's just past fourth street. I'd say can't miss it but you very much could, there's no sign out front. It's the only building that looks like there's someone living in it on that block, though."

"Got it. West Saint Clair, Fourth Street, not-abandoned building." Andromeda repeats the directions to themself as they head towards the front door. "Anything else while I'm out?"

"Nah I'm good, but make sure to grab my keys. That way you can let yourself back in."

"Got it, boss. I'll be right back. Don't burn the place down while I'm gone." They wave before closing the door. Silence falls over the apartment. This is not an unusual state of affairs for his place, but one that he is learning to dislike. The casual flow of conversation with Andromeda had made his apartment start to feel like a home and he doesn't know if he wants to go back to the way it was.

He's not sure what to do with himself. His nervous energy has him entering the guest bed and making sure it's cleaned up and prepared for someone to stay in it. He's not sure how fast they will be able to get Achilles out, but he will need a place to stay once they do and he plans on offering the kid the room.

There's only so much he can do with an already clean and organized room, though, and he quickly finds himself pacing around the apartment as he waits. *What am I doing?*

He turns to head to his bedroom. Pacing helps no one, he might as well try and rest. Andromeda will surely wake him up when they get back. He can take just a quick nap until then.

He curls up on the edge of his bed against the wall. The cool brick helps him regulate his temperature even as he bundles up in his fuzzy blanket. He's running through who the letter might be addressed to in his mind as he starts to drift, succumbing to the bone deep exhaustion that has been chasing him all day.

THE PLAN

THE DELICIOUS SMELL OF kielbasa being cooked greets Icarus as he wakes up. He groans as he rolls out of bed, it has been so long since he's had a decent breakfast. Much less one that was made for him!

His stomach agrees, a rumble joining the distant clatter of cooking from the kitchen. Icarus is convinced that nothing feels better than the snap, crackle, and pops that run their way through his body as he stands up and stretches. Tension seeps out of his body with each crack, it is downright heavenly.

He makes his way out of his bedroom and into the living room while stifling a yawn behind his hand. As soon as the kitchen comes into view he stops. Icarus blinks a couple of times and wipes the crusties out of his eyes to make sure that he is awake and seeing things properly.

Nothing in his vision changes, which is concerning. There absolutely should not be two people in his kitchen cooking right now, and yet.

"What?" he asks, squinting his barely awake eyes at the extra person. They look vaguely familiar, as if he should know who they are.

Damn, my memory is shit. Their white locs starkly contrast their dark complexion. It almost reminds Icarus of Nyx. Nyx? Why is there someone who looks like Mother Nyx in his apartment? Did one of her children break in to... make breakfast?

Nothing makes sense right now, he should go back to sleep. Try this whole 'being awake' thing again later. He turns to head back into his bedroom when Andromeda calls after him.

"Well, look who's finally awake!" he turns towards their way too chipper voice to see them pointing to the new person, "Guess who I found!"

Ah, I'm too slow. He makes his way across the room to sit down on a stool at the island. At least the food smells great, potatoes and kielbasa are one of his favorite breakfasts and nothing beats having someone else make them for you.

He watches the two in his kitchen, how had his life come to this? There are two strangers in his home, one of them he had met just a few days ago and yet they are already an important fixture in his life. The other one he feels he should know, but his brain is still shrouded by the foggy depths of sleep making it hard to figure out who they are. And yet, here they are making him breakfast and chatting with one another. It warms the hole in his chest where a heart should be, it makes his apartment feel like a *home*.

Then it clicks. Icarus knows who that stranger in his kitchen is. He knows because they had met before.

Years ago, hell, years before he even left ATLAS he was introduced to the Reserve Students. He had been in charge of presenting the Elysian Program to these 'troubled prospectives'. It was his job to try and show them why they should try harder to make it into the program proper. The Reserve Students, a body of preteen kids that happened to include one set of twins: Thanatos and Hypnos.

How could he forget?

"Καιρὸς δε, Thanatos," he mumbles as he stretches his arms out in front of him and rests his forehead on the blissfully cool counter.

"And here I was thinking you weren't gonna remember me." Long gone is the shrill and timid voice of a sickly kid, replaced by one of the most soothing and deep tones Icarus had ever heard.

"...Fair 'nuff." The vibrations of a glass hitting the counter top make Icarus look up. A glass of water, just water. He groans, that is not what he wants right now. He's craving the sweet buzz of an energy drink, but that will require him to get up and walk around the island to grab one.

Andromeda chuckles, not moving an inch as they watch Icarus suffer over the glass. "Quit pouting and drink." He drops his head, turning his face away from the glass.

"Oh come on, you big baby. Deja de hacer un berrinche y bebe." They poke his cheek as he pouts. "Mira, food's ready. Sit up and eat."

He sticks his tongue out at Andromeda as he sits up and crosses his arms. Icarus opens his mouth to complain about having to move when Thanatos places a plate of food in front of him. It smells heavenly, he is nearly salivating at the scent alone.

Icarus sends a quick thanks to Thanatos before starting in on the food. Maybe he is being dramatic, but it is damn near orgasmic. It doesn't take much time for Icarus to down the portion of breakfast potatoes and kielbasa on his plate.

"So tell me, Than," he says as he sets his fork down on the emptied plate. "Why are you here?"

"I'm here because you're running out of time, Icarus."

He looks up at that. Running out of time? For what?

"The letter, my guy. Did you read the letter I left on your bed?"

"You mean *you're* the one that broke in?" Oh. *Oh*, of course it was Thanatos that broke into his apartment. That's how he knew where to show up this morning.

"That's not the point—"

"No, no. Back up, bitch. Were you or were you not the one who broke into my apartment?"

"Yes! Okay, yes I was. Can we please talk about actually important things now?"

Icarus grumbles. *Stupid fucking apartment with stupid fucking people and no fucking privacy.* He motions for Thanatos to continue what he was saying before the conversation took a detour.

Thanatos' lip ticks up in a brief sneer. Irritation clouds his voice as he speaks, "The letter I left. From Achilles. Did you read it?"

"Of course I did, what about it?"

Thanatos looks at him as if he had grown a second head. He blinks a couple times, cocking his head slightly to the side and pinching his lips. Icarus can tell that he had fucked up, but he doesn't know how.

The silence is starting to eat at him, if they sit here staring at each other for much longer he is going to go feral. He can't take it.

"What? Why are you looking at me like that?"

"I am waiting for you to tell me what your plans are and why you haven't already gotten him out."

"Oh."

"Oh?"

"Oh, we don't have a plan yet. We just read it last night during dinner."

If looks could kill, Icarus would be six feet under. The glare that Thanatos is sending him is disgustingly pointed.

"What now?" Icarus is becoming irritated. He fucking hates when people do this, it makes him feel so stupid.

"I left that letter for you two days ago."

"Yeah, and I've been a bit busy."

"Busy with what?"

"Well, I don't know, maybe *getting information about who broke into my apartment?*"

Their argument is cut short by Andromeda laughing. Icarus looks at them, takes in their gleeful demeanor. They obviously find the situation entertaining.

"Boys, relax. What matters is that we are here now trying to get him out." A cheshire grin adorns their smug face as they sip on their coffee.

Thanatos sighs as he looks over at Icarus. "You're right. Let's start a plan now, I guess."

Icarus stands up, garnering the attention of the other two. Before they can ask what he's doing, he grabs the plates on the table and takes them to the kitchen. If they are going to plan then they need to have a clean space to work at.

After setting the dishes in the sink he grabs an energy drink. His head is pounding just thinking about the day that's ahead of him and the leftover grogginess from a dreamless sleep won't leave. The extra caffeine should help, it should squash the headache before it makes light painful.

The crack of the can opening sends shivers down his spine. Just the sound is enough to dull the pain, as if his body anticipates the sweet buzz that accompanies it.

"You know those things are really bad for you, right?"

He levels a deadpan look at Thanatos. His eyes rake over their sickly appearance, their sunken eyes and gaunt cheeks. The man looks like he's one sneeze away from his grave and he has the gall to tell Icarus that his habits are unhealthy? That's some grade A bullshit right there.

"I'm dead, what's it matter?"

He doesn't remember Thanatos being such an ass. Sure, Icarus had only talked to the Reserve Students for an hour, but he seemed like a sweet kid. He was direct when asking questions, but never rude. Maybe his twin had rubbed off on him. Hypnos was someone he had to be briefed on before his presentation.

"Why are you being a dick?"

"Why am I—why aren't you working on rescuing someone that I thought was your friend? It seems like I'm the only one who cares."

"Well you aren't," Andromeda curtly responds. "You haven't been here for the past two days. Shit's happened. We are working on getting him out now, so cool it, yeah?"

Thanatos backs down at that, slouching in his seat while the corners of his mouth tug into a frown.

Hopefully Meda stepping in will make him realize that we are trying to help. They need this to run as smoothly as possible if they want to get Achilles out of the program in one piece.

"Earlier you mentioned something about running out of time. What did you mean?" Icarus asks. That has been nagging him, something seems off about the situation. There were no time restraints mentioned anywhere in the information docket.

"They're moving Achilles to isolation tomorrow morning."

The words hit Icarus like a ton of bricks. They're moving Achilles—their golden child, the αριστος αχαιον, their *prodigy*—to isolation? Even worse, they're moving him *tomorrow*? God, he really should have read that letter sooner. No wonder Thanatos is upset.

They need to get Achilles out, and if they want to have any hope of being successful then they have to make their move before tomorrow morning.

"Holy shit," he whispers under his breath.

"Yeah 'holy shit', are we on the same page now? Can we start planning?"

"Why are they moving him to isolation?" Andromeda asks. "Isn't he like their poster child? Why would they do that?"

Thanatos catches Icarus' gaze, purposefully holding it as he answers. "He was acting out. A certain former ginger was antagonizing him, trying to get him to break his engagement."

He scowls, *of course Iapyx is involved in this.* His nose scrunches with barely contained disgust as he imagines the little shit—not little brother, they had never been that close—pestering the blond kid he practically helped raise.

He should have punted the kid when he could've. Now, not only is he too grown for Icarus to drop kick, but he has somehow managed to get their father's love and attention.

"Who's he talking about, Icarus?" Andromeda asks.

Bitter resentment laces his words as he says, "My kid brother." There's no reason for anyone to know of his existence, when Icarus was still in the program he had been slated for the medical ward. He was never supposed to become an Elysian Prospect. *The little fucker.*

Icarus is fuming. Not only do they have to get Achilles out of the program, but they have a limited time frame thanks to the bastard. If he ever sees Iapyx in person it will be on sight.

He can't sink into the rage, they don't have time. He takes a deep breath, puts a mental lid on the burning trash cans of wrath, and changes gears. "So the kid's being moved to isolation. How do I get to him tonight?"

They need a plan. Now.

"Well, lucky for you guys, I already have an infiltration mission planned out."

"Then why didn't you lead with that, death boy," Icarus says through clenched teeth.

Andromeda sighs and rests their face in the palm of their hands. The air is growing thick with barely restrained anger, the tension so thick that it could be cut with a knife.

They can't risk this conversation getting worse. Icarus knows that. Knows that they need the plan that Thanatos has in order to move forward.

He leans back in his chair, crossing his arms and sweeping his hand in front of him as if to say 'go ahead'. He is trying to shove his mounting rage deep down, trying to lock it away until it can be safely dealt with.

With a huff, Thanatos stands up and walks into the living room behind Icarus. He can hear a soft rustling before another manila folder is set on the counter in front of him. He watches as the man walks back to his seat and sits down, mimicking his earlier motion of sweeping his hand out in an invitation to look at the contents of the folder.

That is the final straw for Icarus. He cannot handle this back and forth anymore. Sure, he had started it this time, but it is too much for him. However, he cannot afford to fuck this up.

He shuts down. None of this matters, the only thing he cares about is getting the kid out safe.

Before he can open the folder, a hand grabs it. Andromeda pulls it to them, opening it and laying its contents out across the table for everyone to see. They move their stool next to his as well, that way they can both read the documents.

There is a lot on the pages. Maps, blueprints, dossiers on guards, photos of the building. Thanatos had truly outdone himself.

Icarus squints his eyes, maybe death boy has a use. The idea of not having to collect information himself is nice, especially information this detailed. He wouldn't have to deal with people or his informant again. Well, he might still deal with his informant. They are good for more than just the information they give.

One of the blueprints catches his eye. It's the layout of the academy with a point of entry and proposed path marked out.

"Is this how you're planning to get me to Achilles?" he asks, pointing at the paper and looking up at Thanatos. There is something deep inside him, a burning and protective hatred, that is waiting for the answer and praying that it isn't what he thinks it is.

He will burn that building to the ground if he's right about this. If he is right about them housing Achilles in that room.

He watches as Thanatos nods and says, "Yeah, That's his room. We just have to get you in there."

Icarus is going to *burn them all*. He knows just how shitty ATLAS and the Elysian Program are, but he had thought that something like this was too much for even them.

Out of all the rooms in that gods-forsaken building, they had to move him into the one he would have emotional ties to. Icarus will not only have to face the building in his nightmares, but he will have to go back to his own bedroom. The room that he had abandoned all those years ago. The room that Achilles now inhabits.

Lord knows if they cleaned out the room first. They probably didn't, just throwing the recently abandoned kid into a room full of stuff left behind by the person that abandoned him.

He is going to burn them all.

"When are we making our move?" He is more determined than ever to get there, to get into that building and make their lives hell. They need to move fast. It's not yet noon, though, and they won't be able to do anything in broad daylight.

"I haven't been able to verify this information yet." Than says, seemingly reading his mind. "I haven't had time to verify anything, I had to come as soon as I could."

"What does that mean," Andromeda asks. It's a good question, are they able to trust any of the information that he provided?

"It means that we need to verify it before I send you into the building." Thanatos looks down at the watch on his wrist, shaking it to wake up the display.

"We need to get Achilles out, yes, but we need to be careful. I'm going to need you guys to scope out the building, make sure the guard schedules I have match what's actually happening."

"So... when are we making our move?" Icarus' question still has not been answered and it's irritating him. It's a simple question, why is he avoiding it?

"After I get you guys some phones," he says as he taps the screen of his watch. Icarus' eye twitches at the movement. *What, am I boring him?*

"Okay they've been ordered. I'll head out to go grab those—'

"Why would we trust phones," Andromeda cuts in. "Especially phones from someone we just met?"

They're right. Icarus is irritated that he hadn't thought of the question as he brings a hand up to massage his forehead.

The caffeine isn't enough to stave off the headache mounting in his head from stress and anger. The pressure of his fingers pressing against his eye does help somewhat.

Everything is starting to feel just a bit too much. Shutting down helped for a bit, but now the irritation and anger is bringing back all the emotions and feelings he had ignored. He can't keep pushing for information, he needs to be told what to do.

"Okay, whatever, you'll get us phones and then I'll stake out the building. I can do that."

"I think you mean we can do that," Andromeda says, bumping their shoulder against his.

Right. He doesn't have to do this alone. They'll be there with him every step of the way, even if he's not quite comfortable with their lack of fighting experience.

"You're right, we'll stake out the building."

There's a rustling of papers as Thanatos gathers the information from the table. Icarus watches him, doesn't fight for it to be left with them so they can look it over even though he desperately wants to.

"Where's Achilles gonna stay?" Than asks, his back to the two at the table.

"I have a guest room he can stay in. No one else is using it." It'll have to work, it's all they have unless they were going to put the kid in the living room.

"That works for me," Andromeda says. Icarus looks at them, half expecting them to argue against that in order to take the guest bed for themselves. Sure, they have an apartment in the building, but the way they've attached themself to his hip made him think they would want to remain closer.

That's fine, he doesn't want more people in his apartment than necessary.

"Now that we've got this settled, I'm gonna go grab your phones." Thanatos doesn't linger to say goodbye, instead exiting the apartment as soon as he was done speaking and leaving Icarus and Andromeda to figure out what to do next.

"You need food, especially if you're going to house another person." Andromeda says, turning in their seat to face him. The vibrations of their foot tapping against the footrest on his stool are surprisingly calming, they let him know that Andromeda is there without them touching him.

"I have someone who normally orders my groceries and has them delivered, can we go there?"

"Where's it at?"

"In Ohio City."

"It's quicker to just go to the store ourselves." They aren't wrong, the grocery store is a lot closer to his apartment than Τελεταί is.

"The store and I aren't friends."

"Understood, but what if I'm there to help? It'll be just a quick trip to grab the essentials."

Icarus bites his lip, if it is just a quick trip he might be able to make it.

"We just need food for tonight and tomorrow morning, after that we'll go to your guy and get a whole order put together."

That doesn't sound too bad. Just a quick trip to grab something for tonight. He will have to feed the kid when they get him out, lord knows if the program's keeping him fed properly with the impending transfer to isolation.

Andromeda quietly waits for his answer. He knows they're right, that they do need food for dinner and breakfast. And the promise of a quick trip means a lot to him.

Icarus uses his tongue to push the bar of his smiley back and forth in his mouth as he mentally convinces himself to agree to the trip. It's just one quick trip, the walk will help clear his head from the events of this morning.

"Yeah okay, let's go to the store."

THE GROCERY STORE

THE WALK TO THE grocery store is pleasant. Icarus has his headphones on—blocking out the world—while Andromeda walks next to him. He knows that they were right about him needing to take a step back, but it still feels like a betrayal that the calm walk is actually helping.

He can see them fiddling with the reusable bags they insisted on bringing as the grocery store finally comes into view. It's been so long since he has been inside a shop, what with the whole 'needing to disappear for a few months' thing. Even before that, he had gotten into the habit of having his groceries delivered to the apartment.

His tattoo artist witnessed a store-induced meltdown and made it his job to make sure Icarus had food delivered to him so it wouldn't happen again.

Today, though, Andromeda insists that they go in person. They don't have time to go to Τελεταί and have them ordered and Andromeda will not rest until Icarus has actual food in the apartment.

It is also a way for them to get out of the stuffy apartment, the tension from the argument with Thanatos still hangs in the air.

He is dreading having to physically step into the store though, anxiety is growing and bubbling in him with every step. He knows what awaits him in there; too many choices of food he can't eat anyways, too bright fluorescent lights, too loud conversations with generic store music backing tracks, too many people.

Going grocery shopping is a form of torture, of that Icarus is sure.

And yet, here he is. He's standing in front of the doors with a person who had managed to go from complete stranger to a close friend in just two days. There is no going back now—well, he is sure Andromeda will let him leave if he gets overwhelmed.

He just has to do this. If he can plot to break into one of the most—if not the most—heavily secured buildings in the New World, then he can handle walking through a grocery store.

A sense of impending doom weighs Icarus down, makes him stop just outside the doors. He doesn't want to do this, he feels so much lighter after the walk and he can feel that the grocery store will make him feel bad again.

Andromeda turns around, holding the door open for him. He takes a deep breath, steadying himself before stepping through.

A cacophony of sound greets him immediately and he is glad to have his headphones on. He can faintly hear what might resemble an upbeat pop song filtering through the shitty overhead speakers, but that is overwhelmed by the sheer number of conversations happening around him. They are muffled by the headphones, not that he'd be able to pick one apart from another without them. There are too many noises all at once for him to understand any one.

Icarus glances at Andromeda, silently asking them to take the lead. He's not going to be able to focus on much. Most of his brain power is being diverted to regulating himself under the harsh lights.

He follows Andromeda as they go down the nearest aisle. They turn to show him items before throwing them in the cart, prompting him to give his opinion on each item.

It feels like an hour has passed when they finally make it to the next aisle. Icarus is becoming restless, he has started picking at the hem on his sleeves. Rolling the stitches between his fingers helps distract him.

The sense of impending doom is starting to rear its head again, discomfort and unease prick his skin. He can't handle the number of people clogging the aisles or the decision making he needs to do every time Andromeda picks something off the shelf. It's too much.

He needs to leave.

Guilt nags at him. He can't leave Andromeda in here alone with no explanation, but every time he opens his mouth to try and tell them that he needs to leave nothing comes out.

His vision blurs as he contemplates how to deal with this. He needs to calm down, he can't talk until he calms down. The world around him starts to fade as he focuses on his breathing.

A hand waving in front of his face drags him back into the aisle of the grocery store. It takes a moment for his eyes to focus on the movement and when it does he sees the concerned face just behind it.

He opens his mouth to speak, to ask them to repeat their question, but nothing comes out.

This is frustrating.

He is becoming more and more irritated with each failed attempt to speak. Fed up, he points at the door.

They nod, signing, **GO. I SHOP.**

He blinks, processing what they said and the fact that they know sign language. How had he not thought to ask about that? They said they were in the Elysian Program, of course they would have been taught.

Later. Out now.

Icarus makes his way out of the store as quickly as he can. The crisp Autumn air grants him relief from the suffocating air of the store. He moves to the wall next to the door and leans up against the rough brick.

He focuses on the texture of the brick on his back. It is dulled by the fabric of his hoodie, but still scratches into his skin, grounding him. Each breath of clean, cold air brings him more into the moment. The small sensations return to him; the slight pang of a headache from the bright and harsh lights, the soreness in his throat from the panic, the nausea in the pit of his stomach.

A tap on his shoulder makes him look up. Andromeda is standing in front of him with their arms full of paper bags.

He adjusts the volume of his music, lowering it so he can hear them speak before reaching out to grab some of the bags. Once the lead is split between the two, they start heading back towards the apartment.

The walk is silent, no words are spoken as they make their way through the city.

As they come to a stop at an intersection a bird flies past. Icarus watches it fly down Huron. It's rare to see a bird, even more so in the heart of the city.

Making a split second decision, he reaches out to haphazardly tap Andromeda's arm in an attempt to grab their attention. He wants to follow the bird, wants to see where it's going and what type of bird it is.

He shifts the paper bags in his arms before taking off down the road. The bird is quickly disappearing from his vision. He cannot have that.

"What the—Icarus!" they yell after him. He can hear a rustling before their pounding footsteps join him. The parking garages lining the street are a blur as he keeps his eyes locked on the bird.

Icarus feels light, like running in the crisp mid-day air is releasing something in him. A smile breaks out across his face as he laughs. He feels free.

The sleek black bird disappears for a moment as it turns a corner, but Icarus finds it in the reflection off the mirrored glass finish of the FieldHouse across the street.

He remembers learning about the wildlife that used to live here long ago. History is one of the few subjects they taught at the academy, it was the reason the academy was started. The Elysians were created to heal a dying Earth, to bring the Old Gods back to the land they abandoned. Their history was pounded into every prospect's head.

Animal history was never Icarus' strong suit, but his sunshine loved it. He always had a soft spot for winged animals, he loved listening to the blond boy talk about them.

Icarus went out of his way to learn about the Raven, his sunshine's favorite bird. He doesn't remember a lot about the bird, but he knows that this one is not a raven. It is much too large, even in the reflection he can tell that this is a large bird. The beak is wrong, too. The fact that he can distinguish the beak in the reflection tells him that it is too big to belong to a raven.

What really strikes Icarus as odd as he approaches the small clearing at the end of the street is that the bird was flying alone through the city. There hasn't been a notable sighting of a live animal this far into the city in decades. Hell, he had barely heard of animal sightings *anywhere* since learning that they exist.

The Gods have abandoned them, and have made the world barren. The only surviving nature that he knows of is carefully curated green spaces sprinkled between harsh cement architecture.

So why is a lone bird flying through the city?

He watches through the reflection as the bird lands on the top of a tent in the small green space at the end of the road. He slows down as he approaches, not wanting to scare the bird. This allows Andromeda to catch up to him.

"Why are we running?" they ask, gasping for air after the impromptu sprint.

Icarus points to the bird as it hops along the ridge of the tent. He turns to watch their reaction, this is a big deal.

Their eyes widen and their jaw drops open, they are just as shocked as he is. His smile has not left, though it dulls as their face drops to sadness and grim acceptance. *What?*

"A crow."

Before he can say anything the look is gone. They beam a bright smile at him. "I can't believe you found a bird! That's definitely good luck for us."

But it's not, their reaction sits wrong with him. He squints his eyes, watches them to see if that glimpse of despair will surface again.

When it doesn't, Icarus forces a smile on his face. If they don't want to talk about it then he isn't going to talk about it.

"Sorry for the detour, why don't we head back now?" The unease he feels from the flash of emotion on their face fades into the back of his mind as they start walking.

They make it to the corner in silence. As they stop to cross the street, though, Andromeda proposes a challenge.

"Bet you I'll make it there first," they say. A smug look adorns their face when Icarus looks at them.

"Bet."

He can't help but watch them run off with a smile on his face. He'll let them get a head start, let them think they have a chance to beat him on his home turf.

Maybe things will be okay. If they can smile and have fun on their way home from the store then maybe, just maybe, they will be able to make things work out.

As he starts to chase after them, Icarus thinks about how lucky he is to have the sun shining down on him. The universe has thrown him shit from day one, but today there is no inclement weather. Only sun and high hopes.

And if he lets Andromeda enter the apartment just a few steps ahead of him, then that is between Icarus and whatever higher being watched over him.

THE NEED OF A NAME

THE FIRST THING THAT Icarus sees as he opens the door to his apartment is Thanatos sitting at the kitchen island. He uses his foot to prop the door open, letting Andromeda enter the room before following them.

There isn't any room left on the island to set the groceries down, blueprints and schedules spread out over the surface. He watches Andromeda set their bags on the small section of countertop between the stove and the fridge. *That leaves the sink open*, he sets the bags down in the stainless steel double wide sink.

Andromeda starts to put the groceries away, silently motioning for him to figure out what's next. He shoots them a pleading look, mentally begs them to switch places with him. They do not budge, but instead shoo him to talk to Thanatos himself.

"Whatchya got?" he asks as he sits down on a stool across the counter from Thanatos.

"What, no 'hi! Sorry we ran to the store, we forgot to tell you'?" Icarus levels a deadpan glare at the man. He does not have the energy to argue anymore, not now that the walk to the store knocked the funk out of him.

"Did you get the phones?" he asks instead, hoping that Thanatos will drop the attitude and move the conversation in a different direction.

Icarus digs his fingers into his temples as Thanatos reaches behind him for his backpack. He isn't going to let the good mood he's in be ruined by someone who seems to hate everything he does.

I need to be nice. I need to tolerate his ass. I need to be nice, he reminds himself. If he wants to pull off this near impossible plan, then he will need Thanatos' information. Everything has to be perfect. Icarus can't do it on his own.

ATLAS rules for a reason, they wouldn't have become so powerful if they didn't have everything down to a science. Now, it's on Icarus' shoulders to figure out how to outsmart and infiltrate one of the most secure buildings in the world.

He can do it. He has to.

Rustling in the kitchen fills the tense silence as Thanatos lays two phones on the counter. He slides one towards Icarus. It's a smart phone, one of those old ones that still allows you to take the battery out. Old enough to jailbreak and stay off the radar.

Icarus picks up the device and pops off the back cover, searching for any signs of tampering in the decades old tech. There are no scratches, no weird soldering, no signs that anyone had even touched the phone.

That's good. That means there are no additional trackers hidden in the phone. No, he just has to find the GPS chip—the phone's old enough, it should still have a physical chip—and get rid of it. Without the chip, ATLAS will not be able to track him using the device.

"You won't find it," Thanatos says, breaking the silence. "I already removed the chip."

Icarus runs his tongue along the bottom of his teeth. The sensation of the ridges and sharp edges comfort him as he looks up through his eyelashes as the man.

Thanatos' eyebrow ticks up as he meets Icarus' stare. They silently argue, debate through their eyes whether they can trust each other or not. Icarus' eyes scrunch as he settles on trust.

The phone powers on quickly, the screen burning bright white as it turns on. It's already been set up, Icarus realizes as the home screen appears. It's rather simple; a plain black background with a few app shortcuts decorating the page. Most importantly, there's a small pop up at the bottom of the screen that says:

LOCATION SERVICES DISABLED
PLEASE INSERT GPS CHIP TO ENABLE

"What do I owe you?" Icarus asks. There's no way in hell these were anything less than a grand, there is quite the market for old phones like this. He knows they go for a pretty penny.

A few years back he had tried to get his hands on a phone like this but couldn't, it was way out of his budget. At the time, he just dealt with the loss and reasoned that there was no one for him to contact anyways.

"Achilles' freedom." That's it? That's all he wants for the phones? "The only payment I'll accept is you getting Achilles out of the program."

His lip twitches up as he considers the words. Icarus refuses to let himself be indebted to anyone. Let alone someone with active ties to ATLAS, even if he is providing useful information. Information that they will use to take down the conglomerate, if all things go well.

Sure, Icarus could figure out a way to move his plans forward without Thanatos as an informant. But it will be much easier to have this direct line of communication and wealth of knowledge.

"That's it? Okay, yeah. Deal."

It's not like he's going to walk away now, not now that he knows the kid wants out. The set of Thanatos shoulders relaxes as Icarus agrees to the terms, a breath of relief making Icarus realize that Thanatos didn't trust that he would really help.

He presses his lips together. That stings.

Thanatos drops his hand onto one of the papers in front of him. He doesn't move it at all and Icarus has to lean over the counter a bit to see what it is: a shift schedule.

"According to my information," he says, "There will be a brief thirty minute window where the building is empty."

"Guard change," Icarus whispers under his breath. He remembers the deafening silence that filled the halls of the academy every night at the same time, a time of many wishes and dreams of escape that didn't come true until they did.

"Exactly. Guard change. During this time you will enter the building. The Elysians that are normally posted to the building will be out, too. They have patrol at that time, it should be clear."

"Okay, so we have the when. We'll get in and out within that thirty minute window."

"But where will we get in?" Andromeda's voice next to his ear spooks him, he jumps as goose bumps flood over his skin.

"*Gods*—Meda a little heads up next time," Icarus' voice is breathy from the scare. Normally he'd hear someone coming up from behind him, it's rare for anyone to sneak up on him.

He sees Andromeda shoot him a questioning glance as they rustle his hair before turning back to Thanatos and waiting for their answer. They are obviously not apologetic about the spook.

"I have three possible entry points marked," Thanatos slides a blueprint across the counter as he speaks, "we need to figure out which one to use." The plans have the first floor of the Academy laid out. A room in the center is circled in red. *My room.*

There are three red X's around the perimeter of the building; one on the outside wall of the training room, one in the cafeteria, and one in a classroom. All of them are places that Icarus knows well from his time in the prison.

"This one," he says, pointing at the X in the classroom. That room is seared into his memory, it's in an abandoned wing of the academy. If these are the only three options, then that is the only viable way in.

"I think you should check all three out and decide which one is best instead of making hasty decisions."

"I think you should suck it." Andromeda laughs, then coughs to cover it up. Icarus knows that it's an immature response, but it's his instinct to being patronized. He hates being made to feel like he doesn't know what he's talking about, especially when it comes to the place that he spent the first thirteen years of his life. Really, it's like he's spent his whole life in those damned halls with nightmares.

He's so focused on the sneer of Thanatos' lips that he doesn't see Andromeda grab a marker. His eyes flick to them as they maneuver the blueprint closer to themself, positioning themself to mark down information.

"Since you know the building, Icarus, why don't you tell us what we need to avoid?"

"There's security cameras pretty much everywhere, but the ones that work are here," he points to where he remembers the operating cameras to be, "here, and here. The rest I broke and they never bothered to have them fixed." They circle the areas he points at before shifting their attention to the medical wing.

Once they've marked everything they remember, he points to the main entrance of the cafeteria. "You also wanna mark here and here. That's where the trip sensors are, we'll want to avoid those."

One of the only ways to safely enter the building without being detected is through the windows, not a single one has sensors on them. Everyone thought they did, though, but that's why they were never installed. It seemed too obvious.

With everything marked on the map their path is clear. If they enter through the classroom, they will only have to sneak past one functional security camera. Icarus smirks, of course the entrance he suggested was the best option, he knows that building.

"It looks like the cafeteria isn't an option" Andromeda says, tapping the butt of their marker on the marks denoting the trip sensors. "We won't be able to get past those. What about this other room?"

The training room. "No."

"There's no trip wires, no cameras, it's closer to the room—"

"No. I can't." That's all he's willing to say with Thanatos watching him.

"Got it, so it looks like we're entering here," they tap the abandoned classroom. "When are we leaving?"

"Now, we need to stake out the building for as long as we can." Thanatos starts to tidy the papers on the counter, leaving only the phone he had obtained for Andromeda.

"Great! After lunch, then."

The thought of food makes Icarus' stomach roil. They had already eaten today, do they really expect him to eat again so soon?

As if they can sense his thoughts, Andromeda turns to face him and levels him with the most disappointed glare that he has ever been on the receiving end of. He throws his hands up in surrender, it looks like he's eating again.

"We're eating lunch first," they state, leaving no room for arguments as they turn back to the freshly stocked kitchen. Icarus is left to pout to himself while avoiding talking.

Thanatos does the same, avoiding his gaze as Icarus busies himself with the phone in his hand. He opens the contact list and is greeted by a handful of names: Thanatos, of course, but also Andromeda, Hypnos, Dimetor—*how did he get my artist's number?*—and a mystery contact labeled DO NOT USE with a sun emoji next to it.

Icarus opens his mouth to ask about that last contact—why would he have a contact programmed into the phone that he's not allowed to contact or even know who it is?—when Andromeda returns. They set a sandwich down in front of him, a sandwich that looks like it has cheese on it.

"Dairy-free cheese, it's supposed to taste like provolone. Thought you might like it."

Icarus flushes at the words, it surprises him that they remembered his allergy. He ducks his head and takes a bite of the sandwich. It's delicious, the cheese is a taste he hasn't had in so long. He devours the rest of the sandwich, reveling in the sweet taste and the sweet laughter that fills the air at his antics.

Andromeda and Thanatos talk over the rescue as they eat, cement the details and iron out the kinks in their plan. Icarus doesn't pay attention to them, lets their voices fade into the background as he thinks. There are a lot of things that can—and likely will—go wrong on his end. His mental state is unpredictable at the moment, the lack of sleep will not help him when he enters the building he never thought he'd have to go into again. He thought he was finally free of his past, but there's a nagging voice in his head telling him that if he steps foot in that place again there will be severe consequences.

Icarus' head snaps up as something moves in his peripheries, drawing the attention of both Andromeda and Thanatos.

"Whatchya lookin' at?" Andromeda asks as they glance in the same direction. Icarus swallows a thick clump of fear, but does not look away.

"Nothing. Thought I saw something move. Must have been a shadow or something."

"Huh, weird," they say, turning back to the conversation they were having. "Well, since we have your attention now, there's another piece of information you should know."

Icarus hesitantly looks away from the source of guttural fear, turning towards Thanatos as he speaks, "You know how Achilles mentioned someone named Pat in his letter?"

"Yeah, what of it?"

"Well, Pat is someone we will have to keep an eye out for. He's the kid's Handler."

"Handler?"

"Yeah," Thanatos looks just as uncomfortable with the information as Icarus feels. "Handler."

What the fuck? Why does the kid have a Handler? Only the most troublesome of the Elysians had them, the ones that even ATLAS had a hard time breaking and molding into their perfect toy.

He's having trouble meshing that information with the memory of the kid he has. Sure, Achilles had enjoyed giving his sunshine some trouble but that was just the result of an unfortunate puppy crush. The kid never actually made trouble for the program. Hell, he did everything he could not to get in trouble while under Icarus' care.

What changed?

You left. No, not it couldn't be that. He's been gone for far longer than he had known the kid, there's no way he's still hung up over him to the point of wreaking havoc with ATLAS. *I'm not that important.*

"The issue comes from the way he talks about this 'Pat' in his letter," Thanatos continues, oblivious to the mental turmoil in Icarus' head. "Quote: *Especially not that they've separated me and Pat. Can't get my hopes up now when I'm trying to get him back.*

"I don't know about you, but that's not the way I'd talk about a person that was assigned to keep me in check at all times." Icarus shakes his head. Thanatos is right, he wouldn't talk about a Handler like that either.

"There's something more going on there, we need to find the Handler too."

Thanatos' eyes widen at the words, his mouth gaping as he fumbles out, "No, no there's not enough time."

"I don't care, we need to find them."

"Then you will have to go back. I don't have any information on who the Handler is or where they are being held. Just that they aren't with Achilles right now."

"So we go back," Andromeda says, a fiery determination lacing their voice. "We get Achilles out and use him to gather information on his Handler, then we go back to get them."

They look at Icarus, silently begging him to agree with them. The whole operation hinges on him being able to enter the building for a second time, and he's not sure he will be able to handle that. Still, he can't bring himself to say no. If this person is so important to the kid, then he knows he will go to the ends of the Earth to make sure they are safe.

"Sure. Get Achilles now, go back for Pat. Easy, done deal."

Thanatos huffs, shakes his head at the decision. "You guys are suicidal." He sneers the words as if they are something to be ashamed of. Icarus is not ashamed, would never be ashamed to help someone escape the program. Even if he does not know them.

"Whatever, the next issue is trying to figure out how you guys are going to get Achilles to leave without tearing down the building in search of his Handler. Rumor has it that he's gotten... rough around the edges these past few years." Thanatos locks eyes with Icarus with a veneer of disgust on his face.

Icarus stands up and heads to his bedroom. As he passes Thanatos, he says, "I think I'll be just fine with the kid. I know him."

"Just because you know him doesn't mean he knows you, Icarus. You left a long time ago."

That stops him in his tracks. Those words, though the same as the ones running through his mind, feel different coming from someone else. It makes them more real. He shakes off the uncomfortable realization and continues his path.

"So once we get Achilles, we take the same path out?" Andromeda's voice filters through the air. It's a comfort to hear their voice, helping ground him as he digs around in his closet.

"Yeah. Once you get the kid you guys need to get the fuck out of the building. You should be able to take the same path, but if anything happens I'm sure Icarus will be able to get you guys out."

"Great, and do you have clothes for us to wear?"

"No need," Icarus calls out. He finds the clothes he was digging for: two black shirts, one a long sleeve and one a cut off, and two pairs of black pants. These will work.

The sound of a stool scraping against the floor grates of Icarus' ears, Andromeda soon joins him in his room. He hands the long sleeve shirt and a pair of pants to them. They should fit them pretty well, Icarus buys all his clothes a couple sizes larger than necessary.

"Yeah, that'll work," Andromeda says as they lean back against the frame of the door. They look at him, a questioning glint in their eye—asking a question he is not yet ready to answer. They must recognize the clothes, recognize the make and the fabric of them.

Icarus shakes his head, there's nothing to say. The answer lies in the clothes. Instead, he turns back to his closet and digs out a pair of boots from the very back. Boots he hasn't touched in ten years. Hopefully they'll fit, his eyes search for the tag on the tongue of the boot and is greeted with a size just one smaller than his current boots. That'll be fine.

He doesn't wait to see if Andromeda has left the room, he doesn't much care if they see the galaxy of scars that cover his body as he changes. There are harnesses that he needs to put on before he throws his shirt on, the criss-crossing straps of leather hold his knives.

After struggling to get them situated properly he turns towards the mirror in the corner of his room. Icarus pulls the cloth covering the mirror off, revealing the shattered pieces of glass held together by sheer willpower and spite. Each shard of glass holds a piece of his reflection, and amalgamation in the general semblance of a human. Not that he can recognize himself in the shards. No, he never has been able to.

The straps are easy to adjust when he can see them, it's a matter of seconds before the leather stops irritating him and lays flat on his skin. The sleeveless shirt is thrown on over the harnesses, covering Icarus' sins and flaws until he feels he can breathe again.

The last thing he does with the mirror out is fix his ponytail, tucking stray fly-aways into the tight and neat hairstyle. His hair will need to be tucked up into a hat before they enter the academy, he can't risk anyone seeing it. The red will surely give away his identity.

Once everything is in place, Icarus takes one last moment to look over everything. Anything that could have tied him to his days at the Elysian Program are covered in Elysian Black. His eyes drift to a shard in the bottom right corner of the mirror, catching on an amorphous black blob watching him before he throws the cloth back over the mirror and turns to leave. Andromeda is still standing in the doorway, a soft look on their face. *Pity, I don't need their pity.*

Icarus nods and brushes past them into the living room. It is time to go, time to rescue the kid.

THE RESCUE

IT IS GO TIME. After spending gods know how long watching the building, shift change is upon them. They have only a brief window to get in, get the kid, and get out before the next shift makes their rounds; about thirty minutes if Thanatos' calculations are right.

Icarus looks at Andromeda next to him, his eyes almost missing them in the dark with their all-black outfit. They can do this, they are going to make it in—and out—safely.

They shoot him a thumbs up before pointing two fingers towards the window. That's his signal, the sign that it's time to open the window.

He creeps forward out of the tree cover, making sure to keep low in case anyone looks out over the lawn. His heart is pounding in his chest, it has been so long since he's been in this building. So long since he had left this place and everyone he loved behind.

Icarus' hands are trembling as he reaches up towards the window. He has to find purchase with the bottom of the pane, but his fingers keep slipping.

His breath hitches as a warm hand comes to rest on his shoulder. Andromeda is crouched there with him. They are there, he is not going back into his personal hell alone.

I can do this—we can do this. His fingers turn white where they push against the window trim. Damn, these windows are shut good.

Just when he's about to let go and try a different angle, the window pane slides up an inch. That's all the room he needs as he slides the meat of his hand into that gap and leverages his shoulder to force the window fully open.

With a quick flick of his wrist, Icarus motions for Andromeda to go through the opening. He clambers in after them, making sure to shove a stick into the window track to keep it open while they search for Achilles.

The soft and repetitive *pit, pat, pit, pat* of their steps helps to ease Icarus' anxiety. He is already struggling to remain calm inside the building, a lot of unpleasant memories are tied to this place.

It feels like a punishment for the sins he has committed that they have to enter through the room he and his sunshine would frequently sneak to. The room hasn't changed, the old yoga mats still rest against the back wall next to the window. Just where he had left them last time the two hung out.

There are so many memories just in this room, but he cannot think about them right now. He needs to keep his composure. For the kid.

If it is already this hard for him, Icarus dreads what awaits him in his room. Because *of course* they are keeping Achilles in his old room. Why would they make things easy for him?

At least he knows how to get to the room from here. That is a plus, they don't have time to wander the halls in search of the kid.

Icarus bumps into Andromeda as they stop at the door. He squints his eyes, hoping the apologetic smile is conveyed through the mask he's wearing as he moves to the other side of the door frame. He really needs to be the one leading them through the halls, he's the one who knows where they're going.

A scan of the hallway tells Icarus that there's no guards nearby. He steps through the doorway into the hall, Andromeda follows close behind. If he remembers correctly—and that is a big if given the labyrinthine nature of the corridors—then his room isn't far from here.

Shitty as his memory is, he isn't worried about losing his way, though the halls are mighty disorienting. He's worried that he won't be able to hold himself together as he leads Andromeda through the turns and twists. Icarus has to stop every couple turns, stopping to quell the rising nausea threatening their plans. *Make a left here, turn down this corridor, check for classroom 12A, continue until they hit a dead end.* If he focuses on the directions he won't be able to focus on the memories plaguing every step.

It becomes harder to ignore the tremor in his hands as they pass room after room of memories; first the room that held his classes, then the stairwell he and Apollon would sneak to for some time alone, then the room where he would watch over Achilles, then the hall leading to the cafeteria.

His breath catches in his throat as they come up to a large set of double doors, gilded in the same gold that haunts his nightmares from all those years ago. The training room. The room where his father decided that he wasn't good enough and that he serves the program better dead. The room that changed his life.

Does Iapyx train there now? Is he in there training with our father, receiving the compliments that I should have gotten? Is he being told that he's a prodigy, a natural with fire weapons just like I was told years ago?

Has my little brother completely replaced me? Both as an Elysian and in dad's heart?

A warm, steady hand grabs his trembling hand and tangles its fingers between his. Right, he doesn't have time for this. It doesn't matter if he's been replaced, it was bound to happen. He is disposable in the eyes of his father.

Icarus squeezes the hand in his before turning to continue down the hall. He doesn't let it go, he needs the reassurance that he wasn't walking back into the worst parts of his past alone.

They should be just a one turn away from his old room at this point, he presses on even as the suffocating atmosphere of the building threatens to rip the air from his lungs.

He focuses on the quiet but firm pounding of their footsteps as they make their way through the halls, trying to stop himself from drowning in his thoughts again.

Planning this rescue turned out to be much easier than executing it, Icarus thought it wouldn't be as hard as it had been. Thoughts he would have no issues walking the halls so long as he never entered the training room. How wrong he was.

Every breath in becomes laden with his past, burdened with *What if*'s as they turn the last corner. The hallway is exactly the same as it's always been: long, desolate, *terrifying*.

Doors line the hall, symmetrically dotted down the path. They lead to the rooms holding the next generation of Elysians. The next generation of people who will be lied to and told that they are doing what's right, that they shouldn't question what they are doing and that they can do no wrong.

An undertow of disgust fills in the gaps of his anxiety as they make their way to the last door at the end of the hall. *My room.*

Icarus can see the light from the room creep into the hall as they approach, the door is slightly ajar. He drops Andromeda's hand, stepping between them and the door. **WAIT**, he signs.

There's something wrong, under no circumstance should the door be left ajar. It's one of the academy rules that the door is closed at all times, the students were not to be open and social at any point. Especially past curfew.

Icarus flattens himself against the wall and tries to peek through the crack. He can't see much, just a sliver of the closet and the far edge of the bed.

When that doesn't work, he listens. He doesn't know what he's listening for, per se, but he doesn't expect to hear muffled sobs. No shifting feet, no authoritative voice, just the heart-wrenching echoes of sadness.

The door slides open easily as he nudges it with his foot, revealing more of the bed and the curled up form of a body.

Andromeda joins him at the wall with the flick of his fingers. He's certain there's no one else in the room as he steps through the threshold into his room, leaving them to keep an eye out while he talks to the kid.

The head of the person on the bed snaps up to where he stands. His body moves into a defensive position, the years of training he received here working as they should against a threat as strong as Icarus.

"Relax, kid. I'm here to get you out," Icarus says, pulling his hood back to reveal his face. Hopefully the kid can recognize him, he hadn't thought of how the scar changed his face.

The rigid tension holding Achilles still dissipates as he whispers a soft, "You're alive."

The words set Achilles into motion, he launches himself at Icarus and nearly knocks him to the ground. His strong arms wrap around the trembling kid as he leans into the embrace.

"Yeah, kiddo. I am." He takes a moment to just take in the touch, to really feel the embrace and the comfort of holding his chosen brother in his arms. Tears threaten to spill as a wave of love and guilt rolls over him.

"Now, let's get you out of here." Icarus squeezes the kid in his arms before stepping back, out of the embrace, and turning towards the hall.

"We don't have long before the night shift makes its rounds, we need to get you out now."

"Wait," Achilles' voice is thin, raw. It sounds like he's been crying for a while. "We have to go find Pat."

Icarus was afraid this would happen, afraid that something would go wrong once the existence of the Handler was mentioned.

"Kid, we don't have time right now. We'll come back for your Handler, okay?"

"He's not my handler, he's my fiancée." That... actually explains a lot. Icarus puts a hand on the kid's shoulder, using the other hand to cup his face.

"Achilles. I promise you we will come back for him." Some of the fear seeps out of Achilles' face as he speaks. "But right now we need to get you out, okay?"

His voice is shaky as he responds, "I can't leave him here."

"I get that. I said the same thing years ago. You have my word that I will not make the same mistake twice, we will come back for him." Deep brown eyes widen at his words, fear rushing back in at the prospect of never coming back for his fiancée.

Icarus makes a stupid decision then, one that he prays he will be able to stand behind. "I swear on the river Styx, we will come back for Pat."

Achilles' jaw drops as he flounders for words, truly taking in what Icarus had just put on the line. They will come back for Pat, they just need to get Achilles out first.

Icarus can practically see a wall of determination come down over his face, the αριστος αχαιον has his mission now. Get out, make a plan, come back for Pat.

They step through the door and Icarus turns to nod at Andromeda. He will have to formally introduce the two when they escape, but for now they head down the hall.

Memories blink in the pass of an eye, no longer plaguing him and pulling him under the surface. Not now that he has someone to protect, not with Andromeda's comforting hand slotted with his.

The suffocating atmosphere dissipates with every step they take away from his tumultuous past, the golden gilded doors of the training room aren't even enough to make him stumble. Icarus is leaving his home for the second time, but this time it feels right.

With Andromeda walking next to him and Achilles just a few steps behind, Icarus feels like he's making the right decision for the first time in his life. The memories that haunt these halls seem small, they aren't overwhelming anymore. He feels he can actually face them, stare them down and put them in their place. Tell them that he won't bow to their will any longer.

Relief loosens the tension in his shoulders as the group make it to the room Icarus and Andromeda entered. The window is still propped open, Achilles walks right up to it with no hesitation. He straddles the sill and turns towards the two left inside. Icarus knows something is wrong as his casual grin turns to a look of sheer horror.

It feels like the floor dropped out underneath Icarus, but he schools his expression into a calm acceptance and says, "Go, get out of here. I'll be right behind you."

Then he turns around. There is a lumbering form in the doorway, blocking them into the room. Icarus glances at Andromeda and tilts his head towards the window. He'll take care of this.

And by take care of this he means that he will distract the fucker while they escape.

Icarus groans when he turns back towards the man in the doorway. He recognizes the monstrosity of muscle in front of him.

Sisyphus. One of the top three Elysians, the master of blunt weapons.

Icarus had run into him a handful of times in his childhood, though never without adult supervision. Memory serves him a bone-deep feeling of being under a microscope, a remnant from when he was in the same room as the monster growing up.

Now that he's older and under the same scrutiny by that *thing's* beady eyes, he understands why. It's like he's being examined, being dissected through vision alone. But that would require the monster to have any brain cells, which he clearly doesn't if the lack of a thought behind his eyes says anything. No, no it's more like he is being devoured by the swampy depths of the monster's gaze.

A shiver runs down Icarus' back as he slides into a defensive stance, preparing for whatever the bastard will throw at him. He needs to keep his guard up long enough to allow Andromeda and Achilles to get away, that's it. Just until they get out. Then he will follow.

Icarus watches as a slimy grin crawls across Sisyphus' face, distorting the already fucked up visage. His nose scrunches and he sneers. Of course it had to be him, it couldn't have been literally any other Elysian that found them.

I hope this doesn't last long. Icarus had left fighting like this behind the night he left the academy. He made sure to keep up his training, though, throughout the years.

Countless nights dancing on the rooftop have kept him limber. He can lie and say it was to clear his mind, but he knows deep down that the exercise serves as a pathetic replacement for the rigorous training he grew up doing.

None of those nights compare to the rush of adrenaline pulsing through his veins. The all-too-light feeling of floating through the air as he dodges the first swing of a mace.

It feels like a breath of fresh air to be in the heat of battle like this. Freeing beyond Icarus' wildest dreams as he deftly whirls and weaves out of the way of certain injury.

Icarus isn't trying to fight back, he knows that if he were to engage the monster that he wouldn't make it out. No, he's just providing a distraction while Achilles and Andromeda get the fuck away from the building.

And quite the distraction it will be. Hell, he'll even put on a show for the burly fucker that stands between Icarus and Achilles.

The wind is knocked out of Icarus' lungs as the mace lands a hit. The momentum of the swing easily throws him against the wall. *Ough, that's going to bruise like a bitch.*

The hit serves as a good reminder that he cannot face the Elysian for any longer than necessary. If he spends any more time dancing on the precipice of disaster, he won't make it out in one piece.

He needs to get out.

A quick glance at the window tells him that Andromeda and Achilles made it out, he can't see either of them. Good. It's his turn to escape now.

The mountain of asshole in front of him made that easier said than done, though, as he maneuvers the fight so that he stands between Icarus and the window. Each swing of the mace forces Icarus to take another step back into the labyrinthine halls behind him. *Shit.*

He can't get caught in the halls, he's not sure how long it will be before the night guards make their rounds but he cannot be caught by them.

His attention is drawn back to the monster in front of him when Sisyphus opens his maw, revealing a mouth full of rotten teeth.

"Ya just had to kill my fun, didn't ya." His words stank, the way he speaks reeks of vile and contempt. "Had my eye on those pretty gals you had o'er there, now they gone and left me t' fight yous. I's hoping t' see if they's taste as good 's they look."

Each vile word that comes from that monstrosity's rotten mouth stokes the red-hot pit of anger in Icarus. How dare this disgusting excuse of a human being talk about his friends—no, his family—like that.

"Y'know, after I'm done with ya I'll pay yer gals a visit out there. Can't a gotten far."

His vision bleeds red. It is as if his body is possessed by something as he switches to offense. The only thing left in his mind is a repeating mantra of *how dare he*.

How dare he as Icarus lunged forward, catching Sisyphus off-guard and ducking under his trunk of an arm. The mace is swung just a second too late, slicing through the space he just occupied.

How dare he as Icarus reaches up, grabbing the handle of the still swinging mace. He disarms the hulking giant easily in his stupor.

How dare he as he uses the weight of the mace to sweep the monster's feet out from under him, knocking him to the floor with a loud thud. The mantra repeats in his mind as he uses his new weapon against its former owner, laying defenseless on the floor of the abandoned classroom.

How dare he, how dare he, how dare he, how DARE HE.

THE AFTERMATH

WITH A SHOCK ICARUS realizes the body he is stomping on is no longer moving, no longer breathing.

He staggers back, away from the bloody remains of what was once an Elysian. He did that. *He did that.*

He takes in a raggedy breath and looks down at blood soaked hands—*his* blood soaked hands—and starts to tremble. *What have I done?*

Icarus just killed someone. No, no that's not quite right. Icarus just butchered someone. An Elysian, sure, but that does little to comfort him. That man may have been an Elysian, but he was still human underneath all the grime and vitriol and disgusting filth.

161

His breath catches in his throat as a hand is placed on his shoulder. It's too much. He can't handle it right now, doesn't want anyone to see what he has done.

The slickness of the blood on his hands is revolting, the blood that does not belong to him. The bruises littering his body ache. The mace that caused them lays in a pile of gore next to the unmoving body, never to be used again.

Icarus doesn't want the others to see this mess. It is one thing for them to talk about taking down the Elysians, but another to brutally end their lives.

This was supposed to be an easy break in. They were supposed to get in, grab Achilles, and get out. But he had to be there, he had to try and stop them from making it out. Of course something had to go wrong.

Icarus did what he had to do, but that doesn't mean he wants them to see. Doesn't want them to judge him. He can feel their gazes burning holes into him as he falls to the ground, wrapping his arms around his body in a vain attempt to stop the trembling.

It doesn't work.

The warmth of a body joins him, crouches down by his side. Why haven't they left? Why haven't they run in fear from what he did?

Can't they see the remains, not five feet away from where he has collapsed? Can't they see the blood staining his skin? The filth and contamination flowing through his body?

He hadn't meant to kill the man, but that doesn't mean he hadn't enjoyed it. Doesn't mean that he didn't feel alive for the first time in years as he dodged and danced around the mace as it swung at him. Didn't feel unbridled euphoria as he tore into the body. Just because he hadn't intended to kill the Elysian doesn't mean that he didn't lose himself in the ecstasy and pleasure of causing pain and suffering.

Icarus is a monster, can't they see that?

The anxiety that sits deeply rooted in his gut morphs into something he is better equipped to handle: Anger. He is angry at ATLAS for sensing Sisyphus to the academy when this was supposed to be an easy rescue mission. He is angry at Thanatos for not taking account of this possibility. He is angry at Achilles for making things more difficult for a boy. He is angry at the universe for everything that has led to this moment.

But most importantly, he is angry at himself. He is upset that he let his emotions cloud his judgment. Angry that he couldn't control himself, especially in front of the people that mean the world to him.

And now, he is upset that he cannot contain his anger. Upset as he brings his hand up to repeatedly hit himself in an attempt to make his brain stop. Upset as he uses his other hand to dig into a bruise on his leg, adding his own finger shaped marks to the mottling left by the blunt weapon.

The warmth on his shoulder disappears briefly before two strong, warm arms wrap around him. Icarus can't see anything, the pain mixed with sweat, blood—not his, *oh Gods it's not his blood*—and tears blinds him. And still, he knows who's holding him.

Achilles holds him still as two more hands grab his wrists, pulling them away from their painful targets. Icarus lashes out without the tactile sensation of pain.

Tears stream down his face and he screams into the heavens. He screams and thrashes and lets all his frustrations out at the Gods that should have done something—*anything*—to stop what happened and then screams some more. He doesn't stop until there is nothing left, until his throat can barely produce a whisper.

It is then, and only then, that he can hear a small voice from the body holding him still.

"Please stop. Please, Icarus, you're scaring me, please stop."

He tries to speak, but none of the words make it out of his empty lungs. The kid should be afraid of him, couldn't he see what Icarus had done?

Icarus lowers his eyes from the ceiling, breaking his staring contest with the Gods above to look at the reason they came here. A flash of genuine sadness crosses the eyes of the kid, a look that betrays the shattering of something important.

No, no that can't be right. There's no reason for him to be sad. He should be mad, disgusted, scared. Not sad. Why is he sad?

And why does it make Icarus feel so... empty?

"It came from this hall!" *Fuck, the guard shift.*

"We need to leave. Now." Andromeda's words leave no room for argument as they stand up, pulling Icarus up by the wrists still in their grasp.

As soon as they let him go his knees buckle. The first guard rounds the corner of the hall as he goes down *hard*. There's a crack, a loud sound of something breaking from the fall, but Icarus can't feel anything. He's too far away, there's too much going on.

"Go. Get out," he mumbles. He won't be able to stand, they need to leave. "I'll distract them. Go."

They need to get out, if they don't get Achilles out then this whole mission was for nothing. He would have murdered someone for no reason. No, they need to leave.

Achilles has a different plan as he flings Icarus over his shoulder. It's an awkward squeeze through the window, but they make it through.

Icarus watches Andromeda jump out the window and slam it shut behind them just as the first guard enters the room. He quickly wraps his arms around Achilles' waist as the jostling of movement threatens to make him slip.

The disjointing movement is enough to distract Icarus as they make their way into the woods behind the building. The same woods he had escaped into all those years ago.

Dead leaves and twigs pass in a blur as they make their way further into the dense tree cover. Icarus buries his face into the small of Achilles' back, it is taking everything in his power to keep him lunch in his stomach.

The jostling slows before coming to a halt. Icarus taps his hand against Achilles' stomach, silently asking to be let down.

The world spins as he's settled up against a tree. He doesn't even attempt to stand, he knows that his legs will not support his weight after the fall.

He closes his eyes and leans his head back against the trees. Icarus' head is pounding, the adrenaline of the fight and his outburst earlier has worn off. The aches and soreness is settling deep into his bones.

Icarus is battered to hell and back and his body is going to make him regret it in the morning.

"Why the hell didn't you guys run?" he groans. Not happy with the silence he receives as an answer, Icarus pries an eye open to see Achilles and Andromeda arguing through sign language.

He's too tired to try and figure out what they're saying. Icarus focuses his energy on opening his other eye and sitting up straight instead.

"And leave you with them? After you just killed one of the Top Three?" Whatever argument the two were having seems to be over now that Achilles is speaking. He locks his gaze with Icarus', pausing for a moment as he searches for something in the half-dead glare.

The pity he feels for Icarus is palpable, filling his gaze and making it unbearable to maintain eye contact. He looks to the ground, a small sapling is growing just next to his leg and he focuses on it.

That's enough of an answer for Achilles as he continues, "I can't lose you when I just got you back, Birdie."

"Don't call me that."

Icarus hasn't heard that nickname in a very long time, not since he escaped that night. Not since he was forced to escape alone.

"But that's what I—"

"Don't matter. Don't call me that." Icarus looks over at Andromeda, who has been suspiciously quiet through this conversation. *I can change that*, Icarus thinks, a cocky smirk settling on his face.

"Plus I'm not that easy to get rid of, just ask Mother Dearest."

"Thank whoever is in charge of this fucked Earth that I am not your mother," they respond lightly, running with the change in topic.

Icarus chuckles as he imagines a tired Andromeda chasing small versions of himself and his sunshine around the academy. It would have been entertaining, at the very least.

The laugh makes him wince. *Damn, must've cracked a rib.* They really need to head back to the apartment so he can patch himself up.

To do that, though, he needs to stand up. He quickly finds out that it's easier said than done. Each attempt to stand fails, even as Achilles rushes over to support him. His body just can't support itself with all the damage from the fight. He needs to train more.

This is going nowhere, Icarus realizes. He's not going to be able to walk at all, he's going to weigh down the group. *Shit.*

A shout in the distance accompanies Icarus' thoughts. The guards made it to the woods, they will catch up at any minute.

Achilles doesn't fling Icarus over his shoulder this time, but does crouch before him. Icarus will take what he can, clambering onto the shorter's back with the assistance of Andromeda. Strong hands cup his thighs as he wraps his arms around Achilles' neck.

"Well don't you look cozy, Mr. Koala," Andromeda teases him as they stand and brush the dirt off their knees.

"Shut up," he mumbles as he buries his face in the kid's neck. A wave of exhaustion rolls over him, lulling him into a calm relaxation as Andromeda leads the way to his home.

The rhythm of Achilles' stride—not too fast due to Icarus' weight on his back, but still fast enough to out-pace the guards—and the tune Andromeda starts to hum coaxes him into a fitful sleep. As he fades into unconsciousness, he feels the hands holding his thighs squeeze. As if they are letting him know that he is good to sleep. That they will make sure he is safe.

Icarus is jostled awake as he is set down into a chair. *I'm falling*, his half-conscious brain tells him. He tightens his octopus-like grip on the body holding him.

Achilles taps his forearm, begging to be released.

"You're safe. Stop choking me, I'm not into it," he chokes out.

Icarus loosens his grip enough to let the kid breathe without fully letting go. He doesn't want to wake up, this is only the second time in a month that he's had meaningful sleep and he isn't about to let it slip through his fingers.

"Come on, Icarus." A whisper against his ear, a plea to join them in the world of the conscious.

"We're home, we gotta talk now."

His voice is raspy as he whispers back, "Don' wanna."

"Oi! dejar de ser un bebé." Andromeda calls from... somewhere. Icarus isn't sure where they are in the apartment, but they are far enough away to need to raise their voice.

"'m not a baby, bitch." Icarus lets go, falling into the chair beneath him. After shifting himself into a comfortable position, he reaches back out and pulls the warm body in front of him down to join him. The warmth and comfort of the situation is lulling him back into the clutches of sleep as he whispers, "We got you out," into the head of blond hair that's pressed into the crook of his neck.

"You got me out," Achilles breathes, relaxing as he makes himself comfy in Icarus' hold.

"'m so happy you're okay."

"Talk for yourself," Achilles says, pushing back against Icarus' chest so he can look the man in the eye. Or, look him in the eye as much as possible with Icarus barely awake gaze.

"I thought you were dead, Icarus. They told me you were dead."

"Sorry." He didn't know what else to say, he's too tired to talk about everything that's running through his brain, too tired to actually give the kid a real apology.

Instead, they sit in silence. It's not unsettling, but rather a quiet blanket full of future promises. Promises that come morning, Icarus will talk about what happened and why. Promises that he won't make the same mistake again.

And it's with those promises that Icarus falls back into the loving embrace of the unconscious, ready to face whatever dreams the Gods decide to throw at him.

The Nightmare

A SCREAM RIPS FROM him as Icarus thrashes in his bed. The sheets tangle around his legs as he pushes himself up onto his forearms, his head hanging as he takes in heavy, gulping breaths.

Slowly, ever so slowly, he raises his head and looks around the room. *I'm not there. I'm not there,* he repeats wordlessly as he takes in everything he can in the dim light.

Icarus recognizes his chair, a lump of clothing thrown over the back of it. A breath in. He recognizes the door, a square of cork haphazardly attached to the front of it and dotted with tacks. A slow release of air. He recognized the shadowy outlines of books sitting on the windowsill, illuminated in the soft pink rays of dawn. Another breath in.

He's in his apartment. Not the dormitory, but his shitty apartment.

The panic subsides, leaving Icarus drenched with sweat and uncomfortable. He can feel where his clothes touch him, restricting his movements and sticking to his sweaty skin. He can't take it, it's too much, the sensation is too much.

Icarus sits back on his knees as he flings his cutoff across the room. Then he struggles to unbuckle the knife harness that sits strapped across his chest. The buckles aren't cooperating with him, they're getting stuck and he doesn't have the patience to deal with them. He hears them tear as he resorts to pulling the harness over his head, where it soon joins his cutoff in the corner of the room.

It's not enough, Icarus is still suffocating in the heat of his own panic. The bedsheets twisted around his pants aren't helping, and he decides that they're the next to go. The sheets fight back as he struggles to free himself from them, but in the end Icarus wins and flings them to join the rest of his clothes.

The cool air rushes over him as he lays back on the bed, staring up at the popcorn textured ceiling. His chest heaves with each breath, a small attempt to calm his nerves and keep him from overheating any more than he already has.

As his heart rate starts to slow, he sits up. His forehead burns against his knees, his arms are like molten lava around his legs. God, Icarus hates the nightmares. Every single night has been plagued by them recently, he hasn't managed a peaceful sleep in a week.

It doesn't help that he had to revisit the site of his nightmares to get the kid out. Turns out walking the halls that haunt your subconscious makes your visceral nightmares worse.

Stray tears track down his cheeks as he takes in a shuddering breath. At first the dreams hadn't really bothered him. They sucked, yeah, but they are memories of a life he left behind. Memories he will always carry with him, even now that things have changed.

Now Icarus has people he cares for. People who care for him in turn. He had helped Achilles escape the Elysian program, they're going to reconcile come morning. He has Andromeda, someone who had entered his life recently and made a home for themself despite his reluctance to let them in. He has Thanatos, no matter how rocky their situation is at the moment.

And now, they're planning on going up against the person he sees nearly every night in his sleep. He will have to face that *monster* again.

There's a small part of his brain that tells him that he'll get to see the other face that haunts his dreams, too. The one that hurts in a different way, a more raw way.

Icarus' spiraling thoughts are interrupted by a tap-tap on the door frame. He turns his head to see Achilles standing in the doorway.

"Hey, you okay?" he asks, his voice laced with concern. "I heard you yell."

Icarus now has people in his life who care enough about him to check on him after a nightmare. The tears that never truly went away threaten to spill again at that realization.

Achilles, after not receiving a response, makes his way to the bed. He sits down on the edge of the bed. Close enough to be a comfort, but not close enough to physically touch Icarus.

"What happened?"

How can he answer that? What has happened? He can't say that he had a recurring nightmare about the night he abandoned the poor kid, he can't say that he's reminiscing on the abuse his father handed him daily until he was deemed not worthy of life. He can't burden the kid, he doesn't need to deal with Icarus' issues.

No, Icarus can't do that to the kid. Even if he wants to, the emotion clogging his throat won't let him. Instead, he whispers, "nightmare," before turning to look out the window. Away from Achilles.

A moment passes, a beat of silence, before two arms wind their way around Icarus. It's awkward, the kid clearly hasn't had to comfort someone before. But that doesn't matter to Icarus.

He leans back into the hug, fresh tears making their way down his face and pooling at his chin. The thoughts and emotions are so much, almost too much to bear after living a nearly emotionless life for the past decade.

Icarus roughly wipes away the tears with one hand. He uses the other to grab the hand on his chest, trying to pull it away from him. Put some distance between himself and the body at his back. He shouldn't be seen like this, he needs space to compose himself.

Achilles doesn't allow that, though, as his arms tighten around Icarus. They squeeze away any resistance that Icarus had, the kid isn't going to let him go.

Icarus doesn't allow himself to weep, to show the vulnerability he revealed to Andromeda not that long ago. But he did allow himself the space to ground himself in the hold. His throat burns with the effort of keeping the tears in, his eyes glossed over as he squints the emotions away.

Achilles, bless his soul, doesn't say anything. He doesn't have to, just the act of being at his side is enough. More than enough.

An air of comfort stretches between the two; not silence, but nothing more than a white noise as the rush of cars on the streets below filter through the window.

The peace of the night starts to ease its way into his bones as the tears stop begging to be released, leaving Icarus' throat raw and his eyes sore. Numbness creeps over him as he gently taps the arms around him. They loosen, allowing Icarus to move out of their embrace and stand.

His joints pop as he stretches. There's one elbow that won't crack, he'll have to try again later. The built up pain will eventually become unbearable, but for now Icarus walks over to the chair in the corner. The one with a pile of clothes on it that helped ground him when he woke. If he remembers correctly, there should be a hoodie thrown over the back of the chair. It's rather cold in the room without the clothes he went to sleep in, his boxers provide little warmth.

He grabs the hoodie and holds it up, examining it. The dim light of the rising sun lets him see the details of the fabric; the soft gray material, the embroidered design across the front, the silicone beads tied on the strings. Yeah, this hoodie will do.

The hoodie goes on easily, it's over sized and heavy weight fabric slides easily over his head and drops to cover him down to mid thigh. After it settles, Icarus turns to face a confused and flushed Achilles.

He isn't sure what to say. There are so many things that need to be explained. So many years of information that he needs to tell the kid about.

But Icarus doesn't know where to start.

In a turn of good fortune, he doesn't have to figure it out. Achilles stands up rather abruptly and moves to leave the room.

He pauses at the door, tapping the wood frame as he asks a simple question.

"Roof?"

Icarus nods and follows him out through the dead silent halls of the apartment. No lights are on, the door to the guest bedroom is closed. Andromeda must have stayed after the rescue, hopefully they hadn't been woken up by his nightmare.

He makes sure to grab his keys and lock the door on the way out, Icarus doesn't want another break in to occur. Especially not with someone sleeping in his guest bed.

The hallway is quiet this morning, the absence of muffled noise is disquieting. He keeps himself calm by following the sway of the kid's hair, *back and forth and back and forth,* as they walk towards the staircase. The way the strands would cross each other or bob up and down kept his mind entertained, distracted.

The bang of the door to the roof hitting the brick wall is deafening, it reverberates down the stairwell. Icarus watches Achilles walk to the edge of the roof before settling himself down and looking at the city below. He doesn't follow, at least not at first.

The last time he felt like this was when he first met the kid. Achilles had been so scared when he was dropped off at the academy, his Elysian mother left him there in hopes that the program would 'make something of him'. Poor kid couldn't stop crying then.

At least now there were no more tears. But it feels like the roles are reversed. This time, it's Icarus that was left behind and Achilles is the one trying to put the pieces back together.

Icarus is scared. Scared just as he was that day, a small bundle of tears in his arms.

"Are you gonna come sit down or are you gonna stand there all night?"

Icarus huffs and shakes his head, *what a little shit*. He's right, though, there's no point in standing here—across the roof—and avoiding the discussion that they obviously need to have. He joins the kid, though he can't bring himself to sit down.

"I'm sorry you saw that," he says, fixing his gaze on his feet as he kicks them against the railing. Achilles' gaze burns, but Icarus doesn't look up to meet it.

"What?" He sounds shocked, like he doesn't believe what he just heard. "*I'm sorry you saw that,* my ass! You wanted to deal with whatever that was—"

"It was a nightmare."

"You wanted to deal with *a night terror*—because I don't believe you, that wasn't just a nightmare—alone?"

Icarus isn't sure how to respond to that because, yeah, he does want to deal with it alone. His nightmares are his own, not anyone else's business. Achilles, however, is having none of that.

"No. Sit your ass down, we are talking about this and you are not going to run away."

"Gross."

"Yeah, well, you're gross bitch. Sit down."

With a huff, Icarus slots his legs through the gaps in the guard rail and sits himself down on the edge of the roof. He doesn't move his eyes from his feet, now taking a moment to appreciate the way they swing in the air above the dark streets.

The conversation is out of his hands, he doesn't know where to go from here. He thought that Achilles might accept his apology and then they could move on to talking about why he left, but he hadn't anticipated the kid being so upset about the nightmare.

He can't keep avoiding this conversation. When he was talking to Andromeda, he had managed to avoid talking about the nightmares. Maybe it's time for him to share what's going on in his mind every night when he falls asleep.

Icarus turns to face Achilles, only to be faced with a face full of concern. He can't handle the overwhelming guilt that fills his bones at the look, instead choosing to look out across the city as he attempts to talk.

Only, the words never come. The stress of trying to form a sentence irritates him, and makes him upset. Not at Achilles or the words that need said, but at himself for not being able to say them. Icarus' arms curl into his chest as he wrings his hands, trying to find relief from the irritation clouding his mind.

"This is obviously hard for you," Achilles' voice is soft as he speaks. Calming. "Why don't we start with the elephant in the room. You're alive."

His hands still as the words come back to him. Yeah, he is alive. That's something he knows how to talk about.

"Well shit, kid. I forgot to tell you about that."

Achilles does not respond, though Icarus can feel in his soul that the kid is throwing a nasty look at him. Something that screams 'NO SHIT'.

"That ties into the nightmare, actually. It's about that day." Icarus drops his hands, opening himself to Achilles even if he still can't bring himself to look at the kid.

"Long story short; Daedalus tried to kill me that day after you went to lunch with Apollon."

Icarus hears the sharp gasp Achilles let out at the words. He doesn't want to know what emotions the kid is feeling, doesn't want to risk seeing pity on his face. Instead, he turns his head further away, turns to look deep into the heart of the city.

"When I woke up, Apollon was at my door. He told me to gather my things. That we were leaving." He's not going to cry again, he doesn't think he has enough water in his body to. But that doesn't stop his throat from becoming scratchy.

"He didn't make it out. That's what the nightmare is about. Wakin' up and leaving, but havin' to leave him. Havin' to—" his coughs, dislodging what he could of the overwhelming emotions. "Havin' to leave you behind."

The hem of his sleeve is suddenly very interesting. The rough texture occupies Icarus as he runs his fingers over it and picks at the thread. There's one more thing he needs to say, he swallows and clears his throat one last time to make sure it comes out properly.

"I'm so sorry, Achilles."

It feels good to finally apologize. To finally be able to face one of the people he let down and apologize to them for that. He doesn't expect forgiveness, doesn't feel like he deserves it.

"Don't be." To say that Icarus is shocked would be an understatement. He finally looks at Achilles only to be met with his intensely open and vulnerable gaze. His mouth is set, not in a smile but not in an unkind way. His eyebrows are furrowed, pinching towards the center and accentuating the look of honesty in his warm brown eyes.

"Don't be sorry," he continues, "you did what you had to do to keep yourself alive and that's what matters."

Achilles pauses a moment, reaches out to cup Icarus' face in his hands. Forces him to keep looking at his face, see how genuine he is with the words.

"Do I wish you or Apollon had told me what was going on? Yes." A chorus of *I know, I'm sorry, I'm sorry, I'm sorry* repeats in Icarus' head.

"Do I understand now? Also yes." *Do you? How could you? I'm sorry.*

"It is okay, Icarus."

Warmth runs over Icarus' cheek as Achilles swipes his thumb under his eye. No doubt there are tear tracks stained into his skin with how much he's felt the past few days, and even if they won't go away with the tender touch it still makes Icarus feel better.

"I forgive you, Icarus."

It's then that the tears he thought he had run out of started to fall. Icarus didn't realize that he had been seeking forgiveness for leaving everything behind, but as Achilles says it he knows it's what he's needed all these years. A huge weight lifts off his heart. And while it doesn't relieve all the heaviness, it is more than enough for now.

He allows himself to cry in the hands of someone who cares for him. Someone who—against all odds—found something good in him, something worth forgiving.

The sun peaks over the city skyline as Icarus buries his face into the crook of Achilles' shoulder. Later he will feel bad for crying all over the only clothes the kid has, but for now all he can do is let the tears fall as strong arms pull him into an embrace.

THE ELYSIAN

THE MORNING HUSTLE AND bustle of the city is in full swing by the time Icarus prepares himself to get up. He pulls away from the warm embrace he is curled in and starts to shift back and forth, trying to wake his legs again.

The pinks and oranges of daybreak have shifted to a blue sky, the morning rush on the streets below are on their way to work.

It is nice to finally have a moment of peace. Life has been pounding forward much too quickly for Icarus to keep up with, and this break—as small as it is—had been much needed.

Even better yet, he had the chance to properly apologize to Achilles and spend some time with the kid. There is a nagging part of his brain that tells him he doesn't deserve it. Hell, maybe he doesn't, but the forgiveness has already been extended. That part of his brain can suck it and deal.

With one last glance over the city, Icarus stands up and moves away from the edge of the roof. Using the sleeve of his hoodie he wipes any residual tears from his eyes. There is no doubt in his mind that Andromeda would be awake when they return and he does not need to make them worry by returning with obvious tear tracks.

Warm arms wrap around Icarus as Achilles traps him in another hug. Without a second thought, he squeezes the kid and buries his face in the soft blond hair.

"Gods, I missed having you around kid," he whispers.

"I bet Meda's got a nice breakfast started for us, why don't we head back in?"

Achilles pats his back, squeezing him one last time before letting go and heading back towards the stairwell. Icarus watches him for a moment, drinking up the last moments of the peaceful morning.

Not even the loud band of the door opening ruins the serenity that falls over the two as they make their way inside.

A feeling of déjà vu washes over Icarus as he walks down the hall. The neighbors have finally started waking up, though the muffled sounds of their morning do little to ease his growing anxiety.

As they approach the door to the apartment, he understands why. The door is slightly ajar. Again.

This is just irritating at this point. Icarus misses the days when he would come home and know that no one had been in his apartment. Why can't people just wait for him to let them in? Why must they break into his safe space?

Achilles tenses, likely feeling the irritation coming off Icarus. It best be Thanatos in there and not someone else, Icarus can only handle one person mysteriously knowing where he lives and breaking in.

Not in the mood to draw this out, Icarus roughly pushes the door open. If anyone inside wanted him dead, they missed their chance while he was asleep.

Nothing out of the ordinary. Just an apartment in the exact same state as he left it.

Icarus rolls the tension out of his shoulders and walks further into the apartment. *I fucking knew it,* there, in the middle of the living room, stood Thanatos.

"Why wasn't my door closed?" he asks, looking over at the couch to see Andromeda awake as well. If they let him in, why didn't they just *close the door?*

"Because I let myself in when you didn't answer the door."

"That doesn't answer my question. Why wasn't it closed? Are you incapable of closing the door after yourself?"

Achilles walks over to join Andromeda on the couch, curling up into their side as they throw their arm over his shoulders.

The sight warms his heart, it makes this small shithole feel more like a home.

Icarus looks back at Thanatos and says, "Forget it. Why are you here?"

He doesn't wait for the answer, turning to sit down in his comfy chair next to the couch. Thanatos can stay standing all he wants, but Icarus wants to make himself comfortable for whatever bullshit he's about to spew.

And bullshit it is, "So I got us a boon."

Icarus adjusts himself in the chair, propping his chin on his knee as he adjusts his hoodie. Normally he wouldn't care if people could tell he isn't wearing pants, but something in the air tells him this time is different.

Achilles untangles himself from Andromeda's side and comes to sit on the arm of the chair, using his body to block Thanatos' view of Icarus.

He sighs. By the look of it, Icarus is going to have the kid attached at his hip for a while. Andromeda has the same thought, if the look they shoot at him is any indicator. He shakes his head slightly in response, silently telling them that he will explain later. Then he leans around Achilles to look back over at Thanatos, tilting his head up to acknowledge that he's listening.

"I found someone to get us information. Someone from within the ranks of the Elysians." Icarus can't help but flinch at that. An

Elysian? Working with the people who want to put an end to the hierarchical system that puts them in power? There's no way.

He's just about to voice his thoughts when a figure steps out from his bedroom. Icarus' breath catches in his throat as the person walks into the living room. His eyes slowly leave Thanatos, dropping to the floor.

Each footfall pounds against the wood of the floor, reverberating in his bones and mixing with the erratic beating of his heart. A pair of black boots catch his gaze, *ATLAS issue.* Those damn boots that he coveted for so long but never got to own. Even now, a pang of envy briefly runs through him as he struggles to get his breathing under control.

The footsteps come closer, followed by black-clad legs. Icarus knows he has to look up, has to face whoever this "Elysian boon" is. But he's scared, he's terrified that he already knows.

As the person comes to a stop mere feet away from him, he glances at their hand. A hand he sadly recognizes—and yet doesn't. A hand that is home to scars he has memorized as if they were his own on a hand that's much more rough than he remembers. A hand he desperately wishes he knew the touch of, had dreamed of knowing the touch of, but never got the chance.

A whisper. "Why won't you look at me?"

Icarus had put off facing his fear for too long, the tense air of the room now clogs his throat. His heartbeat refuses to settle on a rhythmic pattern as his eyes graze up a toned arm—one more tanned and packed with muscle than he recalls, yet still spattered with a galaxy of freckles just as they'd always been.

His eyes continue to burn their way up past the sharp collar bones on display just past the edge of a black compression tank. If the situation were different, he would have been all over the delicious stretch of skin there. But the situation isn't different and he still needs to face the one person he desperately wishes he'd never have to see again. The one person he spent years begging and crying for. The one person that shattered his soul without ever so much as speaking to him.

Mentally steadying himself, Icarus slides his eyes up over the curve of his neck and past the sharp edge of his jawline. Icarus' eyes linger there, briefly. Afraid of what he'll see when he meets the Elysian's gaze. Afraid that he'll see a reflection of his own inner turmoil laid out for the world to see. Afraid that he'll have to face the most heartbreaking part of his past, a past he has been running from for ten long years.

"Icarus," the Elysian pleads. "Birdie, please..."

Icarus' eyes snap up at the use of the nickname, locking with the burnished gold ones before him. Eyes that, surprisingly, do not mirror the horror in his own. Eyes that are glossy from unshed tears of disbelief, as if he can't tell if what he's seeing is real.

Any hope that Icarus was clinging onto is gone. He can no longer deny who stands before him. His own personal sunshine has entered his life once again, this time surrounded by a halo of yellow light courtesy of the only light fixture in his shitty apartment.

He can't bring himself to tear his eyes away from the God of a man standing just a few feet away. The overwhelming urge to drop to the floor and beg for forgiveness washes over him, the only thing stopping him from doing so is the chair that he is curled up in.

His gaze is broken by Achilles as the kid stands up, shifting himself further in front of Icarus and blocking Apollon from view.

Icarus shakes his head, his brain frantically tries to process the millions of thoughts and emotions crashing around in his thick skull. A hand cups his cheek, turning his head away from where he knows his sunshine is standing, even if he can't see him.

He's greeted instead with the worried visage of Andromeda. Their eyebrows are furrowed and their lips are moving, but he can not hear what they are saying over the blood rushing in his ears.

I can't hear anything, he realizes. Can't hear the noises of the street from the window, can't hear the voices around him, can't hear himself struggling to speak.

"I'm sorry."

The bubble of static around him pops as he speaks. The sounds of the world come rushing back towards him. He hears Andromeda trying to walk him through breathing exercises, hears Achilles telling Apollon that he has no right to be here, hears Thanatos asking about what's happening.

It is all so much, so suddenly.

Icarus takes in a deep breath with Andromeda's guidance before moving to stand up. At the movement, everything falls to a hush. He would think his hearing has dulled again if it weren't for a muttered, "*whatthefuckwhatthefuckwhatthefuck*," from in front of him.

One foot touches the ground, then the other as he stands up and closes the small gap between him and Apollon. In this new position, Icarus has to look down to meet the ~~beautiful~~ *average* burnished gold gaze. Apollon has grown in their time apart, though he is still considerably shorter than Icarus.

"Why are you here?" Icarus' voice is strong, steady. He's thankful that it didn't betray the mental weakness and desperate need to worship he feels just being in the presence of his sunshine.

"You're alive," Apollon whispers, his gaze sweeping across Icarus' face and coming to rest on the scar that he knows resides on his cheek. The only physical reminder from that day. *He's trying to see if I'm real.*

"Yeah, I am. Not that you cared to know for the past decade." The over-stimulation of everything happening all at once starts to meld into a unified feeling of anger.

"Now answer my question. Why are you here?"

"I'm here to help," his sunshine responds, hushed. "There are rumors of a rebellion. I came to help."

"Why now?"

"There are also rumors of a certain stubborn redhead causing trouble. That he might be the head of this new rebellion." *What rebellion? Why does he keep mentioning a rebellion?*

Apollon raises his hand, moves to rest it on Icarus' cheek the same way Andromeda had held his face earlier. It was swatted out of the air before he could make contact.

Apollon can't just come back into Icarus' life as if nothing had happened. As if he hadn't let Icarus sit alone and miserable for ten years because of a stupid promise. Icarus won't let him.

"Yeah, well, the rumors are true. There is a *certain redhead* out here, but there is no rebellion and he's someone you never met."

Icarus takes a step back—away from Apollon—but the chair stops him in his tracks. He thought he could handle this confrontation, thought the lack of space to run away wouldn't bother him. But he couldn't. Not now.

"I mean," he says with a mocking laugh, "the *redhead* that you knew is dead. Just the way you left him all those years ago."

He looks away from the man of gold, his gaze falling on Andromeda to his left.

"Figure out if he can help us." They nod. "I'm going to get some air."

He doesn't wait for permission to leave. Not that he needs one, this is his damned apartment he can leave whenever he wants to.

Icarus roughly brushes past the Elysian and heads into the kitchen to grab an energy drink. What he wouldn't give for some alcohol right now, but unfortunately he doesn't have any.

He breezes out the front door, not bothering to grab his keys or his knife. He'll be right back and it's not like locking the door will keep anyone from entering anyways.

It's barely a moment before someone else's footsteps join his in the empty hallway. *Andromeda, probably making sure I'm okay,* he thinks. *Or Achilles.* The kid has resolved to be attached to his hip since this morning, if the way he moved to shield Icarus earlier was any indication.

I'll deal with them when we get to the roof. Tell them to go back inside and give me room to think.

What Icarus hadn't anticipated was that it was neither of them, but rather the person he is trying to run away from. He's pushed up against the wall as soon as they make it through the rooftop door. The sound of a can dropping and rolling fills the air as he gasps. His back meets rough brick as he is forced to come face to face with those damned gold eyes again.

"You can't," Apollon rasps, his voice shaking with barely concealed emotion. "You can't just walk away from me. I thought you were *dead*, Icarus. For ten years I thought you were dead."

Every word is spit out like poison, as if it is Icarus' fault that he had apparently been lied to.

"Sorry t' burst your bubble, my guy. But I am very much alive—"

He is cut off by Apollon forcefully grabbing his face and closing the distance between them. There is nothing soft about the kiss as all of their pent up emotions are let loose. All of their pain from years of separation, all of their regret from how they were separated, all of the hurt and betrayal.

There is nothing soft and Icarus wouldn't have it any other way.

He can feel himself practically melt into the kiss, can feel himself give in to something he never dreamed he'd be allowed to have. Something he had regrettably run away from.

Apollon kisses him like a dying man who's only cure is his lips. His hand has not loosened its grip on Icarus' face, holding him in place so that he can not move away even if he wanted to. Another hand comes up to caress his cheek, as if Apollon couldn't decide whether he wanted to be gentle or not.

The tender touch is too soft for Icarus. Being caressed like he is actually important and meant to be handled with care is too much for his broken mind. And yet he can't stop himself as he rests his hands on Apollon's chest, just where he can feel his sunshine's heartbeat. Just where he can feel how much he is truly cared for.

The harsh kiss mellows out and becomes more tender. All of the anger and hatred from Apollon has been poured out and Icarus is too conflicted to be truly angry. Now, it is all soft touches and care.

The loud bang of the rooftop door against the wall next to him shocks Icarus back into reality. He roughly pushes against Apollon's chest, pushing him away before sliding down the wall and curling up on himself. He doesn't want to be perceived, doesn't think he can handle it after what happened.

He pulls his hood up and over his head as Andromeda drops down next to him. They wrap him in their arms, shield him from the world that he so desperately wishes he could hide from.

It's too bad that the world has already seen him and decided to mock him with the presence of a light too bright and blinding. Maybe he could have stood next to that glowing halo, but that was a long time ago. Long before his wings had fallen apart.

It's too much. The pain, the hatred, the *love*. Icarus can't handle it. He can't handle what it *means*. There are too many thoughts swirling around his head, too many thoughts that he isn't ready to acknowledge in voices that do not belong to him.

So, Icarus does what he does best: channels all of the confusion into one source feeling. Betrayal. That is why he couldn't have what he wanted. Betrayal is why he has spent the last ten years alone, why he glares up at Apollon from where he's curled on the floor. Why he spits venom at the man that used to be his sunshine.

"I am not the person you once knew. I have *nothing* to give you."

And he doesn't. The reservoirs of love in his heart are empty. They have been for a while now. He isn't the man he used to be and he doesn't owe anyone an explanation or an apology for that.

The heaviness that was lifted when he apologized to Achilles is back, it latches itself around his heart and refuses to give in to the God before him. He refuses to give what's left of his heart to a man that had thrown it away once before.

If the talk with Achilles had made Icarus realize that he wants to apologize for abandoning his old life and everyone in it, then this interaction with Apollon is making him realize that he might be too spiteful to do that.

Apollon can get fucked for all he cares.

The hatred that has been pooling deep within him since that day has come back to the surface, oozing into the glare that he sends to the Elysian. That is what the man is, after all. An Elysian. A part of the institution that Icarus will burn to the ground, leaving nothing—*no one*—behind.

THE SHUTDOWN

ANDROMEDA ROUGHLY GRABS AT Icarus' face, forcing him to look away from the Elysian. They instruct him to breathe. *1, 2, 3 in. 1, 2, 3 out.* Repeat.

"Five things you can touch," their voice is calm, easy to hear over the yelling in the background but not too loud that it hurts.

"The floor. My hoodie. Your arm. My hair. The puddle of energy drink from when I dropped my can." Icarus reaches out to each item as he lists it, gently tapping it as the shaky words come from his mouth.

"Four things you can see."

"Your ugly mug. The city. My hands. Uh, your sweater."

"Three things you can hear."

"Achilles yelling. You. The cars on the street."

"Two things you can smell?"

"City smog. The energy drink I dropped." Andromeda cocks their eyebrows at his answer. "What? It's fruity."

"And something you can taste."

"Blood."

"Blood?" Their eyes rake down his body, looking for where he might be hurt.

"I think I bit his lip, it's not my blood."

Andromeda looks towards the yelling, leaning forward a bit. A moment of silence passes before they whisper, "Oh my Gods, you did. Good for you."

The smirk that crawls across their face mirrors his own when they look back at him.

"We're gonna sit here for a bit while Achilles takes care of him, kay?" Icarus nods, yeah that works for him.

"Can you let me go? It can't be comfy crouching like that to hold my face."

"It's really not, are you gonna look back over at them?"

"Not if you keep me in the loop on their bullshit."

"Deal." Andromeda drops their hands, leaning back until they're sitting on the roof.

"This is really stupid, isn't it?" Icarus asks.

Andromeda is taken aback, then they let out a full bodied laugh.

"Yeah, yeah this is really stupid. Is that really him?" The rest of their question is silent, but he understands all the same. *Is this really the guy you were crying over?*

"Unfortunately."

The stairwell door slams shut, letting Icarus know that he and Andromeda are the only two on the rooftop. Without another word, he stands up and brushes himself off.

He's mentally rebuilding the walls that had crumbled when Apollon kissed him, painstakingly placing brick after brick in their place. He'll be fine, he has to be.

"Are you good?" Andromeda asks, watching him from where they are still sitting.

"Yeah. I'm good. We should probably follow them in, we still have to talk to Thanatos and make a plan."

If Andromeda hears the waver in his voice, they do not say. He helps pull them up to their feet before they turn to head inside. Their trek down the stairs and through the hall is quiet, only the voices in his head dare to break the silence.

You could kill him. No. *Why not? It would be easier if he were dead, y'know.* No it wouldn't, why would he willingly kill someone? *His blood would be—*

The voice is cut off when they step back into the apartment. There are papers strewn all across the floor, it looks like someone had just dumped a file cabinet on the ground.

I don't wanna. I just don't want to deal with this. But of course, Icarus does have to deal with it. Especially when he sees Achilles, Thanatos, and Apollon trying to organize the chaos.

"What?" Icarus asks. He's tired of this shit, they can figure out what the rest of the question is.

He wants to grab another energy drink since the one he took to the roof had spilled. Before he can, Andromeda hands him a cold glass of water. With a sigh, he takes a sip.

"We started a plan to rescue Patroclus just after you left the room," they say as they settle down on the floor next to Thanatos.

"That is, before we realized that someone was missing," Achilles hisses, jeering at the blond Elysian next to him.

"I know where I was." Apollon coldly responds. He's staring at Icarus, his eyes burning patches into his soul. There is a spot to sit down next to him, but Icarus chooses to squeeze between Andromeda and Achilles instead.

Icarus' hoodie slides up as he sits down, and before he can adjust it he sees Apollon's eyes dip to his thighs as he flushes. Achilles, who has not taken his eyes off Apollon since they entered the living room, puts his hand on Icarus' thigh. He also angles his body so that he is once again between Icarus and Apollon's eyes.

"I know where you should be," Achilles grumbles, returning his attention to the papers in front of them.

Icarus rolls his eyes. He fully checks out of the display of dominance next to him, opting to let everyone around him figure out what they're doing. He trusts Thanatos' planning skills, and Achilles and Apollon both know his skill set intimately. He'll be able to do whatever is decided upon.

It looks like Andromeda is trying not to laugh when he turns to face them. They point at the hand on his thigh, understanding. Icarus isn't *uncomfortable* with the touch, per se, but he does know that people who do not know his feelings towards the kid might read into it in a way that isn't intended. Andromeda knows this, he's certain that they find it hilarious.

"So we're going back for Pat, right Icarus?" Thanatos asks. Oh, he guesses he will have to answer that.

"Yeah."

"Well, we need to figure out where he is first."

That grabs Achilles' full attention, diverting him from his show of testosterone with Apollon.

"Is he not in his room? I know where that is."

"No, he's not." Thanatos sounds agitated. Hell, Icarus probably would be pissed too if he was the information guy and he didn't have the information they needed.

"It seems they anticipated you trying to escape, the moment we got you out they relocated him and hid his location. Even my contacts can't figure out where he is."

Achilles shifts nervously beside Icarus. He can tell that the kid has something he's not saying, makes a mental note to ask him about it later.

"Cool, so we need to find out where he is then. Do you think we can draw him to us?" Icarus doesn't want to go back to the academy. If they can draw the fight to them then he won't have to deal with years of memories distracting him.

"We can try, but how can we be sure that they'll bring Pat with them?" Achilles asks.

That's a great question, Icarus isn't sure how to guarantee that. If ATLAS had anticipated Achilles breaking out, then they likely anticipate him coming back for Patroclus. Which would mean keeping him far away from any buildings that could be broken into and making sure he doesn't go outside.

"We could offer them a trade?" he suggests. They might be willing to work with them if they get something much more valuable in return.

"Like what?"

"Like me." Immediately, Apollon starts to object and Achilles turns to make sure he's not moving towards Icarus.

"No, listen. They think we have a rebellion, right? Use that to our advantage, propose a trade with them. Offer them someone who's supposed to be dead, someone who could turn public perception of them if I were to go public with everything they did to me. They want me dead, offer me as a trade, get Patroclus, and then fight our way out of the trade."

Icarus thinks it's a solid plan, but the look of offense on everyone's faces makes him think they don't agree.

Until, "Or we use me as bait," Achilles offers. Icarus has to admit, the idea of them getting their αριστος αχαιον back might just work. But he won't risk the kid.

"No."

"What do you mean 'No', you just suggested the same damn thing!"

"No, kid. I'm not putting your safety on the line."

"How about we use neither of you as bait? Hm?" Andromeda cuts in.

Icarus groans, that was his only idea. Whatever, they can figure something out then.

He stands up, allowing the group to finish their conversation and he physically removes himself to cool down. He wants to go to his room, but he knows nothing will get done if they can't see him. The kitchen it is.

In the corner of his eye, he can see Apollon move to follow him. Achilles doesn't let him, putting his hand on the Elysian's shoulder and asking him a pointed question.

He only just gets situated on the counter when Andromeda joins him.

"You wanna help me make lunch?" they ask, standing between his knees and resting a hand on his leg. "They don't need our help, we could make something instead since I know you didn't eat breakfast."

Icarus nods and asks, **MAKE WHAT?**

"I think we'll make some soup. It was rather chilly on the roof, it'll warm your insides." They wiggle their fingers as they say 'insides', backing away from Icarus at the same time.

The soup is easy to make, the only thing Icarus has to do is stir it every-so-often. He's sitting right next to the stove, so the task was relegated to him.

Andromeda doesn't try to get him to talk, they let him sit in silence and listen to the bubble of conversation in the living room. It helps him immensely, every nerve in his body begins to relax.

His attention is diverted from eaves-dropping when Andromeda starts to hum. He doesn't recognize the song, but the sway of their hips as they chop celery is infectious. Icarus begins to sway in place on the counter as well, *side to side and back and forth.* It's mesmerizing, the humming and soft movements interrupted every so often by Andromeda clapping and twirling. He could watch them dance and exist joyously all day.

The calm atmosphere is shattered as his attention is drawn to Apollon saying his name. He isn't speaking loud, as if he doesn't want Icarus to hear. But he does, he will always hear his name when it comes from the mouth of his sunshine. Always.

"Why wouldn't you let me help Icarus, you know I know him better than any of you do." He's angry, yes, but worry laced his voice.

"You would have made it worse," Achilles spits back.

"How could I have made it worse!" Apollon's voice briefly raises in volume before dipping to a quiet murmur. "I know how to handle him."

I hate that. I don't need anyone to handle me, I can handle my own damn self.

Achilles seems to agree as he says, "The fact that you just said you can 'handle him' tells me everything I need to know. You would have made it worse."

"Boys, we need to focus," Thanatos cuts in. Icarus has never been so relieved to hear the man's monotone voice.

"We need to figure out how we're going to drag Patroclus out."

A hush falls over the room. The only sounds Icarus can hear are the shuffling of papers and the boiling of the soup on the stove.

A feeling of guilt crawls up his throat, making him feel bad for shutting down like he did. He's ashamed of it, ashamed that he couldn't handle his emotions and made a scene about it. He can feel the stretch of his frown and the furrow of his eyebrows as he delves deeper into the pit of Shame.

Suddenly, Andromeda is in front of him. They are holding his hands, squeezing them. Their thumbs rub circles into the back of his hands, gently coaxing them to release the hem of the hoodie he hadn't realized he was shredding.

They don't try to talk to him. Icarus appreciates it, just their silent presence helps ground him. They stay with him as he draws in shaky breath after shaky breath, trying to calm himself and remind himself that he's not alone. That he didn't make a scene. That he's loved despite his flaws.

"Thank you," he breathes out once the words return to him. Andromeda's face brightens as he says them and they smile as they extract their hands from his.

He keeps his eyes on them as they return to the soup next to him. It has to be nearly finished, it doesn't take very long to make chicken noodle soup. Especially since they were using the pre-cooked rotisserie chicken they had picked up at the grocery store.

Icarus was right, of course, as Andromeda pulled the pot off the burner and tapped his leg. Without hesitation, Icarus slides off the counter. He grabs some bowls and silverware before following Andromeda out to the table.

He can't bring himself to look at anyone in the living room, instead keeping his head down as he focuses on setting the table. If he were to look up, they'd take it as a sign to ask him questions and the rolling waves of guilt and shame in his heart would not allow him to answer.

The chairs scraping against the shitty wooden floor of his apartment hurts Icarus' ears, but it doesn't hurt nearly as much as his heart hurts when he sees Apollon trying to sit next to him. There is a battle in his mind; on one hand he desperately wants the comfort of his sunshine, but on the other hand that comfort isn't guaranteed. No, Icarus doesn't trust him like that anymore.

The thought must be written all over his face as he finally looks up at the blond as he stops fighting Achilles and allows himself to be redirected into a seat across the table.

The pain in his eyes feels like a dagger in Icarus' heart, and he hates that he's the one that put it there.

He can't take it, turns his focus on the bowl in front of him. The soup looks delicious, Andromeda really pulled out all the stops for it. It's too bad that he won't be able to eat it.

Roiling nausea joins the heavy feelings in his stomach, but he's not the only one waiting to eat.

"What did you come up with?" Andromeda asks, using their spoon to mix the contents of the bowl in front of them.

"Yeah, we talked about a couple," Thanatos says, setting his spoon down and pushing the bowl away from him. "We talked about the plans Icarus put forward. We think it's best if we use Achilles as bait, though, since he's worth more to ATLAS and has more of a guarantee of coming out the other end alive."

Icarus sneers, his nose scrunching and lip curling up in disgust at the idea of using the kid as bait. No, he'd much rather keep him out of it. The kid has already been through enough.

"Though if we have to, we can send Icarus in. This would put us as a disadvantage, though. I know you want to do this," Thanatos addresses him directly, "but right now our biggest asset is you and the fact that they think you're dead. We need to keep it that way for as long as we can."

He knows Thanatos is right. He doesn't like it, but Icarus' best weapon right now is ATLAS' ignorance. Even if he were to reach out, they would want to eradicate him. There's no way they wouldn't just kill him on the spot. And why would he be calling in for Patroclus? Icarus isn't supposed to know who he is.

"The last idea is our best shot. We send Apollon back and get him to set up an 'infiltration' mission." Icarus raises an eyebrow as he looks at the blond across the table.

For once he isn't already looking at him, giving Icarus time to actually check out the changes he underwent in the past ten years. His face isn't as full, the puffy cheeks that rounded him out now replaced with gaunt hollows. There is a sharpness to him that Icarus can't help but be drawn to, he was always a sucker for dangerous objects. It looks like he could cut his tongue on the man's jawline.

Before he can look away Apollon turns, catching his gaze.

"If ATLAS approves of a solo infiltration they may be willing to use Patroclus as a show of good faith, a bargaining chip to allow Apollon full access into our ranks. They think we're an organized rebellion, so why not use that to our advantage?"

Neither Icarus nor Apollon move, not wanting to break the contact. This look feels much more intimate than even the moment they shared on the roof. He feels as if he is baring his soul to the man that used to be his partner, mentally laying out all the information they have about the situation and asking him for his trusted opinion.

Because he still trusts him. As unfortunate and unfounded as it is, Icarus trusts Apollon with his life. He knows that he will follow through with whatever Apollon decides, knows that his plan will succeed just as it always has.

"Yeah, that sounds like a plan," Andromeda says, but he knows that their agreement has no bearing on the decision. This is between him and Apollon.

It is decided then, with a look. They will follow through with that final plan, they will send Apollon in to set up a cover mission.

At long last, Icarus breaks eye contact. He turns to see Andromeda facing Apollon, fixing him with a pointed look.

"You will see this through. And when you do, you will retrieve Patroclus and bring him back here *without* putting anyone here in danger. Am I clear?"

Apollon has the sense to look nervous as they speak. Andromeda, as Icarus has learned in the past couple days, can be scary when they are serious. He's glad that he's not on the receiving end of that tone, though his heart does ache at the idea that someone he deeply cares for is.

For his part, Apollon smooths down his hackles and agrees to their demands before returning to the cooling soup in front of him.

With a solid plan set, the nausea that had been plaguing Icarus eases up. It's not gone completely, but just enough for him to be able to eat with everyone.

They have a plan. They know how to move forward. Everything will be okay, it has to be.

The Aquarium

Apollon gets up without another word to the group, leaving his half-empty bowl on the table. Icarus doesn't stop him, doesn't even look up as the blond passes his chair.

There's a lingering taste of resentment in the back of his throat as the front door clicks shut. It tugs at his heart, telling him that he had made the wrong move. That he had done something to make Apollon hate him, and that's why he didn't say anything before leaving.

It shouldn't bother him, not when he is the one pushing the man away. Not when Icarus has done everything in his power to keep him at arms length since he came back into his life.

Thanatos follows suit not long after, pushing his bowl towards the center of the table and heading to the door.

"I need to talk to my mother, see if there's anything else I can do," he says. His voice fades as he walks away from the table. "See if there's any other sources of information I can tap into."

Icarus doesn't look up until the door clicks closed a second time. When he does, he is greeted by Andromeda and Achilles staring at him. He throws his hands up, waiting for them to say something, *anything*.

Andromeda scoffs and shakes their head. They gather the dishes from the table, pulling them all closer and stacking them precariously. Once the stack looks stable enough to carry, they get up and head into the kitchen. Not a moment later, Icarus can hear water running.

Well, that leaves just one person for Icarus to talk to. He turns towards Achilles and quirks his eyebrow in a silent question.

Achilles purses his lips and scrunches his nose, not answering Icarus' unspoken question as he leans back in his chair and changes the non-existence conversation.

"Do you wanna talk about it?"

No. No, he doesn't want to talk about it. His utter disdain at the thought must be written all over his face as Achilles raises his hands in surrender.

Icarus leans forward and rubs the heel of his palm across his forehead. It's calming, grounding. The pressure eases his mind.

What do we need to do now? Nothing? We're just waiting for Apollon to come back with Patroclus, right?

Does that mean we have a free day? Icarus sits up straight at the prospect of having a day where they don't have to do anything. He looks at Achilles, the kid is watching him with curiosity etched into his features.

"You up for an adventure?"

"Depends, what kind?"

"The kind where we go explore an abandoned building that I've been eying for a few years but I've never gone into it because it looks real creepy."

"I'm in!" Andromeda calls out over the sound of running water. Of course they're in, Icarus had no doubt they would want to go. He knew from the moment they met on the roof that they have the same drive to be in places they weren't supposed to be that he has.

Achilles, for his part, stares at him in contemplation. His eyes squint as he considers his options.

A grin crawls across Icarus' face as the kid stands up and turns towards the bedroom. He's a few steps away from the door frame when he looks over his shoulder.

"Can I borrow some clothes?" They really need to get the kid some clothes, maybe they can stop on the way back from the outing and grab him a few things.

"Sure, go for it. There might be a few things that fit you in the back," Icarus replies as he pushes himself into a standing position. The water turns off in the kitchen as he enters, leaning his hip against the island out of Andromeda's way.

"Where are we going?" they ask as they put the remnants of lunch away in the fridge. They kick the door closed and turn to look at him.

"There's an abandoned aquarium across the river. I've been wanting to enter for years now, but I don't mix well with water so I never went."

They nod, likely making a mental note of Icarus' incompatibility with the substance that makes up the lake they live just a few blocks away from.

Without another word they leave the kitchen, patting his shoulder as they pass on the way out. He watches them head into their room to get ready for the day before heading to his own room.

Icarus doesn't stop to think about the possibility of Achilles still changing, and when he walks in he finds Achilles pulling on a pair of his joggers.

"Oh, good choice," he says.

"Those pants are really comfy and easy to tighten." He pulls his hoodie up and over his head, flinging it onto the bed before stepping over the air mattress that's wedged between his bed and the wall.

Icarus can feel the heat of Achilles' gaze rake down his back as he stands in front of the closet. He cocks his hip, preening under the attention. It's about time someone other than his artist appreciated the artwork on his back.

The attention is distracting, though, and not helping him pick out an outfit. He sighs and turns as Achilles grabs one of his flannels and ties it around his waist.

He's wearing Icarus' favorite joggers, his red flannel tied around the waist, and one of his cropped sleeveless turtlenecks. A decently easy outfit, Icarus can match that.

He turns back to the closet, rooting around for a specific set of clothes. Ah! There, his baggy jeans and cropped band tees. That'll do.

Icarus quickly throws the clothes on, briefly pulling the cloth off the shattered mirror as he adjusts the jeans on his hips. He doesn't want them falling off while they're walking. Once he's happy, he covers the mirror back up and turns to face Achilles.

"That's one of my favorite shirts, I normally pair it with a harness though." He digs in the top drawer of his dresser, pulling out a red leather chest harness. Achilles looks at him, stupefied, when he tries to hand it over.

When it becomes obvious that the kid isn't going to put the harness on himself, Icarus moves to put it on for him. He looks at the kid, silently asking for permission before he secures it around his chest. After the last buckle is fastened, Icarus pats Achilles on his bright red cheek and walks out of the room.

Andromeda is waiting for them. They are sitting on the table, one leg crossed in front of them while the other swings freely through the air.

Icarus' eyes rove over their outfit; a cropped hoodie with chains dangling over a black tank, a pair of distressed denim shorts and fishnets. The look is brought together by the boots on their feet, boots that look awfully familiar to Icarus.

"Are those my combat boots?"

"Yeah, I didn't wanna go down to my apartment to grab mine so I'm borrowing yours," they say. Their eyes glide over his shoulder, landing on Achilles behind him.

A look of confusion crosses their face, their eyes flick back to Icarus. He tilts his head, unsure of what they're confused about. They shake their head, hopping off the counter and dusting themself off.

I'll ask them later. If I remember.

"Y'all ready to go?" they ask instead. Icarus nods and heads to the entrance as Achilles says he's good to go.

He grabs the backpack he keeps in the bureau and sets it down on the top. There's some last minute things they'll want to take with them. His riot gear is already in the bag; a small baggie of baking soda, a spray bottle, a mask, earplugs, hair ties, and a small first aid kit with at least some of every medication anyone might need. Icarus throws his blades in there as well before turning to Andromeda.

"Anything else we might need?"

"I've got whatever you don't. We should be good," they respond.

Icarus nods before he zips the bag up. He knows he's being over cautious, but it's better to have something and not need it than to need it and not have it.

The last thing he does is throw on his shoes, a beat up pair of canvas high tops, before they head out the door. He makes sure to lock the door, even as the voices in his head make sarcastic comments about how the lock is useless at this point anyways.

The small elevator feels cramped with the three of them in it. No one speaks, the air sits heavy and stale between them.

Gods, we need this fucking break. This is unbearable.

It is a small blessing when they step out into the crisp autumn air of the city. At first they walk in silence, Achilles and Andromeda just following Icarus as he leads them down the sidewalk towards Nautica.

Traffic slows to a crawl on the streets beside them as they near the Flats, business men leaving their stuffy offices to go grab lunch at one of the many restaurants that line the river.

It isn't long before the buildings start to spread out, becoming more run down and unkempt as they enter Irishtown. This area is one that Icarus knows well, its food is amazing and its residents are some of the best people he's met. A shame that ATLAS refuses to help them, instead choosing to leave them to their own devices.

Maybe I can talk to a few people down here, they've gotta have a grudge against ATLAS too.

As they approach the drawbridge, Icarus can't help but talk. He's not sure his companions are listening as he rambles about the history of the area they're in, and he doesn't much care. He had learned a lot from the locals and he loved rambling about it.

It's been a very long time since the drawbridge was in use, no one rode down the river anymore. The gears are rusted shut, at least the ones Icarus can see as they cross the bridge. The metal echoes under their footsteps. As much as Icarus doesn't like the water, he must admit that it feels freeing to walk over it like this. Almost like he's flying.

The Aquarium sits proud on top of the hill, abandoned but no less imposing. From this side of the hill, the amphitheater isn't visible. But Icarus knows it's there, it's where he took dance lessons after he escaped the academy.

Ever since he started those classes and learned about the building next door, he's wanted to check it out. He remembers the tales that were whispered between the other kids in the class; stories about mutated animals and monstrous deep sea creatures. He's not sure how anything would survive in an abandoned building for decades, but they were fun stories used to spook the kids and keep them from entering unsupervised.

They walk up to the chain-link fences that surround the building, dotted with caution signs and "Do Not Trespass" placards from decades long past. They hold no weight in the system set up by ATLAS, there was no legal system to be concerned about so long as they did not earn the attention of the Elysians.

Icarus scales the fence easily, straddling the top as he looks down at the two still standing at the base of the fence. Andromeda follows him up, quickly starting their ascent up the chain links. But Achilles hesitates, looking up at Icarus with big brown eyes full of concern.

"What if we get caught?" he asks.

"We won't," Icarus replies. He's sure of it, in the many years he spent hanging around the Pavilion he had never seen an Elysian check on the building. He can't guarantee that nothing's changed, but he feels it deep in his soul that they are safe here.

Achilles digests Icarus' answer for a moment before climbing up the fence in front of him. They drop down on the other side together, the sound of gravel crunching under their shoes scratching something in Icarus' brain.

The doors are locked, of course, but that doesn't stop Achilles from pulling on the door and throwing a fit when it doesn't open.

Icarus walks up in front of him and reaches for the pocket on the harness. Achilles stops fussing with the doors as he pulls a lock pick from the pocket with a grin. That's really why he recommended the kid to wear the harness, it's his go-to for exploring and holds all kinds of goodies.

He ignores the way Achilles' cheeks flush, instead turning back to the door and squatting in front of the lock.

"Only you would have a fucking lock pick stashed somewhere," Andromeda laughs.

The lock falls from the door as Icarus responds, "Gotta be prepared for everything." He stands up and gently pushes the door open before gesturing for the others to go in ahead of him.

He doesn't return the lock pick to the harness, he's not sure if they'll need it again. The tool slides into the pocket of his pants as he follows Andromeda into the building.

Icarus isn't sure what he expected, but it sure wasn't a pristine lobby. The building, desolate and crumbling from the outside, stands in near perfect condition on the inside. The linoleum floor is worn, sure, but it is polished to a shine and as clean as it can be. There's not a single cobweb in sight, not a speck of dust. It's pristine.

It's like they stepped through to a time before the Elysians existed. It feels wrong.

"I thought you said this was an abandoned building," Achilles says, looking around with the same confusion Icarus feels.

"It looked abandoned from the outside," Andromeda chimes in. Their face lights up as they head down the hallway to their right. "Wait, does this mean that there might still be living animals here?"

Icarus laughs as he follows them. Who knows, maybe all those stories from when he was a kid were real. If the building looked this nice after years of desolation, there might just be some living creatures inside still.

They pass into a room with running water exhibits and dioramas of the area. Icarus recognizes the map of Ohio, but he doesn't understand why so much of it is green. According to the map, most of the state has been covered in forest and National Parks and he doesn't know how to mesh that information with what he was taught at the Academy.

"Icarus, come look at this!" Achilles calls from the next room over.

He takes a photo of the map with his phone, making a mental note to check it out later, before jogging into the next room. Andromeda is already there, looking at what Icarus assumes Achilles wants him to see.

There's a large round table in the center of the room. Or, no, not a table. It's a glass pool, the clear sides allowing you to see the contents easily.

Andromeda leans halfway into the pool, with Achilles standing next to them and watching over their shoulder.

As Icarus walks closer he can see why, there's something in the pool. In the clear water, there is a brown... thing.

It looks like a very large rock but as Andromeda reaches for it, it moves. It scuttles along the floor of the pool, puffing up sand in its wake.

"What the fuck is that?" Icarus asks, confused and a little disgusted. He doesn't like the creature at all, it sets something off in the back of his mind that screams '*UNSAFE, UNSAFE*'.

"According to the information over there," Achilles points as a pedestal on the other side of the pool. "It's a horseshoe crab."

"I wanna touch it." Andromeda wiggles their grubby hands as they walk towards where the horseshoe crab disappeared.

Icarus grimaces, they can touch that thing all they want. He wants to get out of the room, though.

"How the fuck is it alive?" he asks as he slowly moves towards the exit. Achilles shoots a weird look at him, probably judging him for his reaction towards the creature, and just shrugs in response.

"Who knows but look how cool it is!" Andromeda says as they hold up the now caught crab.

Icarus' stomach drops at the sight. There are so many legs on the bottom of that thing. There has to be hundreds! And they are moving and *oh he's going to be sick.*

He heaves, not able to stand the sight of the creature, and makes to run out of the room.

"Wait, come back! He's just a friend, he just wants to be your friend!" Andromeda calls after him.

"Absolutely not, he can be your friend." His words are accompanied by Andromeda's laughter, they seem to really enjoy his suffering.

As soon as he enters the next room, Icarus empties his stomach into the nearest trash can. *That damn crab and it's stupid fucking legs,* he can't seem to scrub the image from his mind.

It's not long before his hair is being pulled back, Achilles talks to him but he doesn't pay attention to what is said. He's reduced to dry heaving, the painful retches wreak havoc on his body.

By the time Andromeda joins them in the new room, Icarus is slumped against the wall and trying to calm his breathing. Gods, he hates throwing up. It's one of the most unpleasant feelings in the world.

He pouts up at Andromeda when he notices their presence and they stick their tongue out at him.

"Why is this room a mess?" Achilles asks, drawing his attention to the room he had stumbled into.

Huh. Now, this is more like what Icarus had expected of the entire building. There is a glass tunnel in front of them, riddled with cracks and fissures along the top. It looks like it may have once been fully submerged in water, but not now. Now, the water sits around waist high on either side. It's murky, still clear enough to see the dying plants and coral through, but not clear enough to see the other side of the room.

The feeling of wrongness from earlier settles deep into Icarus bones. Why is this room different? Why isn't it in the same pristine shape as every other room in the building? What were these tunnels used for?

He starts towards the tunnel, Achilles falling into step beside him. The kid is trembling like a leaf and it does nothing to ease Icarus' racing thoughts. There is something deeply wrong about this place, but he can't put his finger on it.

The tunnel is oppressive. The further they go into it, the more it feels like something terrible is going to happen. Icarus hasn't ever had a reaction this bad to a place, not even the terror of the training room at the Academy could compare.

By the time they reach the halfway point, the group is running. Icarus doesn't care to spend any longer than necessary in what is undoubtedly a death trap, and he can hear Achilles' and Andromeda's thundering footsteps just behind him.

They break through the door at the end of the tunnel and into the light of the pristine lobby once again. Icarus' breath is labored as he collapses in the middle of the floor. Andromeda stands over him, lightly nudging his side with their boot.

"Wanna get out of here?"

"Fuck yeah let's leave," Achilles agrees from behind them. Icarus doesn't know how they aren't out of breath, but he quickly waves off that thought and gets up off the ground.

He doesn't say anything, just turns and walks out of the building. They can unpack that later, right now they have to worry about walking home in... total darkness?

It was just past noon when they arrived at the aquarium, but the sky is pitch black when they leave. That's weird, Icarus doesn't feel like they spent that much time there.

The group walks in silence laced with terror and dread, and Icarus thinks that maybe it was a mistake to come.

Maybe, as they return to the apartment and go to sleep without talking to one another, he should have let the legends live. Was the trip worth it?

Thoughts of the bone-chilling fear Icarus felt in that last room cradle him as he falls into a fitful sleep. There are some things that should remain a mystery, and Icarus thinks that the aquarium is at the top of that list.

THE DANCE

IT'S NIGHTS LIKE THESE that are the hardest to get through. The nights where he can't sleep. Not when Icarus knows that the moment he closes his eyes he will relive a nightmare again. No, he can't go to sleep knowing that.

He doesn't want to live through that pain again, he's already done so more times than he can count. Even worse than that is that his nightmares don't just affect him anymore.

Achilles is sleeping on the air mattress next to his bed, Andromeda in the room just across the apartment, and Apollon on the couch in the living room. If he were to have a nightmare it would wake them all. They don't deserve that.

It's difficult to get out of the room without waking Achilles. The kid refused to leave him alone and he understands why, appreciates it even, but it makes it hard to get any alone time.

He carefully leans off the end of the bed, over the air mattress the kid is sleeping on, to grab a pair of sweats from the clothing chair in the corner. It takes a few tries to reach without feeling like he's toppling off the end of the bed, but with sweatpants in hand he maneuvers himself towards the door.

Each step through the apartment is slow, silent. He knows just how light of a sleeper Apollon is, and his heart is pounding in his chest as he inches towards the front door.

As Icarus passes the bureau he eyes his keys. He should lock the door... but if anyone were stupid enough to break in this time they'd be met with two of the best fighters in the state. Yeah, they'll be fine if he leaves the door unlocked.

He does grab his headphones, though, before stepping out into the hallway. The soft click of the door closing stresses him out briefly, it might be loud enough to wake any Elysian. He hopes it's not.

The halls are silent, it's far too early for any of his neighbors to be awake. Hell, it feels like the whole world is asleep around him. Hopefully, he'll be able to join it in peaceful rest soon.

Icarus slides the headphones on and connects them to the phone Thanatos gave him as he enters the stairwell. He splurged when he got them, opting for a pair that would not only fit over his piercings but also had active noise canceling.

He can feel the reverberations of the rooftop door slamming open, but can't hear it as he throws on a random playlist.

Now that he's away from his apartment, he can actually put on the sweatpants. There is no one on the roof, just as he hoped and expected. No one to see him—*perceive him*—as he begins his stretches.

It has been so long since he's felt the pleasant burn in his muscles. The soreness that he has accumulated over the past few days evaporates with each movement, leaving room for only agility and motion.

Icarus made it a habit to dance whenever he could after he had left the academy. It was one of the only things he could do as he was healing from that night, he couldn't train as he normally would without a sparring partner and the wounds on his legs begged for rest any time he tried to run. And with everything that has happened as of late, he just hasn't had the mental energy or willpower to get up and dance.

That is going to change. He refuses to let these inconveniences get in the way of something he loves doing for himself. He may have a rebellion in the works—not one he wanted, but one that was handed to him by necessity—and plans to deal with the cruelty of the Elysians, but that won't stop him from taking care of himself.

A deep breath in, shake the tension out, and move. It's the same routine he always uses, it allows him to glide into the song without hesitation.

He wants to feel. Feel his body move freely through the crisp autumn air. Lungs breathing in the sweet and tangy scent of the city as he breaks free—as if he has been standing still his entire life.

Feel the rough texture of the concrete roof with each step—grounding him and reminding him of where he is; on the rooftop in the dead of night while the city sleeps peacefully. Occasionally his hand kisses the cement as he prepares for a jump, stinging in the most satisfying way.

Feel the release and flex of the muscle as each of his movements blends together. His body moves to the melodies that are pumped directly into his soul through his headphones. Not a thought crosses his mind, he trusts his body to know how to carry him from one note to the next.

Feel the sweat that starts to prickle the skin of his forehead from the exertion. The salty stickiness that makes the loose material of his cutoff stick to his athletic frame. The sweat that reminds him that no matter what happens, he is still human.

Still human in the way his body expresses frustration. The tug of his scowl as words are carelessly thrown around him. Express frustration in the way that he can give all that he is to one person and in the same breath refuse to do so for another. Express frustration in the way that he picks and chooses what he says to get the most visceral reaction from the people he cares about just to know that they do care for him in return, in the way that he isolates himself to see just how far that care will go.

Still human in the way he can unintentionally frustrate others. Not knowing what to say or what to do in order to make things better. Actively making situations worse because he doesn't understand things the way everyone else does.

Still human in the way he moves. Not a care in the world as he dances in the night where no one can see him. No one can see how he lets out the emotions from the deepest pits of his soul with each and every step, each and every movement.

The only thing that matters is the beat of the music and the scrape of his feet against the rough concrete of the roof.

Icarus dances to each song as they play, whether he has a set routine for them or not. Some of the songs he has been practicing for years, he had found his favorite choreographers through them. He lets the harmonies of the songs take him over, lets his body do what it needs to in order to purge his frustrations and sins.

Eventually, a song he knows intimately comes on. It is the first song he had learned, the first song he had poured his soul into. Each step feels like stepping into the arms of a loved one, like being wrapped in care and contentment.

Only for that blissful feeling to be ripped away from him as his footing slips, suddenly needing to take into account another person. It's only a second before they move in tandem, Icarus' body seamlessly working around Apollon as if the blond was simply an extension of himself.

His eyes roam as they dance, grazing over the warm tan of Apollon's skin and cataloging his blemishes—reminders that he, too, is human.

It looks like Apollon came to the roof not long after waking up. The remnants of sleep stick to the corners of his eyes, slight bags accompany them. Even the way he moves is ever so slightly sluggish, in part from not being able to hear the music they are dancing to.

Icarus is torn on how to feel. He has been trying to distance himself from this reminder of his past, this reminder of the love he used to be able to feel. And yet, a part of his brain is glad that the blond is there. It tells him that this is the most complete he will ever be.

As the song comes to an end, Icarus slows but does not move away from Apollon. Their breaths are ragged and labored between them.

"I didn't know you danced." Apollon's voice is raw and filled with so much adoration that Icarus does not want to deal with.

Icarus doesn't respond—can't respond—as he fights to reign in his shuddering breath. His head is reeling from every thought, every emotion, that had run through his head before he was interrupted. What should have been a cathartic release was cut off early. The Fates really couldn't let him have a peaceful night, could they?

"I want to apologize. I shouldn't have forced myself on you earlier and I see that now." The adoration falls into regret as he speaks, "I didn't know you were in a relationship. I hope I haven't caused an issue."

Icarus' eyebrows scrunch up and he tilts his head. Last he knew he wasn't in a relationship, but that still doesn't mean Apollon should have kissed him. Not now, not when he had become everything they said they never would.

"Who am I dating?" Icarus asks, clearing his throat before saying, "I'm not dating anyone."

"You're not? I thought you were with Andromeda. You two seem really close."

A laugh erupts from Icarus, he can't believe it. The thought of dating Andromeda—one of the only people who has cared for him in the way a family member would—is hilarious.

Andromeda had wiggled their way into his life on this very rooftop. Had kept running into him and making sure that he was doing well. Had held him as he wept when his heart was broken over the very person standing in front of him.

They have become an integral part of who Icarus is. A true cornerstone that he cannot see himself living without.

And yet, he has never once thought of being attracted to them. They are a soulmate in the truest sense of the word, a piece of him forever more. But he will never see them in that light.

"Nah, I am going to tell them that you said we were together though. They'll get a laugh outta that."

As he calms his laughter, Icarus looks down at Apollon. His face is wrought with confusion, his eyebrows furrowed and an adorable pout on his lips.

"Wait, you're serious? You actually think we're together?"

"Well, what else am I supposed to think?" Apollon explodes. "You pushed me away and spit venom at me only to immediately look at them with a kindness and gentleness that I haven't seen in years."

"That sounds like a you problem," Icarus can't contain the snarl of his lips, the distaste is nearly tangible to him. "You see, I actually like them and care for them."

Icarus makes a show of flicking his gaze down Apollon's body as he says, "Can't say the same for you."

"Why?" Apollon asks, moving to close just a portion of the already small gap between the two. He looks away, instead focusing his gaze on Icarus' shoulder. "What did I do?"

"*What did I*—Apollon, look at me," Icarus demands. He waits for Apollon to look up before cupping his cheeks and forcing him to maintain eye contact.

"*You* never came after me. *You* became an Elysian. *You*," he pauses, dropping his hands as if they had caught on fire where they sat.

"You broke my heart."

"I broke your heart?"

"Yeah, you did. You said that you would find me. What happened to that?" Icarus takes a step back as he speaks, tries to create room so that he can breathe.

"I—Icarus I did find you. I am here right now, even after I was told that you were *dead*." Apollon doesn't let that stand, taking a step back into his personal space.

"That night we got you out, I was told that they found you and—and they killed you." His voice breaks, as if the thought of Icarus dying still hurts him even when the man is standing in front of him.

"Well they didn't." Icarus snaps. He came up to the roof to let some energy out, to find peace so he could sleep. This is anything but.

He needs to leave.

As he turns to make an escape, Apollon reaches out and grabs his wrist.

"If I had known you were alive—"

"You could have." Icarus turns his head to look at the hand that tightens around his wrist.

"You could have looked for me, like you said you would. I made it easy for you, I stayed in the city all this time hoping, praying that you would find me."

Icarus snatches his arm back as he makes his way towards the door. He doesn't stop, not even as he says, "If you cared for me at all, you would have found me. I was right here waiting for you."

The night is silent as he flings the door open, entering the stairwell and leaving Apollon on the roof. Anger crawls up his throat and irritates his eyes as he returns to the people who do actually care for him and his apartment.

The world is silent around him as he makes his way to his home. The only sounds to be heard are the chorus of voices in his head screaming one on top of the other until even Icarus can't tell what they are saying. That is, until the door to his apartment flings open, a very ruffled looking Achilles in its wake.

"Where were you?" he asks frantically. Without waiting for an answer, he steps forward and wraps Icarus in a warm hug.

"Sorry, I didn't mean to worry you," Icarus wraps his arms around the kid, reciprocating the hug. "Couldn't sleep, so I went to the roof to dance."

Achilles' arms tighten around his waist as he buries his face in the space between Icarus' shoulder and his neck.

Footsteps echo down the hallway that make Achilles tense in his arms. Icarus sighs, *Apollon*. Achilles doesn't relax again until the elevator dings and the doors slide shut.

"I really did go up to dance. Didn't get to finish dancing, though," he reassures Achilles.

"I believe you. Bed time now?"

"Please. I want this day to be over." Icarus disentangles himself from Achilles. He gives the kid a smile before pushing him back through the threshold of the apartment. They can talk about what happened when they wake up in the morning.

Sadly, they do have to work with Apollon for the foreseeable future. They can't risk Achilles threatening the man.

For now, though, they can sleep. The kid makes his way towards his air mattress in the corner of the bedroom when Icarus grabs the back of his shirt. Tonight he needs someone to be there with him. Someone to hold him and quell the nightmares he knows are going to come.

"Listen, I know you have Patroclus and I'm not looking for anything. But I need... y'know, someone to be there. You're gonna be that someone."

Achilles nods, setting himself down on the edge of the bed. Icarus crawls over him, nestling in against the wall before opening his arms and beckoning the blond to lay down. They situate themselves, adjusting until both are comfortable in each other's arms.

In the dark of night, Icarus lets himself mourn what could have been with Apollon. What he could have had if things were just ever so slightly different. Icarus could have been in his arms right now, but he isn't.

And in the morning, he will have to act like that doesn't bother him. Tomorrow, they will begin the next step. Move to get Patroclus, plan how they are going to burn ATLAS to the ground, plan their futures.

For now, though, he grieves. He grieves the love that blossoms under impossible circumstances. Grieves the death of that impossible love as their paths diverge in a way that cannot be fixed. Grieves the future they could have had together.

It's with these thoughts of grief that Icarus falls into a dreamless sleep.

THE NEXT MORNING

THE SUN IS BLINDING as it shines through the window directly over Icarus' face. He tries to roll over but is stopped by an unfamiliar weight holding him in place. Groaning, he cracks his eyes open to see the blurry shape of Achilles asleep in his arms.

Fuck, Icarus' head falls back on his pillow as he realizes that he is tangled in the kid's limbs. He wishes he could stay there and enjoy the morning, but his joints are protesting with the need to move.

Limb by limb Icarus extracts himself from the koala grip that Achilles has him in. The kid is deep asleep, he doesn't rouse even as Icarus moves him in his attempt to get out of bed. He's glad the kid is able to get rest—glad that he himself has gotten rest—and he exits the bedroom with a bit more energy than normal and a smile beaming wide across his face.

That, however, doesn't last long. As soon as his eyes land on the three people sitting at the table Icarus knows he's in for a long day. He closes the door to the bedroom before heading to join them, a yawn threatens to escape that he covers with the back of his hand.

As he walks to the table, Andromeda cracks open a can that was sitting in front of them and sets it next to them.

"Good morning, Sleeping Beauty. How'd you sleep?" they ask. There's a teasing lilt to their voice that his brain—still trying to wake up—cannot fully process.

He sits down in the chair next to them and picks up the can to examine it. It's an energy drink, but not one of the flavors he keeps in the kitchen. It'll work just fine, though, and he gulps it down in the hopes that it will help him become semi-functional for whatever fresh hell this conversation is going to be.

"That can't be good for you," Thanatos says, a disgusted sneer on his lips.

Icarus is about to retort something rather unsavory when Andromeda asks, "When is Achilles gonna wake up? We need to talk."

"Your guess is as good as mine," Icarus' voice is rough from sleep. "He's dead asleep and I'm not waking him, kid needs the rest."

It seems he won't have to wake the kid. As soon as the words leave his mouth, Achilles throws open the bedroom door. He is disheveled, looking around the room frantically until his eyes land on Icarus. Only then does he visibly relax.

"You have *got* to stop disappearing on me," he exhales. Achilles adjusts the hem of the hoodie he is wearing—*my hoodie*—as he joins the group at the table. It's giant on him, absolutely swallowing him in the excess fabric and falling mid-thigh. It would be cute, hell it should be cute. But there's a voice in his head telling him that his clothes are on the wrong person. That it should be someone else, someone he has spent years yearning for, in his hoodie.

Icarus tears his eyes off Achilles as he reaches up to pull his hair into a ponytail, instead choosing to look over at Apollon across the table.

It should be Apollon wearing his hoodie. Not Achilles.

"What did you want to talk about?" Icarus asks Andromeda, sliding his gaze to look at them. Now that the kid has joined them, they can address the shit show that's brewing in the atmosphere of the apartment.

"We were trying to figure out what to do next and I didn't think it was fair to leave you two out of the discussion. What do you have planned for ATLAS?"

"Nothing." The word feels sticky in his mouth and it causes his eyebrows to furrow. Icarus doesn't have anything planned, nothing outside of a vague wish of burning the corporation to the ground.

Icarus has never been much of a planner, he's much more comfortable acting on impulse. This is especially true for the past few years, ever since he realized that he has no hope of actually toppling something so ingrained in society as the Elysian Program is.

Icarus is just one man, he might be able to do some lasting damage to their reputation but toppling the program? There ain't a chance in hell that he could do that alone.

Plus, he had just gotten a family. Achilles is with him and safe, they found and incorporated Andromeda and to an extent Thanatos. *I guess Apollon is here too.*

He doesn't want to risk them all in a suicide mission like that.

"You don't want to go after your father for that night?" Apollon asks, his voice is brutally cold. Icarus doesn't like how hollow the words sound, it's not right.

Icarus reaches up to touch the burn scar on his cheek. The rough skin that shouldn't be there, and yet it is and it stands as a reminder of the fact that he will never be good enough in the eyes of the one person that is supposed to love him unconditionally.

If it were just Icarus, he would come up with something and say that he wants revenge. But he can't—and won't—risk the lives of Achilles and Andromeda just for his own petty revenge fantasy.

"No, I won't get you guys killed for something that happened to me ten years ago."

Something softens in Andromeda's eyes as he speaks, something that warms him and tells him that he made the right choice in accepting them into his circle. But then it's gone—blinked out of existence in the matter of a second.

"I want revenge," they say. "You won't take your own, but that doesn't mean I can't take it for you. It doesn't mean I don't want my own vengeance for the hell that program put me through."

Icarus nods. Petty revenge is a nice color on them.

"Yeah, I'm in too. Those bastards will pay for every single thing they've done to us," Achilles chimes in. Icarus doesn't look at him, his eyes stopping on Apollon. He is glaring at Achilles with a look that Icarus has never seen in his eyes before.

"I know I never got to experience the trauma first-hand, but I would also like to beat some sense into the people that run the program. Show them that they shouldn't overlook people just because they are disabled."

Icarus' eyes roll over everyone at the table. This is so much larger than he realized, and even if Apollon isn't saying anything he knows deep down that the man wants revenge.

He may want to keep his friends safe and out of the hands of ATLAS, but it is becoming incredibly apparent to Icarus that the only way to do that is to help them make a plan. At least then he knows he will have done everything in his power to keep them safe.

"Okay," he says, leaning back into his seat. "If we're going to do this we need to be careful. Really play to our strengths and stay out of the Elysians' line of sight."

There are only five of them—*soon to be six with Patroclus,* he reminds himself. That's nothing compared to the hundreds of Elysians across the country. Nothing compared to the endless wealth and power that ATLAS has in its clutches.

They will have to be extremely careful, play by ear, and hide in the shadows.

"What can we do to ruin their reputation? Can we turn the general public against them?" he asks.

"I don't see why we couldn't with the right information," Thanatos says. "It will be difficult, the Elysians have been idolized for as long as they've been in power. But, I don't think it would be impossible."

Something moves in the corner of Icarus' vision, drawing his attention away from the conversation. A little shadow darts around his peripheries, but he can't seem to find it when he looks over. Something feels wrong.

There is a nagging feeling in his gut that he just can't shake. He doesn't know what it is, but every nerve in his body is on fire. He feels uneasy, like he's being watched. They can't continue the conversation here, it's not safe.

Icarus stands up and stretches, trying desperately to act normal even as his heart beats ruthlessly against his chest.

"I think I could use some fresh air and a good stretch after last night, what do you guys think?"

He catches the glare on Apollon's face morphing into vehement disgust in the corner of his vision, but when he looks at the blond it's molded into an intense look that screams *MINE*.

It makes his heart flutter, the thought that Apollon is pinning him with such a look. Not that Icarus is paying attention to that, though. No, no he wouldn't do that.

The settled paranoia flares up again and reminds him that they need to leave.

"We can talk on the roof, yeah?"

Andromeda nods as they stand up. They're the first one to head to the front door, though Achilles soon joins them. He turns around to look at Icarus after he reaches their side. There's something unreadable in his eyes, something that confuses Icarus. Before he can say anything, though, Apollon scoffs and draws Icarus' attention. His chair scrapes loudly across the linoleum floor as he aggressively makes his way towards the door.

The last person to stand is Thanatos, who silently follows behind Icarus as the group makes their way through the dingy hall towards the roof.

The prickling sensation of being watched fades as they put distance between themselves and the apartment. The paranoia subsides. Icarus isn't sure why the shadow makes him feel so seen or why they are present at all. They've been following him around for a while now, but this is the most obtrusive they've been.

It must be because of what they're discussing. That's got to be it.

The mid-day air is chilled as the group makes their way out into the sunlight. Or, what should have been sunlight if the smog didn't nearly block out the sun's warm rays. This is fine, at least Icarus doesn't have to worry about getting sun-burnt.

Icarus wastes no time settling down with his back to the city skyline, his legs spread out in front of him as he reaches for his right foot. His muscles are tight and protest the movement as he leans his head as far down as he can.

"The Elysians hold no power if we take out their support, right? Their power comes directly from the public if I remember correctly."

As he waits for a response to his question, he switches to stretching his left leg. Icarus is able to touch his forehead to his knee on this side, a reminder to work on the flexibility of his right side some more.

The silence is thick as he moves back to center. Icarus looks up to see why no one is answering to find Andromeda and Thanatos locked in a heated mental debate, their gestures large and angry. Apollon is huffing and shuffling his feet as he pointedly looks away from everyone else on the roof and over Icarus' shoulder. *A great help he is.*

Achilles looks lost, like he isn't sure if he should interrupt the silent argument to his left. *He can help me with my stretches.*

244

Icarus leans forward and taps the kid's foot, quietly asking him for assistance. He leans forward, stretching his arms as far as they can go as Achilles pushes him with his knee. The kid doesn't stop pressing his weight forward until Icarus' forehead rests against the concrete.

A groan escaped Icarus' lips before he could stop it, it's been a long time since he had anyone to help him stretch like this and the pleasant burning of his muscles has him sighing in relief.

The shifting of feet in front of him stops and Apollon's voice fills the tense air, "How do you plan on changing the public's opinion?"

"That's a good question. I don't know." His voice is strained as he responds, Achilles pushing down just a bit more to get him into a deeper stretch.

"You're right though," the kid chimes in, "The Elysians only hold power because the public allows them to. I remember learning about the insurrection in class, legally they have no authority. But no one's spoken up because they didn't have a reason to."

"Don't have a reason to my ass," Icarus mutters under his breath. There is plenty of reason to speak up, plenty of reason to expose the abuse the program inflicts. The general population just doesn't want to pop their comfortable bubble of protection because it's not their kids that are being torn piece by piece and reformed into mindless abominations.

The disgust is potent on his tongue, and Icarus will do anything he can to make sure that no one else will know its taste.

"I know there's been some grumbling within the ranks," Thanatos says as Icarus sits back up. He leans back against Achilles' legs as he listens to the man speak. "People are upset that they got skipped in line."

Icarus looks at Apollon as the accusation hangs in the air. Apollon did rise the ranks quickly, of course it caused a disturbance among the Elysians he had overtaken.

"There's also been chatter underground. I heard some rumors a while back that people are starting to get locked up for trying to speak out." Andromeda adds. "They're booking them under acts of treason."

"What?" Icarus doesn't know what to make of that. "They can't commit acts of treason against a corporation?"

"Well, they can if no one will stop them."

Icarus groans, it doesn't surprise him that ATLAS would do something like this. It really doesn't. But yet, it feeds the boiling rage that has been slowly building since he first met Andromeda and started down this path.

"So what can we do?" Achilles asks, his voice hushed as the reality of just what they will be going up against hits him.

"I can spread more rumors in the underground." Icarus nods at Andromeda's words. He could help them, talk to Dimetor and see if he will help them too with his extended client base.

"That sounds like a great idea," Thanatos agrees. "If you can do that, I can start sowing more discomfort in my networks as well. Maybe even see if I can't get us some top level shit to fan the flames."

"Then what?" Achilles sounds almost defeated, and Icarus does not like that sound at all. He leans his head back to look up at the kid's face, only to be greeted with concerned eyes. *He's looking at me, is he worried about me?*

"What do you mean?" Icarus asks.

"What happens after we spread the rumors? Once the public starts turning on the Elysians, what then? They have a chokehold on the government. How are we going to change that without losing anyone?"

"That's where I come in," Apollon says. Icarus' eyes slide forward to see the glaring at Achilles. "I'll take care of everything from within the program."

Icarus rolls his eyes. It's not that he doubts Apollon's abilities, more that he thinks it's such a douche move to swoop in the way Apollon is. *'I'll take care of everything?' Nah, that's literally the most nauseating thing he can say.*

He adjusts himself, scooting slightly away from Achilles so that he can cross his leg and rotate his back. If he's going to listen to the pompous ass talk, he's going to get a full stretch in.

"I was thinking that I could start a new rumor, tell them that ATLAS is skimping on them and that they deserve more power—"

Apollon is cut off as Andromeda and Achilles start yelling at him. A mixture of Spanish and curse words is thrown around before Icarus gets their attention by whistling.

"Let the man speak, I think he has a decent idea."

"As I was saying," Apollon continues, "I will tell the lower ranks that they deserve more unrestricted power. They'll latch onto that and I'll tell the upper ranks that there are rumors of a coup among the lower ranks."

I'll be damned, this actually is a decent idea, Icarus thinks. He really just said it to get everyone to stop being so loud, but they might actually have something here.

"That could cause a rift in the ranks and maybe even one between the program itself and ATLAS." Icarus' eye twitches, why hadn't he thought of that? Get them to turn on themselves and it will be easy to overtake them.

"What then?" Achilles asks again. "After we topple ATLAS, what happens?"

"Then we attack them directly. Make sure they're out of the picture for good." Thanatos sounds so sure of himself as he speaks, as if he knows that everything will go to plan.

"When they don't have public favor it will strain their relationship with the government. They will look bad on all fronts and they decide at that point to fight with a kid they declared dead ten years ago? That will be it for them."

"But that means that Icarus will have to go public, go back into the limelight. No, we'll have to find another way." It's adorable how much the kid cares for Icarus and his well being, even if the care is misplaced.

"Nah that's alright, I'll gladly go public if it means defeating them." Icarus crosses his legs and props his head up on the heel of his hand, throwing a lazy smile towards the kid.

"It'll be fine, kid. It's about damn time they found out I'm alive and kickin' anyways. They got a lot to make up for."

Icarus blocks out the rest of the conversation as the plan is finalized. He instead lays back on the concrete roof and looks up at the clouds above him. *Everything is going to be okay.*

It isn't until Achilles lightly kicks his leg that he sits up. As he stands, he pats Achilles' shoulder, thanking him for bringing him back into the present.

His legs feel much looser than they did when he woke up, he really should have stretched last night before going to sleep. Icarus knows better than to go to bed right after dancing, but it had escaped his mind with everything else going on.

As he follows Andromeda towards the door to the roof, however, he hears Apollon say something that makes his blood run cold.

"You're cheating on Patroclus with Icarus, aren't you?"

THE ARGUMENT

As the words drip from Apollon's mouth everything comes to a halt. Not a sound can be heard, not a move is made, not a breath is taken. The world has come to a still as the accusation hangs in the air.

Icarus can handle a lot, he has been through immense physical pain before. Hell, he's been on death's door more than once. He has been separated from a life of love and friendship only to be reunited with the people he left behind thinking he was dead. While settling into his new life, Icarus had been called every name under the sun: whore, tranny, faggot. He can handle shit being thrown at him.

This, however, is something else entirely. This isn't an attack on Icarus' character, it's a direct accusation against Achilles.

Icarus' eye twitches as Apollon starts to spew nonsense. He isn't sure what the man is saying, he's changed his focus to Achilles. That's what matters right now, making sure the kid is okay.

Achilles, the person who was always there for him. The person who heard a rumor that he might not be dead and reached out on his own faith. The person that helped him even as he was losing control. The person who held him close as he was breaking. The person who was slowly helping to glue himself back together one fragile piece at a time. The person who had wiggled his way into Icarus' heart and taken the place of little brother.

Achilles, whose eyes are starting to flood with tears as he avoids Icarus' gaze. A gut-wrenching pain contorts his face, his eyebrows are furrowed and he looks like he's seconds away from crumbling where he stands. Icarus takes a step towards him, but the movement breaks him from his thoughts and he bolts to the rooftop door.

Icarus watches the kid disappear into the shadow of the stairwell before turning to face Andromeda. He doesn't have to say anything, just tilt his head towards the door. Andromeda nods and heads inside to check on the kid.

With that taken care of, Icarus turns to face Apollon and levels him with a look of pure, putrid hatred. Every ounce of vitriol in his body is pinned on the man as he contemplates just how much he wants to hurt him. Just how much Icarus wants to give in to the voices in his head begging for vengeance.

Apollon's voice wavers as Icarus steps closer, but does not cower. He does not show weakness, even as he has to tilt his head up to look Icarus in the eyes.

Icarus trains his attention on what Apollon is saying just in time to hear, "I'm right, aren't I?" The words are accompanied by a smirk. It infuriates him, what right does Apollon have to patronize him?

"You're sleeping with him," he chuckles, his smirk morphing into a disgusted grimace.

"Even though he is engaged," he stresses, pausing to give more emphasis to the word, "you're sleeping with Achilles." Anger pools deep in Icarus' gut and its twin hatred rears its ugly head.

"*Gods*, Icarus," Apollon spits, "I know you make bad decisions but this is unbelievable."

Icarus snarls, a deeply guttural thing, and his lips pull back into a sneer. He takes a step forward, crowding into Apollon's personal space and forcing him to take a step back.

That doesn't stop Icarus from pushing forward again, and again, and again, until his back hits the brick wall of the building. For his part, Apollon does not cower, even as Icarus blocks him there and leans in so their faces are mere inches apart.

Who is he to say these things? What right does he have to come back into my life after ten years of nothing and dictate who I sleep with?

"You know, you could have been more subtle." There is a shake to Apollon's voice as he speaks, "Maybe don't parade him around in your hoodie after coming out of the same room in the morning. Maybe don't let him get all touchy-feely with you in front of other. I don't know, maybe at least *try* to hide that you're fucking him."

Icarus needs him to shut up for just one gods-damned minute. Just one minute of peace and fucking quiet while he figures out how to deal with this situation without risking their only chance to get Patroclus.

But he doesn't get that. And as Apollon opens his mouth to speak again, Icarus grabs his jaw. His hand covers Apollon's mouth, silencing him.

"You shut your fucking mouth. You know *nothing* about who I sleep with." Apollon tries to pry the hand off his face, tries to free his mouth so he can respond—to no avail.

"I do not owe it to you or anyone, but you really hurt the kid. So I'm going to say this once and once only, okay?"

Apollon's eyes blow wide, the pupils swelling and devouring the beautiful gold of his eyes as he nods. It makes Icarus sick, this should not be pleasurable for him. He tightens his grip on the blond's face, really digs his fingers in knowing they will leave bruises.

"I sleep with whoever the fuck I want to sleep with." Each word is wrapped in barbed wire and drips with poison. "The kid is not one of them. Neither are you, frankly."

Apollon swallows, causing his throat to bob under Icarus' finger. He knows the issue has been dealt with, that he should back off, but the glimmer of adoration in Apollon's hazy eyes makes him want to puke. Or stomp it out, crush it under his heel until Apollon finally understands that there can never be anything between them. Not again.

"At least Achilles looked for me," comes out of his mouth before he can think about what he's saying.

Maybe, if the Fates were a bit more kind, things could have been different. But they aren't, and Icarus resents that fact as he drops his hand and turns to leave.

He needs to check on the kid and make sure everything is okay. Maybe they need to find Achilles separate sleeping accommodations. The thought of sleeping alone again makes Icarus want to scream and rage, but he will do whatever needs to be done to make sure the kid is okay. Especially since they're trying to get Patroclus back. Icarus does not want him coming to the same—albeit incorrect—conclusion that got them into this mess.

Before Icarus can take even a single step towards the door, he is spun around. His back hits the rough brick wall next to where Apollon was just held and his eyes flick up to the arm next to his head—bracing him in against the wall—as another hand wraps around his throat.

Icarus tries to speak, to demand that Apollon let him leave, but the words die on his breath as the hand around his throat tightens. He can't help but lean his head back against the wall as he desperately gasps for air.

"And just who have you been sleeping with, then?" Apollon asks, his voice is hot against Icarus' ear.

He's too tired for this. Too tired to deal with the saccharine sweet words coming from the person he oh-so wishes he could have slept with instead of Alkibiades. It's not like it's any of Apollon's business, anyways, and Icarus would rather not have his sexual habits on display.

He pushes forward—against the hand that restricts his breathing—and rasps, "Wouldn't you like to know, weatherboy?"

A deep red blush spreads across Apollon's gorgeously tanned face. It stains the tips of his ears as he barely contains a whimper. *He's almost cute like this, maybe I should tease him more often...*

Icarus runs his tongue over his lips as he thinks about how he wants to hear that pathetic sound fall from Apollon's beautiful lips again. His thoughts are interrupted as he's pushed back against the wall again.

"No you don't." Apollon's voice is hoarse with need, it is down right *delicious* to Icarus' ears. "I asked you a question, pretty bird."

His eyes snap up at the name. It's a new one, he's never been called pretty bird before and *Gods* is it doing things to his resolve. Icarus smirks, his tongue busying itself with the sharp tip of his broken canine tooth.

"I didn't know you were a kinky bastard, wanting to know all about who fucked me and how they fucked me." Icarus can see the moment his words affect Apollon, his burnished gold eyes darken and his breath hitches.

"Yeah, I'm not so sure you want that, sunshine. I always thought you were more of a..." Icarus searches for the words he wants to use, the words that will get the most reaction out of the blond, "*hands on* learner."

"Oh," Apollon groans. "You are such a fucking tease."

He loosens his grip on Icarus' throat, instead choosing to run that hand down over his chest and stomach before grabbing his thigh and pulling it up to rest against his hip. Every piece of skin that he touched burns, as if the sun itself were tracing its fingers over him. And maybe it was, maybe the man—no, the God—in front of him was the sun and Icarus had flown too close to his heat.

The searing heat of Apollon's hand slides up to where his thigh high socks end, an airy '*fuck*' accompanies the movement. Icarus' breath stutters as Apollon digs his fingers into the soft muscles, decorating his thigh with bruises and marks.

"Did you wear these just for me, birdie? Just to provoke me? You must know how crazy they make me." He leans his forehead against Icarus' as he continues, "how crazy you make me."

What a selfish ass.

"News flash, dick," Icarus responds. He wraps his arms around Apollon's neck, subtly pulling the blond as close to his body as he can as he buries a hand in the soft golden locks. "The world doesn't revolve around you."

Apollon's lips are just a hair's breadth away. Icarus slides down the wall so that he has to look up into Apollon' heavy-lidded eyes. If either of them were to move, they would lose themselves in the endless abyss of want.

The hand that sat next to his head moves off the wall now that Icarus isn't trying to escape. Burnished gold eyes follow the path his fingers trace over the curves and dips of Icarus' body. The touch is delicate, intimate as he takes his time to trace out each and every scar and blemish he comes across.

Icarus lets out a shaky moan as that torturous hand suddenly gropes his ass. He instinctively pulls at the hair in his hand, searching for any way to remain in control of the situation as he is fondled and manhandled.

The world fades away around them. Only Icarus and his sun exist in the moment, lost in a battle for dominance. The only thing he can hear is their labored breaths fighting for space in the mere centimeters between their mouths.

This is dangerous for Icarus. He has spent so long building a wall between him and his sunshine. If this goes much further, he isn't sure what would happen. He is standing at the precipice of διαφθορά and *Gods* is he ready to throw himself over the edge.

He's not sure who makes the move, who closes the distance between them, but suddenly his senses are flooded by the man. Apollon's lips are sickly sweet on his.

Icarus tightens his leg around Apollon's waist, pulling the man flush to his hips as he devours every ounce of lust that is given to him.

He can feel more than hear when Apollon moans into the kiss, it sends pleasant vibrations through his body. The hand on his thigh creeps up to his ass, working in tandem with the other hand to knead the flesh there.

The move elicits a moan from him, giving Apollon a chance to lick his way into Icarus' mouth. It doesn't last long, though, before Apollon breaks the kiss with a stunned look on his face.

"Is that a piercing?"

Icarus bites his lip, showing off the piercing in question. He tends to forget about his smiley, the two spiked ends aren't that noticeable if you aren't looking for them. However, they are very apparent in situations like this.

Apollon gapes at his mouth, seemingly excited about the existence of the piercing if the twitch Icarus feels against his is anything to go by.

And *oh*, if that doesn't excite Icarus as well. But that's not going to happen. At least, not today. Icarus pushes hard against Apollon's chest, shoving him away as he stands up to his full height.

"I believe I said I wouldn't fuck you, no?"

Golden eyes meet his as Apollon's eyebrows furrow in confusion. He must have though Icarus would give in, that Icarus wouldn't have the willpower to withstand the display of dominance.

Icarus simply looks down at the blond in front of him as he tries—unsuccessfully—to school his expression.

"Achilles will be taking your sleeping accommodations." That's all he gives the man before he pushes past him and makes his way towards the stairwell door. Who could say if he makes a show of it, if he purposefully stretches his arms above his head to make his shirt ride up to show off his bruised ass.

He changes his mind at the last minute as he stalls with one hand on the doorknob.

"You're a smart boy, aren't you?" he purrs. "You'll figure it out."

Icarus doesn't look over his shoulder as he descends into the darkness before him. He doesn't want to know just how much he affected Apollon, doesn't want to get close to the edge of disaster again.

He may have been able to play it off as being unbothered, but each step he takes away from the roof makes it harder for Icarus to breathe. He had the world in his fingers and he had *walked away.*

A singular tear rolls down his cheek as he rounds the corner and exits the stairwell. This is for the best, he can't be distracted right now. He needs to be on his A game for Achilles. That's what matters right now, Achilles and by extension Patroclus.

It doesn't matter how many times he reassures himself of that, though, as the voices in his head pick at the cracks of his reasoning. They remind him of what he could have had, the love he desperately wishes to have.

It doesn't matter. Icarus slaps his cheeks to bring his mind back to the task at hand. He needs to clean up the mess that Apollon created, even if he doesn't want to see the wreckage that awaits him on the other side of the door.

THE MELTDOWN

THERE IS NO SCREAMING coming from the apartment as Icarus steps through the door, something that he is immensely grateful for.

Hopefully, that means that Achilles isn't destroying everything. Hopefully.

The first thing Icarus sees as he rounds into the living room is Andromeda's back. They are standing with their hands in the air, a sign of surrender. *That can't be good.*

He looks around them to find Achilles tearing around the apartment. Pillows are being thrown, papers are strewn across every surface, and every item that had been neatly piled on the couch has been ransacked. Achilles has even changed his clothes, no longer wearing Icarus' hoodie but the clothes he escaped the Elysian Program in.

Icarus stands there for a moment, his mind racing as he takes in the rather tame carnage before him. It's clear that the kid is looking for something, and Icarus has a sinking feeling he knows what for. *No, he would have shared information like that.*

"What are you even looking for?" Andromeda sounds frustrated, their voice a pitch higher than normal and raspy. "Why don't you sit down so we can talk about this?"

They're pulling every strategy that they know, every strategy Icarus recognizes from the mediation classes they had to take at the academy. But they aren't working.

It's almost as if Achilles can't hear them as he continues to destroy the couch and the surrounding area. It isn't until he turns around and sees Icarus standing behind Andromeda that he stops.

He looks rough and it hurts Icarus. He's been crying, the tears have dried up but his face is blotchy and his cheeks are shiny. He stands still, but his small frame heaves with every gasping breath he draws in. Icarus wants nothing more than to comfort the kid, to hug him and tell him that everything will be alright, but he isn't sure it would help.

A sharp pain twists itself into Icarus' heart as his hands start to twitch at his side. He doesn't know what he should do, the situation is like nothing he's ever been in and he's so afraid of making it worse.

What if he hates me? I'm the reason Apollon said what he did, what if the kid doesn't trust me?

Icarus' train of thought is broken as the wind is knocked out of his lungs by a weight barreling into him. The kid burrows himself in Icarus' hold as they fall back onto the ground with a painful thud.

Achilles' pain echoes through the apartment; he unleashes everything into Icarus' chest. He's screaming about how it's not fair.

It's unfair that he's out here but Patroclus is still held captive by the program. It's unfair that he has everything he's ever wanted on a platter in front of him because of that. It's unfair that Icarus is doing nothing to stop him, nothing to put distance between them. It's unfair that no matter what he does, Icarus will never see him as anything more than a little brother. It's unfair that he still feels this way despite ten long years of separation, despite loving Patroclus with his whole heart. It's unfair that he feels he's being unfaithful even though nothing has happened. It's unfair, it's unfair, it's unfair.

Each word is accentuated by a fist pounding Icarus' chest and burrowing into his skin, winding their way around his very soul and leaving their mark. His eyes are wide and unfocused as he takes each burning stab.

He's right, it is unfair. Of course, life isn't fair. But if Icarus had known that this is how Achilles felt then he would have stood up to Life and forced them to level the playing field just a bit, if only to ease the kid's burden.

But he didn't. He didn't know and there's nothing he could do about it now.

Icarus raises his eyes to Andromeda's. They are livid, the intensity of their gaze sets the fear of the Gods into him. *They're mad at me, oh Gods they're so mad at me. What—I—*

DO WHAT? Icarus isn't sure what they mean, are they asking what they should do about the situation? He shakes his head, whatever they have in mind will have to be talked about later.

YOU TAKE-CARE fs-APOLLON? That question is easier to answer and he nods. Yeah, he had taken care of the bastard.

CAN I PUNCH? He can't help but smile at that question before mouthing 'please'.

HE OKAY? Another nod. Not the full truth, but the kid will be okay. Icarus is sure of it.

YOU NEED ANYTHING? Icarus shakes his head. No, he doesn't need anything right now, all he needs is to make sure Achilles is okay. They can talk about what happened on the roof later after he figures out what happened himself.

ME GO CLEAN NOW. He nods to acknowledge what Andromeda signed before they turn and head into their bedroom.

Icarus shifts his attention back to the mass in his arms. The kid had stopped pounding his fist against Icarus' chest a bit ago and the screams had morphed into quiet sniffles.

He finally moves his hands from where they sit locked together against Achilles' back, raising one to brush back some of the hair that had come loose from the kid's ponytail.

"Hey kid, talk to me," he requests.

"I hate you." Achilles' voice is raw from the screaming and crying, but that doesn't mean the words didn't hurt.

"Yeah?"

"And I hate that I love you."

"Yeah." Icarus hates that word. *Love. It's nothing but a tool for manipulation.* Still, he cups the kid's cheek and cradles his head against his chest.

"And I'm tired of waiting for Apollon," he spits the Elysian's name as if it were poison in his mouth, "to bring Pat to us. I just want my fiancée."

Icarus makes a noncommittal humming sound in agreement. He can empathize, can understand how Achilles feels without the love of his life at his side.

"And I'm gonna go get my fiancée. Apollon clearly has other priorities right now so I'm gonna do it myself."

"Wait."

Achilles does not wait as he pushes himself out of the embrace and stands up. He looks down at Icarus—his arms still held out as if he were still holding the kid—as he speaks.

"No. I'm done waiting."

Icarus leans around Achilles and finds Andromeda poking their head out of their room. They're shaking their head, clearly not approving of what's going on but not wanting to step in and make things worse. They're right, Icarus should stop this and make the kid change his mind. But he won't. He knows just how stubborn the αριστος αχαιον can be. At this point, the only thing he can do is insert himself into the plan to make sure that he can keep Achilles safe.

He swallows and nods, sending a small apology to Andromeda before he looks back up at Achilles. The rough texture of the carpet bites his palms as he leans back onto them, making it easier to keep looking up.

"Okay."

"And I don't care if you tell me no—wait."

Icarus shrugs, "Okay. I need to get dressed but I'm down."

"I was expecting you to fight back. Tell Me that it's a stupid idea." Achilles' arms drop to his side, defeated.

"Well, it is a stupid idea but it beats sitting here waiting for someone I can't trust to do what he said he'd do." Icarus stands up as he speaks. "Plus I'm tired. Like really tired. And I'm not gonna sleep if you're out there being reckless so I might as well join you."

Andromeda reaches him before he gets to his room. They grab his arm to turn him around as they say, "Wait, what do you mean you can't trust Apollon?"

He frees his arm from their hold and heads into his bedroom, leaving the door open so he can catch them up on what happened on the roof. Achilles follows him in, setting himself on the bed while Andromeda leans against the door frame.

"So, as soon as y'all left the roof I cornered Apollon and threatened him, right?" Icarus starts as he rifles through the clothes in his closet. He's searching for a long sleeve shirt, something he knows he has to have but doesn't know how far back it is.

"Well, it turns out he's a freak and not in the good way." It's all the way in the back corner, now he needs to find a clean pair of pants.

"He kept trying to pry into my love life, find out who I've been sleeping with. It was weird, especially since I told him that it's none of his business."

Icarus turns around and sets the clothes on the bed. He rolls down the thigh high socks, careful not to flip them inside out.

"Hell, I even told him to his face that I wouldn't fuck him and he kept pushing that boundary too! Like, I get that we were a thing when we were younger but I haven't seen him in ten years!"

Andromeda is nodding along to his story, Achilles' eyebrows are furrowed and he looks confused. It was then that Icarus realized this is probably the first Achilles has heard of him and Apollon being together. It was a secret at the academy and they were damn good at keeping it under wraps.

"So I took control of the situation and told him again that I wouldn't fuck him," Icarus continues as he pulls on the clothes. As soon as the long sleeve shirt is settled, he takes it off again. No, no he can't do that sensation today.

Instead he grabs a tank and rummages around the room for his compression sleeve. It has to be here somewhere, he had worn it when they broke in to get Achilles.

Ah! There it is! Icarus picks it up off the ground and puts it on, covering his tattoo once again.

"I might have also told him that he isn't someone I'd ever want to fuck, just to get my point across."

Andromeda barks out a laugh at that before quickly stifling it behind their hand. He's glad they appreciate the humor in the situation, because it is clear that Achilles doesn't.

Icarus turns to his dresser and grabs a ball cap and mask from the top drawer. He situates them as he says, "So yeah, that's what happened up there." Then, he turns to Achilles.

"I also told him that you would be taking his sleeping accommodations to avoid a mix-up like this again." Achilles nods, still unsure what to make of the situation.

The mask covers his face, slightly obscuring his voice as he says, "That's why I don't think he's inclined to help us at the moment. Or anytime soon. I don't think he'd give us up, though. That would require him to tell his bosses that he fucked up a potential infiltration mission he created because his supposedly dead ex told him that he's not their type."

Andromeda does not try to stifle their entertainment this time as they double over laughing.

In between cackles, they say, "I can't believe you told him he wasn't your type after you broke down crying about him the like third time we talked!"

"Listen! The bastard deserves to be knocked down a peg or two!"

Icarus smiles behind the mask as he looks back over at Achilles. The kid is smiling and quietly chuckling as well, Andromeda's laughter is truly contagious. Icarus is glad, it's good that the kid isn't pouting anymore.

Hopefully that smile will stay once they get Patroclus out. Speaking of which, "So how are we going to get your boy back?"

Achilles sobers up immediately, Icarus knows he hadn't thought of a plan but his silence confirms that fact.

"Why don't we use one of our earlier plans? One of the hostage plans," Icarus suggests. The kid nods, clearly handing the reins over to Icarus.

"I'm not quite ready to reveal myself in case Apollon tries to sell us out, so you'll be my hostage."

Andromeda nods before they speak. "That works, let me go get ready and we'll figure out—"

"No, you'll stay here," Icarus interrupts them. "You're the only one of us that can reliably tend to wounds. We'll need you when we're done."

"You make a good point. But I hate it."

"You can hate it from inside the apartment. Achilles and I should probably head out soon if we want to get this done in daylight."

Achilles gets up and heads into the living room without another word. Icarus really hopes that Patroclus will help get the kid out of this funk, it's scary to see him so... quiet.

Andromeda leans back and looks out the door before pushing themself off the frame. They walk up to Icarus, whispering, "Are you sure you'll be okay? This is a really bad idea."

"Yeah we'll be fine," Icarus replies, his voice hushed to match theirs. "I'm anticipating a fight though, it's why I want you to stay here."

They nod, it's clear that they do not want Icarus to follow through on this plan. But they both know it's too late now.

"I don't know who we're going to meet out there or what state Patroclus will be in. We just have to pray that he's still alive."

Icarus pats their shoulder as he leaves the room. They won't need to take a lot with them, really just themselves and their weapons.

He grabs his baseball bat, swinging it in hand before sliding it through a loop on his pants. Right next to the bat was a handkerchief and he grabs that too, he can use it to tie up Achilles' hands.

They don't need any extra bulk, Icarus mentally crosses stuff off his mental list. No keys, no bag, nothing that could expose his identity. He sets his phone on the counter and turns back towards the kid.

"I'm good, you ready to go?"

Achilles nods and the two head out. Andromeda sees them off, their face disappearing as they close the front door.

It's now or never, I suppose.

THE EXCHANGE

THE STREETS ARE BUSTLING with life as Icarus and Achilles make their way through downtown. The air between them is tense, nearly thick enough to cut through.

Icarus is silently worrying. *Everything will be okay,* he tells himself. But he doesn't quite believe it.

Sure, he had been the one to come up with their plan. He had been the one to say that it was okay and that they would make it out. But now that they were actually headed into what would surely be a fight, he's questioning it. Questioning his own sanity after what happened with Sisyphus.

Anxiety buzzes in the back of his mind as he assures himself that everything will be okay. It will be, it has to be.

"I can hear you thinking, spit it out," Achilles says beside him. He's walking with his head down, eyes focused on the cement at his feet. His hands are stuffed into his pocket and his back is hunched. The kid hasn't looked at Icarus since they left the building.

"It's nothing. I'm just worried," Icarus admits. He doesn't know what else to say. They have their plan, they just need to make it work. Icarus just needs to keep the voices at bay. Easy.

"What are you worried about? The plan?"

"Nah, we've got that locked down. Go to Playhouse, 'trade' you for Pat, get the fuck out."

Achilles hums. "So what, then?"

"Well..." Icarus trails off. He doesn't know how to tell the kid about his mental crisis. Doesn't know if he wants to even if he could. So he thinks of any other reason to worry, "I'm just not sure who we're going to face. There are a number of Elysians in this area, what if we can't handle them?"

Achilles stops dead in his tracks, causing Icarus to turn around and look at him. The kid's dark brown eyes are boring holes into his soul, pinning him in place as he speaks.

"You, the best of the best in the Elysian Program. You, who were born and bred to be number one. You, who has the αριστος αχαιον at your side. You're worried about fighting them?" The tone of his voice is incredulous, as if he can see through Icarus' pathetic excuse of a worry.

"Well, when you put it like that it sounds stupid," he automatically replies. He knows it sounds stupid because it is stupid. He couldn't have come up with something more convincing?

"That's because it is stupid. They could put Daedalus himself in front of us and we would still walk away victorious. We will be fine."

He knows that Achilles is right. He knows it. And yet those voices in the back of his head are telling him that everything is going to go wrong. That he hadn't thought of something.

Icarus takes a deep breath in, nods, and turns on his heel. They're almost at Playhouse Square, the harsh lights of the district can be seen even in the bright afternoon sun. They can't turn back now.

According to legend—the legend of academy gossip, that is—Playhouse Square used to be a theater destination. It used to house shows from all over and people would flock to the neon lights in their fanciest clothes to watch.

Icarus wishes he could have seen the area back then, the metal archway feels disappointing in its current state of disrepair. The letters no longer light us and the metal filigree has long since turned to rust.

Now the district is used for Elysian business. Negotiations, planning, generally showing off their might. This is where that happens. It's why Icarus and Achilles chose to come to Playhouse Square. If they're going to get ATLAS' attention, they might as well walk right up to their front door.

Icarus falls into step behind Achilles as he grabs the handkerchief from his pocket. He uses it to lightly bind the kid's hands together with a loose knot. He needs to make it look like he's holding the kid captive without actually holding him captive.

From here on out, Icarus should not speak. His voice has dropped considerably from his time on testosterone. Unfortunately, that means he sounds quite a bit like his father and Gods forbid if anyone were to recognize that.

As they enter under the neon lights Icarus puts a hand on Achilles' shoulder, makes it look like he's guiding the kid. His other hand wraps around the grip of his baseball bat and he swings it idly through the air at his side.

They stand under the rusted metal sign and Icarus watches the crowd, scanning for an Elysian. They're always easy to pick out, what with their over the top outfits. Each Elysian took a design course while in the Academy, a course dedicated to creating the perfect Elysian Persona down to the very clothes you'll wear while in public.

While scanning, Icarus notices that the crowd is becoming nervous around them. People are starting. Passers-by no longer look at them as they walk past, instead giving them a wide berth.

Good. It's good that they are staying away. I don't want civilians getting caught up in this.

He's starting to get antsy, his eyes flit over the crowd and he shifts to tap his foot against the ground.

"Stop fidgeting," Achilles whispers under his breath.

Icarus huffs as he readjusts, shifting his weight so that he can't kick his foot anymore. The nervous energy still needs an outlet, though, and he starts messing with his smiley piercing behind his mask. At least no one will be able to see that.

Eventually an Elysian will come to them. He knows they will. Icarus is willing to bet that one of the uneasy pedestrians had already called for help.

Before long a voice booms through the warm afternoon air. Loud and commanding, it says, "Turn around and step away from the hostage."

Icarus listens, at least partially, and turns around. However, he uses the movement to wrap his arm around Achilles' neck and hold him in a headlock.

It takes everything in Icarus' power to keep himself from groaning as his eyes land on the Elysian. The hair might be different and the baby fat may have long since disappeared, but Icarus would recognize his own face anywhere.

Iapyx. *Of fucking course* his little brother would be the Elysian to find them.

It's a good thing Icarus brought his bat with him instead of his blades. The Gods know that Iapyx would have recognized the engravings as well as the way he fights with them. There is no chance that he wouldn't, they have to share the same technique from training under the same guy.

Iapyx is itching for a fight, the way his hands twitch at his side gives him away. He's about to make a move for something at his side—*probably his blades*—when Achilles speaks.

"Stop!" His voice is shaky, Icarus knows it's anger masked as fear. But it seems to work on Iapyx, as he stops moving and shifts his attention to the kid. "They said they'll let me go if you give them Patroclus!"

Gods, I hope this works, Icarus prays. Everything relies on this.

"And why would we do that?" Iapyx responds. He takes a step forward, throwing his hands up in front of himself when Icarus tightens his arm around the kid's neck.

The urge to speak is killing Icarus, but he can't risk it. Not when it's his own blood in front of him, someone who would definitely recognize the timber of his voice.

He lets the kid talk, negotiating his own trade. He's not sure how much he would be, anyways. Each word that comes out of Iapyx' mouth brings a surge of thoughts and emotions over Icarus.

Didn't Iapyx just graduate? Why is he out patrolling alone? It's normal for new graduates to be out, but they must be under ranked supervision. Why is his skin so perfect? Didn't he train under

Daedalus just as I did? Why was he allowed to live? Is he **better than me?**

"Don't the big three want me back?" That question brings Icarus' attention back to the negotiations in front of him.

"Of course they do, Achilles! I just don't know why we'd hand another member of ours to a terrorist group," Iapyx sounds incredulous. *Terrorist group? Man, we've barely even done anything.*

Before Achilles can respond, a harsh tone rings through the air. Iapyx doesn't take his eyes off them as he reaches into his pocket and pulls out a phone. The noise must be his ringtone, why does it not surprise Icarus that the bastard would take being annoying to the next level by assaulting people's ears.

"Yeah, okay. Send him out."

They know, Icarus panics. *ATLAS already knew we were coming.* The thought sinks like lead in his stomach. How did they know? This plan wasn't even fully fleshed out until they were walking over, how did they know about it?

Maybe Apollon told them, a voice in his mind taunts. *They're alllways waaatching,* another hisses. *You think you can outsmart them?* The voices pile on top of the other until Icarus can't tell them apart.

His vision blurs as he tries to reign in the voices that are screaming in his head, trying to be heard over one another.

They're watching— What if— THERE HE IS— The golden child— KILL HIM—

Icarus can't make it stop, why won't the voices just SHUT UP?

Then it's silent. The only thing Icarus can hear is the ringing in his ears as the voices suddenly fall quiet. He doesn't have time to question what's happening as Achilles starts shaking in his grip.

He looks down at the kid, trying to see what's wrong and is horrified to see him struggling against his arm. He loosens his grip immediately and looks towards Iapyx, who's turned away from them. *Thank the Gods.*

"I am so sorry," he whispers in the kid's ear. He wants to apologize more in depth, explain what came over him, but before he can Achilles gulps and speaks.

"Not now, that's Pat."

Icarus looks back up and finds Iapyx facing him with another person at his side. He is horrified as he takes in every detail of the guy—*Patroclus.*

He's leaning heavily on Iapyx, his shoulders curve in on himself. He looks like he's in pain, cuts and torn bandages litter his dark skin. One of his eyes is swollen shut and his lip is bleeding.

Patroclus looks like he's been through hell, like he shouldn't still be standing. They must have held him in Tartarus, there's no way he would look like this without visiting the torture chambers there.

Icarus wants to shield Achilles' eyes, hide the horrific sight from him. But he can't, he's supposed to be holding the kid hostage. He can't coddle him.

The disgust and horror morph into anger as he looks at the smug grin on Iapyx' face. The bastard is *proud* of what they did, *he's fucking proud.*

He doesn't move, holding Achilles in place. He will make them come to him. It may just be a small amount of power, but Icarus will take any leverage that is handed to him.

The closer they get, the more Achilles fights against his hold. It pains Icarus to hold him in place, but this has to go right. They can't mess it up right before they get Pat safely in their hands.

Icarus locks eyes with Iapyx as they initiate the exchange. Neither of them back down, it would be admitting defeat.

It's a simultaneous exchange, Icarus has one hand on Achilles' bicep while the other one is on Patroclus' shoulder. The poor kid is trembling under his hand, he needs medical attention as soon as possible.

As soon as Iapyx lets go of Patroclus, Icarus pulls him back. He knows he's being a bit rough on the kid as he throws him, but he doesn't stop to think about it as he grabs his bat and drops into a fighting stance.

Next to him, Achilles rips his hands out of the ties. He wastes no time in grabbing Iapyx' hand on his shoulder and twisting the wrist until Icarus hears a sickening crack. The kid turns to grab Patroclus but is met with another Elysian.

Icarus loses track of them as he focuses all his attention back on his brother in front of him. The kid will make it out and take Patroclus with him, of that he has no doubt.

"I fucking knew it," Iapyx spits in front of him, dropping his broken hand to his side.

Icarus clocks the minute movements his brother is making; the slight shift of his weight onto the balls of his feet, the slight turn of his hand—angling it towards his hidden blades, the way he tilts his head down. Iapyx is going to attack.

He's right, and as his brother darts in he swings his bat in front of him, using it as a physical barrier between them. Iapyx's blade hits the metal of the bat, scratching it and creating a disgusting noise that makes Icarus gag.

Iapyx uses that small distraction to his advantage, swiping Icarus' feet out from under him.

Icarus goes down hard, the stray pebbles on the concrete dig into his back. His bat clatters to the ground beside him, rolling just ever so slightly out of his reach.

He stretches, reaching for the bat. His fingers are just millimeters away from the base of the grip when he abandons the attempt, instead focusing on Iapyx as he bears down on him.

His brother is straddling his prone body, holding him down. The heel of his broken hand is pressing into Icarus' bicep and he turns to look at it just as his other fist connects with Icarus' mask.

The mask cracks from the hit, knocking Icarus back into motion. He wraps his legs around his brother, swinging his body to the side and dislodging Iapyx from on top of him.

Icarus immediately crawls towards his bat, the metal gleaming in the sun as it rolls further and further down the gentle slope of the concrete. He doesn't get far, though, as a hand wraps around his ankle and pulls him back towards Iapyx. His skin burns as holes are torn in his pants, the rough concrete unforgiving under his knees.

"Who are you?" Iapyx hisses as he tries to climb on Icarus' back and pin him. He's successful in pinning Icarus' arms to his side, and Icarus grimaces as his mask hits the concrete below him. The plastic crackles as the cracks grow larger.

Icarus kicks back, finding purchase and causing Iapyx to yelp and let him go. This time, he gets to his feet as he scoops up the bat.

It's a matter of time before backup arrives, he has to end this now. He swings his bat over his head, coming down on Iapyx's shoulder with a delicious crunch.

There's a soft roar in the back of his head at the noise, a sound of unanimous approval. He raises his bat to swing again but Iapyx rolls out of the way before it can land. The metal of the bat clangs against the concrete, the end of the bat caving in on itself.

Icarus turns to face his brother again, but is met with another punch landing on his cracked mask. This time, the plastic shatters. Some shards embed in his scarred skin while others rain down on the sidewalk. Icarus licks his now exposed lips and smirks as the man.

"So that's the reason for the mask. To hide your ugly mug," Iapyx jeers. It makes Icarus' blood boil. "Why don't you take off the rest and face me, man to man. Or are you too ashamed to show the world your disfigurement? I bet the rest looks disgusting."

KILL— He's right— BLOOD— You're disgusting— Spill his guts— KILL HIM—

Icarus drops his bat. It will be of no use to him now. No, now he wants blood. Iapyx's blades should be in the same places his were if he had trained under Daedalus. He darts in, surprising Iapyx as he reaches for the back of his boot.

His fingers graze the looped handle of a throwing blade, *bingo*. Icarus pulls it out of its hidden sheath and wraps his hand around its paracord hilt before sinking it in Iapyx' side.

Iapyx screams, the sound feeding the voices in Icarus' head as he watches the dark red blood pouring down his brother's side. Icarus pulls the blade out and plunges it into Iapyx's shoulder—the one that isn't turning a mottled purple color.

He's transfixed by the blood, the dark red beckoning him forward. *Delicious— Taste it— BLOOD— Run—*

Sirens wail in the distance, snapping Icarus out of his head. He's too late, backup has arrived. Fuck. He was supposed to have made a run for it.

Iapyx is still screaming beneath him as another Elysian rushes towards them. They're carrying one of Daedalus' weapons, it's spewing fire. The crackle of the flames ignites something in Icarus' memory, leaving him gasping as he turns to flee.

Not fast enough. The flames boil the skin on his arm as they trace their way up towards his shoulder. He can't tell if he's screaming or if it's the voices in his head and he keeps running.

NO FIGHT— Run— KILL THEM— BOOOOO—

He doesn't look back, but he knows they're chasing him. The pounding of his heart syncs with the pounding of their boots on the concrete. He can still feel the flames dance across his skin, devouring his arm even after they stopped physically touching him.

He hopes and prays that the kid got Patroclus out of the area, that they headed back to the apartment. This had to be a success, especially since Iapyx had seen his face. It didn't seem like he recognized the burn, but someone will. Someone will know who he is.

Icarus ducks into an alleyway and heads north towards the lake. He can't go directly back, there's no doubt that the Elysians will be tracking him. He can hear them calling after him. His only option is to lose them before heading back to his place.

Every step Icarus takes wears more of his adrenaline, he's slowing down. He won't be able to run for much longer. In the distance,

Icarus sees the sign for the Wolstein Center. *Perfect, I can hide there and rest.*

The doors are held shut with a chain. He doesn't have time for this. Instead, he rushes across the street and ducks behind some abandoned buildings.

There are shattered glass bottles strewn about in the crevice he hides in, but that doesn't bother Icarus as he slides down the brick wall. He just needs to catch his breath. That's all.

Sweat drips into his eyes as he leans his head back against the brick. It mingles with the blood trailing down his cheek, stinging in the wounds there.

His arm burns still, and when he looks down he is met with the sight of melted polyester and blood. Shit, his compression sleeve. That has to come off, now, before the fabric fuses with his melted skin.

He rips his hat off his head, balling it up and stuffing it in his mouth as a make-shift gag before starting to pry the fabric off. Screams tear through his lungs as he pulls each molten piece off. Skin comes off with them, creating a pile of viscera at his side. As he's pulling the last piece off, he hears sirens fly by.

Tears are pouring down his face, mixing with the blood, as he calms himself and listens. He can hear the footsteps of a ground patrol pass by his hiding space. Icarus silently prays that they will not double back.

He waits as long as he can to see if anyone else is in the area. Nothing. Good, he needs to get back to the apartment as soon as he can. He has nothing to bandage his wounds and his burn needs taken care of immediately if he doesn't want it infected.

The Wolstein Center is a good ways away from his place, especially if he can't take any of the main roads. His body is running on autopilot as he turns down an alley.

Every ounce of Icarus' remaining energy is put into getting him home, even the voices in his head stay quiet. He doesn't know what alleys he turns down, here he's going, other than knowing that it will take him home.

The sun sinks behind the city skyline, his vision blurring as everything becomes dark. He can't see the brick of the walls anymore, but it doesn't affect him. Truth be told, he hasn't actually seen anything as he ambled through downtown. He's not sure how he's made it this far, doesn't know where he came from. All that matters is that he's hobbling his way through the lobby of his apartment building.

I made it.

THE PAIN

IT IS WELL PAST dark when Icarus stumbles through the front door of his apartment. He doesn't remember how he got here, the only thing on his mind was making it home.

Relief immediately floods his every nerve as he realizes he's safe. He's home, he did it. Icarus crumbles to the floor, not caring to announce his entrance.

Safe? You may be safe, but what about them? You are the danger.

Icarus looks up as the ground shakes with footsteps. He is met with Andromeda's concerned face, Apollon hovers close behind.

His eyes stay on the blond, taking in his furrowed eyebrows and scrunched nose—tell tale signs of anger. They don't last, though, as Apollon's eyes rake over Icarus' wounds.

He's disgusted by you, look at how horrified he is.

I am safe here, Icarus reminds himself. *They will take care of me.* It's as if the words give him permission to fall, the pain drags him down into inky darkness.

Voices melt together around him before fading away altogether, instead being replaced by taunts and jeers. Warm hands run along his skin, the only indication to Icarus that he is still conscious.

Nausea roils through him as pain causes the world to tilt. Icarus swallows hard as he tries to keep the rising bile at bay.

Listen to us, you're going to hurt them. You need to leave, you should have killed him— SPILL HIS BLOOD— he touched— RU-INED HIM—

The voices fragment apart, surround Icarus in the eternal depths of his mind. He doesn't have the energy to mentally round them up and quiet them, instead allowing them free reign to terrorize his mind. It's not like they're wrong. Icarus should have killed Iapyx. The bastard deserves to be a stain on the concrete for the pride he held in what ATLAS did to Patroclus.

Icarus drops his head back against the cool wall, taking a deep breath in to combat a sudden wave of nausea. The heat of the hands has concentrated in one spot: on his arm.

Look what he did— BURNED YOU— You're a monster— He BURNED us—

The voices vibrate closer and closer together, congealing into one reverberating mass as they scream. **YOU ARE A MONSTER,** they say, **THIS IS A MARK OF YOUR SIN.**

Flashes of images accompany their words, and if Icarus weren't desperately trying to hold himself together he would have sarcastically congratulated them on the new party trick.

At first Icarus doesn't know what he's supposed to be seeing. The images disappear within seconds. But then, then he sees himself—his fingers bending and cracking, his teeth growing sharp and jagged, his arms elongating—and he *knows*.

Icarus opens his eyes, but the images are still there. He covers his mouth with his hand, desperately trying to keep himself from heaving, but is met with a gooey substance. Pulling his hand back, he sees a thick black sludge oozing through his fingers. He can feel that sludge leaking from his eyes and his nose and his mouth and it chokes him. It drowns him.

They were right. Oh Gods, they were right to call him a monster.

He's gasping for air, clawing at his throat with black-coated fingers in an attempt to get the disgusting sludge out, when a warm hand wraps around his wrist. Another grabs his face, being careful not to cover his mouth as it forces him to look down.

His vision is still blurry but he knows it's Apollon. He would recognize his touch anywhere, even after all this time apart. It is as if his soul yearns for it.

Icarus focuses on the man in front of him to the best of his ability. The voices make it hard, they roar in defiance as he does.

He uses the hand on his face as an anchor, uses it as a guide to pull himself out of the murky black depths he's been drowning in.

The room spins as he nears the surface of the black waters in his mind. Hands are reaching for him from the depths, the voices call him back into the shadows. But now another cuts through the rush of the waters.

"Ick—!" his lifeline calls. His voice is so far away, muffled by the ooze that surrounds Icarus. "Come— to me— Ple—"

It isn't until he breaches the surface that he can make out what Apollon is repeating. "Icarus please! Listen to me, come back to me!"

Icarus lurches forward as he vomits, no longer able to hold it within him. The meager contents of his stomach splash over the hand on his face and the tile next to him. It's black. He can't breathe, his lungs restrict under the pressure of his dry heaves. *It's black.*

Apollon forces him to look away, pulls him back into his gaze. His watery gold eyes search for any hint of recognition in Icarus' cold gray ones.

"Birdie," his voice is timid as he speaks, "can you hear me?"

Icarus parts his mouth, tries to respond, but he can't as he gags on stale air.

"I'm taking that as a yes." Apollon looks away from him then, nodding to the person next to him. "We need to move you, okay?"

Apollon doesn't wait for a response as he pulls his hand away and leans back. Icarus chases the touch as it leaves, yearns for the heat it was giving him. His mouth parts—what for, he will never know. To yearn, to beg? No, he would never stoop to that level—when something chalky and fruity is slid between his lips.

He accepts the sugar tab and bites down as strong arms slide across his back and under his legs. Icarus winds his arms around Apollon's neck, buries his face into the Elysian's shoulder as he is carried across the room.

The counter is cool beneath his legs as Icarus is set down, though the chill is quickly chased away by heat. Apollon hops onto the counter next to him before pulling Icarus into his lap.

His train of thought is diverted as a glass is pressed into his hands. The texture of the glass is calming as he runs his fingers over it. Calming, but not distracting enough as his thoughts drift back to the warm body behind him. The body that pulls him flush to it's chest, the body that seems to fit to his perfectly. As if they were made to hold one another.

Icarus begins to hyperventilate, his every sense is drowning in Apollon; his warmth is all encompassing, his touch is fire, his scent is home.

There is a small part of Icarus' brain that tries to remind him that they hate the Elysian, that he lost his chance. But that voice is quickly neglected as the room closes in around him. Icarus groans and rolls the mounting pain out of his tense shoulders.

Strong hands begin to knead the taut muscles, thumbs pressing deep into the bundle of tension just below his neck. It hurts, but not nearly as much as he knows it will in the morning.

The hands disappear for a moment before reappearing around the cup in Icarus' shaking hands. They stabilize his hold on the glass.

Icarus leans his weight back into Apollon. He allows himself to be cared for, something that he hasn't had in Gods knows how long, and it does something for him.

In a way, he gives his control over to Apollon and he would be lying if he said it didn't make him a little hot. That forfeit of power mixes with the mind-numbing pain that's rearing its head, and boy does it do wonders for Icarus.

His groans start to taper off, beginning to sound more like moans. They don't last long, however, as Apollon raises the glass in their hands to Icarus' lips. The cold water shocks him, cools every inch of his body as he greedily downs the glass.

The shock of the cold water wakes his senses, makes him much more aware of the situation he's in. More aware of the body pressed flush against his back, more aware of the way Apollon cups his hands as if they are the most precious thing he's ever held, more aware of the way he could just move his hips back ever so slightly...

"What are you doing?" There is an amused lilt to Apollon's voice as he hooks his chin over Icarus' shoulder. His breath tickles the shell of Icarus' ear as he speaks, something that makes his heart warm just a tad.

Icarus moves the glass away from his mouth, setting it down next to him as he goes to respond. The words never leave his mouth, though, as they morph into a blood-curdling scream. Pain slams into Icarus' body like a freight train, every ounce of fear and adrenaline he has been running off turn back on him with a vengeance.

It hurts, *everything hurts.* Icarus reaches up and behind himself, burying his hand into soft golden locks as his back arches and his muscles convulse. His very nerves are on fire, burning him from the inside out.

He can't hear anything, his screams mask any other noise that may be happening around him. He can't breathe, Oh Gods he can't breathe and he can't stop screaming and it hurts *it hurts **it hurts IT HURTS.***

—

The counter is warm under Icarus' cheek as he wakes up. He doesn't want to open his eyes yet, doesn't want to deal with the fact that it is too damn bright in the apartment now. At least the blinding pain is gone, that is definitely a good thing. Though, it has been replaced by bone deep weariness.

He is nearly lulled back to sleep by someone—Apollon, it has to be Apollon—playing with his fingers. Without thinking, Icarus grabs the hand holding his and presses it against his forehead.

"Mornin Birdie, how are you feeling?" Apollon asks. His voice is rough and raspy, he must not have gotten any sleep.

Icarus doesn't answer him verbally, debates pretending like he didn't even hear him. That doesn't last long, though, as his joints start to ache. He groans as he pushes himself up, and Apollon is quick to help him.

"Hey, Andromeda?" Apollon calls, just loud enough to have his voice carry through the apartment without blasting Icarus' pain-addled mind.

The first thing Icarus sees when he opens his eyes is the God standing before him. Apollon is looking out into the living room over his shoulder.

Icarus takes a moment to study him. To study the way his eyebrows crease, causing an adorable frown line to appear between them. To study the subtle bags under his eyes, evidence that he had kept watch over Icarus instead of sleeping. To study the way his nose twitches and his jaw clenches as he waits for the one person with thorough medical training to join them. To study the way his normally glowing tanned skin seems hollow, as if Icarus himself had leeches the life from the galaxy of freckles.

His eyes trace constellations on Apollon's cheeks, bouncing from one freckle to the next to the next until he's met with intense gold eyes staring directly at him.

Time stops for a moment as Icarus gets lost in the deep burnished gold. It's one of his favorite colors, has been for as long as he could remember. Heat floods Icarus' cheeks as he looks away, breaking eye contact. He slides himself towards the edge of the counter, prepares to hop down, but is stopped by Apollon stepping between his legs.

"Let me up," Icarus mumbles. He lays his left hand flat against the Elysian's chest in order to push him back. When that doesn't work, he adds, "I'm fine. Let me stand up."

"Stay here," Apollon whispers into the space between them. "Let Andromeda check everything over, make sure everything's okay."

Icarus sighs, he does not have the mental capacity to deal with this bullshit right now. He really just wants to curl up in bed and sleep, but he needs to check on the kid before he can do that.

He pushes against Apollon's chest one more time, to no avail, before his patience snaps.

"I said I'm fine." His voice is hushed, but pointed as he grits out, "Now let me get the fuck up or I will shove my foot so far up your ass that—"

A cough cuts off his threat, letting Icarus know that Andromeda has joined them.

"Hey Apollon," they say, their voice saccharine sweet. "Why don't you run and grab us some more gauze. We're almost out and Icky baby here will need plenty if he wants to keep his wounds from getting infected."

A fake smile is plastered across their face. They're remaining as civil as they can, but Icarus can see the flame of anger burning in their eyes. They are pissed.

Apollon tries to argue, tries to give them a reason for him to stay, but Andromeda gives him no ground to stand on. The protests peter off as he gives in to their request, turning to exit the kitchen and grab what he needs for the errand.

Icarus and Andromeda watch him in silence as he grabs his jacket and heads to the door. Before he leaves, he turns and sends Icarus an undecipherable glance. Well, undecipherable may not be the best word. Icarus knows what that glance holds, but he refuses to acknowledge it as Apollon heads out into the hall.

He waits for the door to click shut before turning to look at Meda. They slide into the spot that Apollon had just left moments before.

Ugh, I still can't leave.

"So you're fine, huh?" they snidely remark as their eyes scan over Icarus' wounds. They tap his right wrist, acknowledging that they need to look at it more before shifting their attention to his face.

A pen light shines into his eyes as they check Icarus for signs of a concussion.

"Yeah, I'm fine. I feel fine and I would like to go check on Achilles." Andromeda waits for him to stop speaking before instructing him to open his mouth and stick out his tongue. They produce a tongue depressor from somewhere, torturing Icarus with the awful taste and texture of the stupid thing while checking for Gods know what.

"For sure. I'm real inclined to believe you after you screamed so hard that you passed out." Their voice drips with sarcasm, but even still he can admit that they're right. He isn't fine, but that doesn't mean that he won't fight to get off the damned counter.

Their glare softens as they look down at the bandages around his arm. They look fresh, Andromeda must have tended to his burn after he passed out. There is no staining, no blood seeping through the gauze. Should be fine for now, especially if they are running low.

"Here, take these," they instruct him, handing Icarus three small red pills. He doesn't question what they are, popping them in his mouth and dry swallowing them as Andromeda turns to grab him a glass of water. The look of disappointment on their face is a punch to his gut when they realize and set the glass on the counter beside him.

"They're pain meds. I gave some to you when you woke up earlier but it doesn't hurt to take more." They sound exhausted. Hell, they probably are after dealing with everyone's injuries. Icarus prays that the kid came back with nothing more than a scratch, but between Patroclus and himself he knows that Andromeda has a lot to tend.

That doesn't stop him from trying to leave, though. "So, can I leave now?"

"Not until you eat something." The exhaustion is masked by determination as they turn towards the fridge. "I'm going to heat up some chicken nuggets. Just eat a couple and you're free to go, okay?"

Icarus whines, he really isn't in the mood to eat right now. That earns him a pointed glare, telling him that there is no way he is getting out of this. He raises his hands in front of him, a show of compliance even as his face scrunches up from the thought of eating.

"I trust that you will eat these," Andromeda says as they dump a handful of dino nuggets on a plate and pop it in the microwave. Icarus nods when they turn to him.

"Good. I'm going back to check on the children."

They leave without another word, leaving Icarus alone with his thoughts and the droning hum of the microwave.

He closes his eyes and leans his head back against the cabinets. This is the first chance he's had since the fight to think through everything that's happened.

The voices he has grown accustomed to aren't bothering him, but he knows they are still there. They lurk in the abandoned corners of his mind, wait for him to slip up and give them something to feed on.

Icarus doesn't know what they are or where they came from. He isn't sure he wants to know at this point. They've firmly cemented themselves in his psyche, becoming something he will just have to live with.

The drone of the microwave begins to lull him back to sleep, the tension of everything that has happened starts to melt off his shoulders.

BEEP. BEEP. BEEP. Before he can drift into unconsciousness he needs to eat. He told Andromeda he would.

Icarus painfully peels his eyes open, sleep grates on them like sandpaper. Gods, what he wouldn't give for some proper rest.

His legs can barely support his weight as he finally hops down off the counter. It feels like he might collapse at any moment, his knees buckle with the effort of keeping him standing.

Using the counter as a crutch, Icarus slowly hobbles the three steps over to the microwave. As he grabs the plate, he considers how he is going to make it to the table to sit down and eat. The distance between the counter and the table doesn't look terribly far, but there is nothing for him to lean his weight on. He's not sure he would make it with both the plate of nuggets and the glass of water intact.

Instead, Icarus decides to set the plate down on the counter and eat where he's at. The first nugget goes down easy, he's more entertained than anything. The second is a bit harder, the food hits his stomach and he starts to become nauseous. By the third, Icarus is done. He can't eat any more.

Hopefully that's enough to avoid Andromeda's anger. Icarus slides the plate with the rest of the nuggets back into the microwave before grabbing the glass of water and downing it.

At long last Icarus turns and makes his way out of the kitchen, using the counters and any available surface to support his weight. He wants to curl up in his bed and go back to sleep, but as he heads towards his bedroom his brain tells him that he has just one more stop to make first.

THE VOW

THE FIRST THING ICARUS sees when he hobbles into the living room is blood. Blood soaked bandages are draped over the back of the couch and blood stains cover his beige carpet.

The dark red sludge is enticing. It makes his mouth water, something that both excites Icarus and freaks him out. He's so engrossed in the conflicting feelings that he doesn't hear Apollon entering the apartment.

The plastic bags he's carrying rustle as he walks towards Icarus, the bright white draws his attention as they're set down on the table next to him.

"Was he injured that badly?" Icarus asks, his voice barely over a hush. He turns himself around so that he can lean against the edge of the table, give his weary legs a bit of a rest.

Apollon looks over at him. His eyes dart from blemish to wound and back again, checking that nothing new has happened since he's been gone. They linger for a moment on his lips before looking over his shoulder into the living room.

Icarus follows his gaze, turning his shoulders away from Apollon so that he doesn't strain his neck. He watches Andromeda as they kneel down next to the couch, a bottle of antiseptic and a wad of cotton balls in their hands. They set the cotton balls in a dish on the coffee table before soaking one in antiseptic and dabbing it along a particularly nasty looking gash on Patroclus' leg.

Patroclus doesn't react to the burn that Icarus knows he must be feeling. Actually, now that he looks closer, it looks like Patroclus is out cold. It's the best time to run antiseptic over his wounds, when the poor guy can't feel it.

It doesn't look like a peaceful sleep, though. His eyebrows are furrowed and a frown is etched onto his face. The poor kid's in so much pain that he can't escape it even in sleep.

That tugs at Icarus' heart, nearly as much as the sight of Achilles cradling his fiancée's head does. He's sitting at the end of the couch with his hands tangled in Patroclus' hair. His fingers tug at the coils, pulling them out before smoothing them down and pulling them out again.

Hell, even Thanatos is over by their new addition. He's hovering over Andromeda's shoulder, providing them with an extra set of hands as they need it.

"He's not doing well," Apollon whispers. "At least the blood isn't his."

Icarus whips his head around to look at the blond. His eyes scrunch as he tries to understand what Apollon means by 'the blood isn't his'. Was someone else bleeding? It doesn't look like Achilles is hurt, there weren't any visible bandages on the kid. And sure, Icarus himself had gone through the ringer last night, but he hadn't been bloodied.

At least, he hadn't been bloodied by the time he returned to the apartment. Not as far as he could remember.

"What?" Icarus manages to ask. He doesn't know exactly what he wants to ask, but Apollon understands him anyway.

"The blood isn't his. None of it is. He may have been tortured, beaten, and broke, but he wasn't bleeding by the time he got here."

That clears up nothing for Icarus, and the intense gaze Apollon has him under is making him incredibly uncomfortable. He breaks his gaze away, turning back towards the group by the couch.

This time Icarus really hones in on the blemishes littering Patroclus' dark skin. It's hard to see in the poor lighting of his apartment, but Icarus knows that bruises color every inch of his body.

There are lumps and shiny raised ledges—inflamed lacerations—that tell Icarus everything he needs to know about the kid's time in Tartarus. How long had he even been in there? It can't have been that long, they had just broken Achilles out of the Academy the day before last.

Each and every blemish that's visible to Icarus makes him more upset. The voices help him keep count, they taunt him as he catalogs every spot where Patroclus was hurt.

It's all your fault. A contusion on his cheek. *If only you had forced Apollon's hand.* A ladder of stitches on his collarbone. *If only you had gone back into the Academy to find him after grabbing Achilles.* A painful stutter of breath as Patroclus breathes around undoubtedly broken ribs. *If only you hadn't left the Academy at all.* A stark white bandage across his chest. *If only you had never met Achilles.* Red blood dripping down his thigh.

Icarus is suddenly ripped from the jeering voices in his head by a searing pain in his arm. It feels as if there are large claws digging into the already damaged and sensitive flesh, but when he looks over he sees nothing. Apollon is sitting close enough to bump his arm, but he's preoccupied with the new package of gauze in his hand.

What the fuck was that? What the actual fuck, holy shit it hurts. Why does it still hurt?

"Are you feeling okay?" Apollon asks, looking up at Icarus. His eyes overflow with care and concern, so much so that it's painful for Icarus to look at.

"You look pale, do you need anything? Food? Water?"

Icarus grimaces at the phantom pain wreaking havoc on his arm. It is taking everything in his being to keep from screaming out. Something is wrong, but he doesn't understand what and doesn't know how to make it stop.

"Yeah, I'm fine," he grits out. He doubts that Apollon believes him, but he hopes that the man has enough common sense to let it drop anyways.

"If Patroclus wasn't bleeding then where did all that," Icarus gestures at the red mess in the living room, "come from?"

For a brief moment, Apollon looks hurt. The look is gone within a second, though, instead replaced by a detached look of disinterest. "It came from you."

There ain't no way. Icarus' jaw drops as he does a mental check of his own wounds. Third degree burn? Check. Lacerations on his cheek from broken plastic? Check. Bruises from punches? Check.

That's it. That's all the injuries he had received last night. None of which should have been bleeding after the trek across the city, and even if they were there was no way they could produce that much blood.

"You asked, I'm just telling you what I saw." Apollon's voice is cold, distant. Icarus doesn't like it. It feels like Apollon is holding him at an arm's length and it's putting him on edge.

Maybe it's for the best, I shouldn't be so attached to him anyways. Icarus isn't so sure he believes himself, but that's not something he needs to deal with right now.

He looks away from Apollon, shifting his attention back to Andromeda as they finish tending to Patroclus' wounds. They secure the tail end of a bandage around his leg before rocking back on their feet and standing up.

They look over at him, flicking their eyes to Apollon just past his shoulder then settling on him. Icarus tilts his head towards his room, silently asking them to meet him there.

As they pass by the table they nod, they will meet him there after doing what they need to in the kitchen. Icarus doesn't wait to see what they're doing as he pushes himself off the table and onto his shaky legs.

Apollon does not look at him even as he struggles to move, even as his knees threaten to buckle under his weight with nothing to support him.

That's okay, Icarus can do this. Fuck Apollon, he doesn't need a man to help him get to his bed.

Each step is marginally easier than the last, until he's moving at what might be considered a normal pace. Icarus does not stop moving until he is next to his bed, where he finally allows his knees to give out. He flops onto the soft mattress, lying still until he hears Andromeda walk in and set a glass on his night stand.

"I'm setting these here for you to take when you wake up," they say as Icarus shifts his body weight so that he's sitting up against the headboard.

"How are they?" Icarus asks, watching Andromeda as they sit down on the edge of the bed facing him.

"Physically or mentally?" they scoff. Icarus doesn't respond to that question, either would work for him but he has the feeling that they're both intertwined. Silence stretches between the two, a battle of patience as Icarus waits for them to continue and they wait for Icarus to answer.

"Never mind," they say, looking out into the living room. "That doesn't matter. They aren't doing great. I mean, you saw Patroclus. Poor kid passed out as soon as he was set on the couch and hasn't woken up since."

Icarus hums. He had figured as much, but hearing it from their mouth was something else entirely.

"Icarus." They sound so small with their voice stripped of all the sarcasm and annoyance, it doesn't sit right with him. "We were such a mess when they showed up last night.

"I was yelling at Apollon for this whole mess happening and I told him that any blood spilled is on his hands. The Gods sure do have a sick sense of humor, sending an inconsolable Achilles covered in blood through the door with a semi-conscious person on his back right after that."

Andromeda looks back over at him, their eyes scan his face and gauge his non-existent reaction. Icarus is too tired to force anything other than a dead-pan look onto his face.

"And Achilles, man, we were scared about him. At first we thought the blood coating him was his own. I tried helping him first since Patroclus was out like a light as soon as we laid him down, but the kid wouldn't let me. He swore up and down that there wasn't a single injury on him but with that much blood I didn't believe him, made him prove it to me by washing off the blood and changing into clean clothes."

An air of disbelief falls over them as they dramatically throw their hands up in a wild gesture. "You'll never believe it, but he didn't have even a single scratch on him! Not one! I'm scared to find out where the blood came from, what poor soul stood in his way."

Icarus grins, that doesn't surprise him. Achilles is such a brat of course he'd show up looking like he was on death's door when in reality he didn't have a single scratch on him.

The smirk drops off his face, though, when he sees a somber look of regret cross Andromeda's features. "I feel like such a dick. I shouldn't have said what I did to Apollon. It really hit him hard, especially after you came back and tried to tear yourself open."

"I did what?"

"You don't remember? You stumbled through the door and blacked out for a bit, then you started ripping at your throat and chest." They reach out to tap the bandages around his throat.

"We couldn't get you to stop, it was like you couldn't hear us. Good news is you keep your nails short, so you weren't able to puncture your own skin."

Anger floods his body, he knew that something was wrong with what Apollon said earlier. He knew the bastard was lying, that the blood in the living room hadn't come from him. The blood out there is still red, it's untainted. It couldn't have come from his monstrous veins.

But why would he lie? Something isn't adding up, but Icarus is too angry to think about it.

"It was a scary time, do you remember any of it?"

Images pop up in his mind, flashes of scenes provided by the writing black mass in the corner of his vision. They make him nauseous, but those are all scenes from his dreams they didn't actually happen, right?

Icarus shakes his head and purses his lips. No, those were pain induced dreams. He doesn't remember any of that actually happening, especially not last night.

Now that he's trying to remember, Icarus realizes that he can't recall anything that happened from when he left the Wolstein Center to when he woke up on the counter of his kitchen. *What did I do?*

His confused gaze lands on Andromeda. He can practically see the gears turning behind their eyes as they add another piece to the puzzle that is Icarus and his health.

He needs to divert them, change the conversation away from himself. "So, how is Patroclus now?"

They take the change in topic, thank the Gods. "Better, I'll give him that. I don't know if he's surviving on love or spite, but whatever it is it's strong. He shouldn't be breathing and I think Achilles knows that, whatever they did to the guy is enough to kill any other man."

Icarus picks up on the forced tinge of positivity in their voice, the way that they phrase their answer to make it sound like everything will be alright. But just below it lies a waiver of uncertainty that tells him the full story. Nothing is set in stone yet and Patroclus will have a long road to recovery ahead of him if he pulls through.

"Icarus, I don't think he was supposed to survive the trade." Andromeda looks at their hands as they speak, their tone laying bare a deep seated fear. "I'm doing everything I can, but I think they planned on Patroclus dying once they handed him to us."

That makes sense. In some twisted part of his mind, Icarus imagines that he would plan the same outcome if he were in AT-LAS' position. They wanted him to be the blame, wanted him to be their scapegoat so they could win back the trust of their golden child.

That realization makes his skin crawl. What kind of depraved people run ATLAS? And how could they toy with someone's life so easily?

Monsters just like you, the black mass in the corner of his vision hisses. *They're monsters, but so are you. Why don't you show them what a **real monster** can do?*

Icarus snaps his head up as Andromeda rests their hand on his shoulder.

"I don't know what's going through your head, but I want you to know that none of this is your fault. You did the best that you could given the information we had."

Pity. They are pitying him. Icarus hates it, he doesn't want their pity. He bites back the scathing response that comes almost as second nature to the feeling.

Of course Icarus knows it's not his fault. He didn't capture and torture Patroclus. Even if the voices try to convince him it is, even as guilt gnaws at his stomach. If his life had been just a little bit different then this wouldn't have happened, but that doesn't change the fact that his life isn't different and the torture that Patroclus went through at the hands of ATLAS did happen.

Andromeda sighs and drops their hand as Icarus remains silent. They mumble something that he doesn't catch before standing up.

The room falls into a silent darkness as they leave, drawing the door partially closed behind them. It's cracked just enough that he can see what's going on in the living room, but not enough to let the light pour into the room.

Icarus' eyes do not leave Andromeda's back as they walk up to Apollon. It's a brief moment before the blond stands up and follows Andromeda past Icarus' line of sight.

He turns his gaze to Achilles on the couch, only to find that the kid is already looking at him. Grief is etched into every facet of his face. He looks exhausted. No, past exhausted. He looks like he could drop at any moment.

Icarus can't change what has happened, but he can do everything in his power to make sure that he never sees that expression on the kid's face again. Voices start to buzz in the back of his mind, it sounds like they're laughing. It angers him, what is there to laugh about?

ATLAS has crossed a line. Icarus could put his past behind him, he could focus on keeping his friends and his family safe. But they fucked up. They hurt Achilles, and Gods forbid they see the light of another day without learning what that means.

Icarus will stop at nothing to make sure that his family is safe from harm, and if that means personally assuring that the Big Three feel every ounce of pain that their orders inflicted on Patroclus, then so be it. Icarus will fall, but he is going to drag them down into the pits of hell with him.

[REDACTED]

A PHONE BUZZING. THIS couldn't be a more inopportune time for a call. Everyone is otherwise occupied, but that doesn't mean they aren't listening.

"What?"

"You found him." The voice is grainy, they must have called from a burner phone.

"Yeah, I did. You were right."

"I told you he didn't die in a fire. Did he tell you anything about it?"

"No."

"Find out what you can. There's something hiding just under the surface, figure out what it is."

"I will. Now stop calling me, I told you I would reach out to you when I can."

The crackly voice on the other end of the call laughs. "Okay, talk to you later. I love you."

The call ends with a beep. Tonight Icarus will sleep, but tomorrow he will talk. He can't keep his secrets forever.

Index of Greek Terms Used

Achilles: The Aristos Achaean, the best of the Greeks. He is a warrior of myth that played a large part in the Trojan war and an even larger part in Homer's Iliad. He is an exceptionally strong fighter who had to be humbled by the gods themselves before he singlehandedly ended the Trojan War years before Troy was destined to fall.

Aeacus: A son of Zeus and the father of Peleus and Telamon. He was said to be so just in life that he became a judge in Hades after death.

Andromeda: The daughter of Cassiopeia. She was beautiful, which lead to her mother boasting that she was more beautiful than the Nereids (sea nymphs). The Goddesses did not take this well and had Poseidon torture Andromeda by chaining her up on a rock at the edge of the ocean, where Cetus (a sea monster) would be sent to ravage her. She was saved by Perseus and ended up marrying him and founding Mycenae with him.

Apollon: best known as the God of the Sun by people today, Apollon is the brother of Artemis and child of Leto and Zeus.

When he was born he declared godhood over three things: The Lyre (a stringed musical instrument), the tripod (a symbol of divine prophecy), and archery. He is notoriously not able to be in love as all of his love interests in myth meet terrible fates. He was later synchronized with Helios, the God of the Sun.

Ariadne: The daughter of Kin Minos of Crete. Fell in love with Theseus when he came to slay the minotaur and helped the hero in his task. Then, he abandoned her on the island of Naxos, where Dionysus found her and fell in love with her.

Αριστος αχαιον: (aristos achaion), a term used in reference to Achilles in the Iliad. It means 'best of the Greeks' and is used as a title to show just how important Achilles and his fighting prowess is to the Greeks in the Trojan War.

Asphodel: One of the realms of Hades. It served as the middle ground between Elysium and Tartarus where the souls of ordinary people could go.

Atlas: A titan in Greek myth. He did not side with the Olympians in the Titanomachy and as punishment he must bear the weight of the world on his shoulders.

Cassiopeia: The mother of Andromeda and Queen of Ethiopia. She believed her daughter to be more beautiful than the Nereids and as punishment Poseidon forced her to sacrifice Andromeda.

Chthonic: Of the earth, meaning a patron of the Underworld.

Daedalus: The father of Icarus and renowned inventor. He created the Labyrinth for King Minos, who then locked him and his son inside as a way to stop them from sharing the details of the construct.

Διαφθορά: (diaphthora) An Attic Greek word meaning 'destruction'.

Dimetor: An epithet given to Dionysus meaning 'twice-born'. This stems from the myth that Dionysus was originally born as the son of Persephone, but that he was slain and born again as Dionysus.

Elysium: One of the realms of Hades, Elysium was a paradise where the souls of heroes could reside.

Hypnos: The twin brother of Thanatos and son of Nyx. He is the god of sleep and father of the god of dreams.

Iapyx: A mortal who is considered a favorite of the god Apollo. He was given a blessing by the god, but instead of a more violent gift he asked for the gift of healing so that he could prolong his father's life. His familial line is uncertain, though it is stated in Strabo that he may have been the son of Daedalus.

Icarus: The son of Daedalus. He was imprisoned in the Labyrinth with his father and escaped. Before they took flight, he was told to fly the middle road, neither climbing to the sun nor dipping to the sea. Once they were in the air, however, Icarus could not resist the sunlight that he had been deprived of for years and flew towards it. This melted the wax holding his wings together, leading him to fall to his death in the aptly named Icarian sea.

Minos: The King of Crete and son of Zeus. He commissioned the Labyrinth from Daedalus to serve as a prison for the Minotaur, then had Aegeus select sacrifices to send in annually. After death, he became a judge of souls in Hades.

Nyx: The Goddess of the Night. She is a primordial Goddess, existing far before both the Titans and the Olympians.

Patroclus: A character from Homer's Iliad. He was very close to Achilles and was considered the compassion to Achilles' rage. When Achilles refused to fight in the Iliad, Patroclus dawned his armor and pretended to be the Aristos Achaean to lead the troops into battle. He was killed in battle because of this.

Rhadamanthys: Another King of Crete and son of Zeus. He is the brother of both Minos and Sarpedon, and after death he became a judge of souls in Hades.

Sisyphus: A terrible King who sought to cheat death by chaining him up. This meant that no one was able to die, leading Ares to search for the captive daimon.

Tartarus: One of the realms of Hades. Tartarus is the deepest pits of Hades and is considered to be eternal imprisonment. This is where people who do unspeakable acts go the be punished. (eg: Ixion being bound to the flaming wheel, Sisyphus pushing a boulder up a hill for eternity, Tantalus always being within reach of food and water but any time he reached for it the food and water would be just out of reach)

Τέλεται: (teletai) Ceremonies of purification, which were celebrated at Agræ, prior to full initiation at Eleusis. Later became associated as a word meaning 'Mysteries'

Thanatos: A Δαιμονες (daimon) and the personification of Gentle Death. Thanatos is a Chthonic deity and a psychopomp. He is the son of Nyx (night) and twin brother to Hypnos (sleep). He ruled over non-violent deaths, death that felt like entering into eternal slumber. There do not exist many historical records of Thanatos in myth as he really only appears when the children of Nyx are mentioned.

Acknowledgements

I don't even know how I want to start this. There are so many amazing people who have helped me get to the end of this book: Clanky and their threats to my safety for what I did to Icarus (/affectionate), Doom and their excitement to read this book, Rafiq and his everything really. I would be remiss if I left out The Shit Show. Natsume, Locke, Cryptic, Feral, Koumori, Alec, Alex, and Scaley: I love you all. Thank you for being by my side since day one. So many amazing people, and so many more to come.

I do want to go out of my way to thank my mom, though. Thank you, Mother Dearest, for always holding me to oppressively high standards in every aspect of my life. Thank you for telling me that I need to go to college for something that actually matters and not "those silly little stories". Thank you for pushing me down the road to a place where I feel safe enough to vent my frustrations on paper and share it to the world. You did the best you could in raising me and even with the hiccups along the way I wouldn't trade that for the world.

Lastly, I want to thank every single person who stood in front of me and told me that I couldn't possibly be autistic because I did something with my life. Let this book serve as a giant middle finger to you.

ABOUT THE AUTHOR

Andromeda Ruins (he/him) is a queer punk from the Middle of Nowhere, Ohio. He is currently in the last year of his under-graduate program and intends on going to grad school to study with a hopeful Classics major and Folklore studies concentration. Andromeda works full time as well, having gotten himself into a career where he looks at telephone poles all day and makes sure they follow safety criteria set forward by the government.

In his free time Andromeda reads books in dead languages, explores the haunted forests that surround him, and writes. He is queer, disabled, and neurodivergent, sitting comfortably in the 'I don't know what's going on' category in just about everything. This leads to him writing a lot about fucked up queer, disabled, and neurodivergent characters.

For more information on the cover artist, check out Sarah Mason Art: https://www.sarahmason.art/

ALSO BY ANDROMEDA

Call Me Icarus
Δάιος

Grief Short Stories
Death Comes For Us All
Wait For Me

Milton Keynes UK
Ingram Content Group UK Ltd.
UKHW011330310124
436997UK00002B/4